BLUE HALO SERIES BOOK EIGHT

LIAM

NYSSA KATHRYN

LIAM

Copyright © 2023 Nyssa Kathryn Sitarenos

An NW Partners Book
Cover by L.J. Anderson at Mayhem Cover Creations
Developmentally and Copy Edited by Kelli Collins
Line Edited by Jessica Snyder
Proofread by Amanda Cuff and Jen Katemi

❀ Created with Vellum

She's looking for a fresh start...she finds him.

Nylah Walker knows what it's like to be protected. You don't grow up with five brothers without having someone close by, watching your back at all times. She craves independence, and Cradle Mountain is her fresh start. Her new beginning. But fate has a terrible sense of humor, because during her first shift at a new job, not only does she meet overprotective, sexy former Marine Liam...she also finds herself in unimaginable danger.

Liam Shore knows danger. He lived and breathed it during his time in special forces, then again as a prisoner to Project Arma. He thought living in a small mountain town would mean leaving peril behind. But suddenly, he and his friends are hunted men. Protecting his team is his first priority...until the danger overflows onto others.

When the threat shifts its sight to the new woman in town, the one with ice-blue eyes who captured his attention without even trying, Liam is determined to protect her, despite how hard Nylah tries to resist her savior. Because losing Nylah isn't an option.

ACKNOWLEDGMENTS

Thank you to my book team; Kelli, Jessica, Amanda and Jen. You take my book to the next level. None of my stories would be what they are without you.

To my ARC team, thank you for being the first readers and my greatest fans.

To every person who picks up and reads this book, thank you. You make sure the next gets written.

And to the two most important people in my life, Will and Sophia, thank you for your support and love. You are my world.

CHAPTER 1

Nylah Walker adjusted the collar of her crisp white shirt, her gaze moving over her reflection in the mirror. As uniforms went, this one wasn't terrible. At least she got to pair the shirt with high-waisted black pants and not some uncomfortably tight skirt.

Heck, she'd even go so far as to say this outfit was cute...kind of.

She shifted her attention to the small clock on the bedside table. Okay. Time to go.

Nerves rattled inside her belly. Her first event in the new town, Cradle Mountain. The job wasn't optimal. There were few shifts at the event center, and only weekend work. But she'd just arrived in Idaho two days ago, so it was lucky she'd found anything. Tonight, she was working an engagement party.

She couldn't help smiling. Because not only was this a new town, it was her first time living anywhere other than Misty Peak, the town where she'd grown up. The first time living anywhere without family watching over her every move.

They did it with love, but God, she craved a bit of independence. A bit of freedom.

Almost on cue, her phone rang. One side of her mouth lifted when she saw Cody's name pop up on the screen.

With a sigh, she lifted the cell. "Got nothing better to do on a Saturday night than call your big sister?"

They were twins, but her father had let slip that she was born seventeen minutes before Cody...and she wasn't going to let him forget it.

He chuckled. "I'm on break at the bar and had a wild urge to talk to someone who'd chew my ass out."

The bar—their father's bar. The one she'd worked at her entire adult life. The one everyone had assumed she'd take over after he died.

Her lips twitched. "Kayden could have done that in person."

"Ah, but Kayden's out rescuing some sad soul from the forest."

Oh, she could just imagine. Misty Peak was in Tennessee, with the beautiful Smoky Mountains running through it. Her oldest brother was a former military pararescueman, which made him perfect to work in search and rescue. Except, of course, he chewed out every unlucky soul who came across his path.

Nylah looked out her condo window at the woods beside the apartment building. It was a bottom-floor condo in a group of twelve. The living room only had a view of the parking lot, but at least the place was different. New. Two things she desperately needed. "Well, I'm sorry to tell you that I'm just heading out, so I don't have time to do much ass-chewing."

"Exploring Cradle Mountain?"

"Actually, I got a job."

Her brother whistled. "Already?"

"Don't sound so surprised."

"I'm not. I'm happy for you. What's the job?"

"Working at an event center. It's not ideal, but..."

"That's great, Ny. You deserve to be happy, and I hope you find that there."

Her heart softened. God, she loved her brother. All of her

brothers. Yes, they were suffocating at times, but it was because they loved her.

"When will Paisley be getting home and joining you?"

The condo was her best friend's place, and the entire reason Nylah moved was because Paisley was away for work and the condo was currently empty. "Her retreat goes for a couple months, so not for a while."

Her friend was a Pilates and yoga instructor. She was away running a retreat in Bali right now.

"You sure you're okay out there by yourself?"

She rolled her eyes. There was the brother she was so used to. She'd like to blame his protective nature on his time in Delta Force, but that would be inaccurate. All her brothers had been like that since the day they were born.

"Yes. I'm great, Cody. You take care of Dad's bar, okay?"

"Always. Call if you need anything. And when I say anything, I mean—"

"Anything. I know. Thanks for being such an awesome twin." And he *was* awesome. He'd bowed out of the military six months before their father's health had taken its final turn for the worse, and he'd been everything the family needed since.

"I love you, Ny."

"Love you too."

The moment the call ended, she wanted to call Cody back again. She should be used to being apart from him after his time in the military, but this was different. He wasn't off saving the world. He was back home, in Misty Peak. And she wasn't.

It was strange, this tug for independence that battled with a love for family and home.

But this was what she wanted.

With a straightening of her spine, she slid her cell into her back pocket and slipped out of the apartment. Paisley's condo was cute—two bedrooms, two bathrooms, bright and clean. The living areas were small but cozy, and the surrounding woods made for a lot of peace and quiet. Exactly what she needed.

When she reached the parking lot, she unlocked Paisley's Ford Maverick pickup and slid behind the wheel. It wasn't until she was driving to the event center that a certain set of gray eyes flashed in her mind, causing a shiver to run through her.

Liam's gray eyes.

She cringed at the memory of bumping into the stranger earlier today. She'd literally walked straight into the man's back as she'd been setting up for the function, dropping about half a dozen glasses to the floor in the process.

The embarrassment had only lasted for, oh, about two-point-five seconds before her gaze had collided with his. Then, of course, she'd lifted a piece of broken glass and promptly sliced her finger. The second he grabbed her wrist, she'd felt his touch down to her bones, and she'd thought her heart would pound right out of her chest.

Just her luck, she'd see him again tonight. Because he was part of Blue Halo Security, and this engagement party was for one of the guys on the team.

Her belly did a little flip.

She pulled into the event center's employee lot, then jogged to the back door, which led to the kitchen. She was so damn on time, she was bordering on late. Crap.

She was about to step inside when a man barged out, and she almost ran into him.

Nylah jumped back. "Sorry!"

He gave her a tight smile that didn't reach his eyes—so dark brown, they seemed black—before continuing on his way.

She frowned. Not even a "that's okay"?

Shaking her head, she entered the busy kitchen. The cooks were scurrying around, setting tray after tray of cocktail food onto a long counter, while the servers helped arrange the food and set up trays of drinks.

Music drifted in from the ballroom, the steady flow of voices already loud.

Quickly, she slotted her bag into a cube before clocking in and lifting a tray of king crab leg bites. She smiled at her boss as she passed, a middle-aged man who had a fatherly way about him, then stepped into the ballroom.

A band played at the front of the room, while a bar was set up in the back. It was still early, so the room wasn't completely packed, but the number of military men in attendance made it feel more crowded than it was. God, they took up all the space.

With slow steps, she moved further into the room.

Having five military brothers, she could pick them anywhere. They held themselves differently than others. Scanned their surroundings like they were constantly looking for a threat.

She recognized several of the guys from online news reports. They'd been all over the media when information about Project Arma was leaked to the public a couple of years ago.

She couldn't imagine going through what they'd endured. Kidnapped. Given experimental drugs. Having their DNA altered, and in effect, their lives irrevocably changed.

Busy scanning faces, she almost ran into a cocktail table in her path—would have, if strong fingers hadn't wrapped around her forearm and tugged her to a stop.

With a gasp, she looked around, finding those beautiful gray eyes she'd been thinking about all afternoon.

"Hey! You again." The words came out too breathy.

He was tall. Maybe...six-three? Six-four? He certainly towered over her five-six. And he was broad, with light brown hair her fingers twitched to run through.

Man, she was losing her goddamn mind.

One side of his mouth lifted. "We've got to stop meeting like this."

Awareness sparked in her belly like little fireworks, not only from his deep, gravelly voice but the way the heat in his touch seemed to penetrate through her clothes to her skin.

She swallowed, trying to force her voice to work. "You mean with me not watching where I'm going and you saving me?"

"Fortunately, I like saving people."

Oh yeah. He looked like a savior. "Well, thank you. And to show my gratitude, I can offer you a king crab bite."

Slowly, his fingers unwrapped from her arm, but not before she felt the smallest caress of his thumb against her pulse. Or maybe her mind was making that up? And God, why did she want to pull his hand back to her?

"No, thank you. But come past me again in case I change my mind."

She gave him what she hoped was a cool, calm, collected smile, but in reality, probably bordered on crazed. "I'll be sure to do that."

She moved past him, whispering, *Do not fall or walk into anything* in her head the entire time.

She wasn't usually so clumsy, but apparently around him, she was.

Why was she so fixated on the man? Cradle Mountain meant long-awaited freedom. Independence. Not finding a guy. Certainly not one like Liam. He had "protector" written all over him, exactly what she was trying to get away from.

She stopped at a small group of women, two of whom had large pregnant bellies. "Hi, ladies. Can I offer you a king crab bite?"

"Oh my gosh, yes, please. I'm starving!" One of the pregnant women grabbed two.

A woman with long red hair chuckled. "Sure, I'll have one."

The pregnant woman groaned as she ate the crab in one go. "These are amazing!"

The other pregnant woman laughed. "Well, now I *have* to have one."

The redhead smiled. "I'm Lexie. The starving pregnant woman is Evie. The slightly less starving pregnant woman is Samantha. And this is Sage. I feel you should have our names because you'll be seeing a lot of us tonight."

Nylah grinned. "It's nice to meet you. I'm Nylah. And call me over as much as you need."

The second pregnant woman, Samantha, let out a groan. "You're right, Evie. These are—"

"To die for," Evie finished.

"Let's not go dying just yet," a male voice said, before strong arms slid around Evie's pregnant stomach from behind.

Nylah straightened. Another man she recognized. She was pretty sure he was one of the men who'd been part of Project Arma, but he lived in Marble Falls, Texas, with his team.

"Luca," Evie sighed, leaning into him.

Three more men joined the group, each touching one of the women. God, they were all so big—well over six feet. Definitely the Marble Falls team.

"We were just making friends with Nylah here," Samantha said as she also leaned into her guy's front. "She's going to look after us tonight. Nylah, this is Kye, Luca, Asher, and Mason."

God, she was never going to remember all those names.

The guys dipped their chins while Kye gave her a smile of gratitude. "If you keep our women fed while they grow small humans, we'll be eternally grateful."

"Small?" Lexie scoffed. "Nothing will be small about them. Not with your genes."

Nylah smiled at them. "I'd be happy to keep everyone fed. I believe there are some sweet and tangy meatballs in the kitchen that I can bring out next."

There was a ravenous groan, but she wasn't sure if it came from Evie or Samantha or both.

Sage nodded. "Bring them. All of them."

Nylah laughed and nodded before moving away.

They were so friendly. For some reason, she'd expected the people who'd been part of Project Arma to be arrogant. Or maybe standoffish and closed off. They'd basically become celebrities for what they were now capable of—incredible strength and speed, quick healing and the ability to hear things they shouldn't. All because of an unsanctioned military experiment they hadn't even known they were part of.

She visited several more groups before returning to the kitchen. Her phone vibrated in her back pocket as she stepped through the doors.

Was that Cody again? Or was it Kayden this time? Hell, it could even be Eastern. He'd just announced to his siblings that he was leaving the military and moving home to spend more time with his daughter.

She entered the kitchen and lowered her tray to the nearest counter, then checked her phone.

Eastern.

She canceled the call and sent a quick text.

Nylah: Sorry, I can't talk right now. Working. Chat later.

Quickly, she slipped her phone back into her pocket, lifted the tray of meatballs, and headed back into the ballroom. Something pulled her attention to the right, and she almost stumbled at the sight of Liam. He was standing with a small group of guys—but his gaze was on her. It was hot and intense and so fixated, her breathing just...stopped. It was like her lungs couldn't get air.

She forced her eyes away, beelining for Lexie's group.

Over the next hour, she continually moved around the ballroom. Time passed quickly, and whenever she grabbed a new tray, the food just seemed to vanish.

She was dropping off her tray for what felt like the tenth time when her phone vibrated with another incoming call. Kayden this time.

Jesus Christ, she was going to kill her brothers! All of them. Slow. Painful. Deaths.

She wasn't supposed to take a break, but if she ignored her older brother's call for too long, he'd just call nonstop. This would have to be quick.

She slipped out of the back French doors onto a wide deck, cold air brushing over her face, then, finally, answered the call. "Hi, Kayden."

"Hey, Ny. I just wanted to check in."

She wrapped her fingers around the railing and scanned the parking lot. "Thank you. I appreciate that. I'm working, though. Plus, I've already received a call from both Cody and Eastern tonight."

Okay, those words probably came out a bit short, but God, she hadn't been here for half a week and there hadn't been a night without her brothers contacting her. They worried because it was her first time away from Misty Peak, but she needed space.

There was a heavy pause before he finally said, "Too much?"

Despite everything, the corners of her lips lifted. "Yeah, Kayden. Too much. I love all of you, but I need some time away. Some space to breathe on my own."

He blew out a breath over the line. "We're suffocating you."

"Maybe, but…it's a loving suffocation."

He gave a small chuckle. "I get it. I'll let the others know to back off."

Relief washed over her like a blast of fresh air. She hadn't realized how much she needed to hear that until her brother said it. "Thank you."

"Cradle Mountain treating you well?"

She ran her fingers over the railing. "Well, I've only been here a couple of days, but so far it's great."

"Not as great as Misty Peak, though."

She grinned. "Time will tell. It's got pretty big shoes to fill."

"It does. Okay. I'll leave you to it, then. Maybe talk to you in a week. Remember to watch your back, okay?"

"Always. Love you, Kayden."

"Love you too."

The second the call ended, she pushed her phone into her pocket and wrapped both hands around the railing. Then she closed her eyes and let the dry air fill her lungs. The air of a new town.

She was just opening her eyes again when the door opened behind her.

CHAPTER 2

*L*iam looked around the busy ballroom. People were scattered throughout every inch of space, drinking, talking, laughing. Most were locals from here in Cradle Mountain, with his team woven throughout the crowd.

Seven other men with whom he'd been through the hell of Project Arma. Men he now considered brothers.

Each of them had found their person—a woman they loved and wanted to spend their life with. And fuck, he was happy for them. They deserved love. Hell, they deserved to be happy for the rest of their goddamn lives after dedicating so many years to the military, only to be held hostage for years.

His gaze caught on Eden and Bodie, two of the eight men from Marble Falls, Texas. Their entire team was here tonight too. The men who'd saved Liam and *his* team. Men Liam would be indebted to for life. It felt good to have everyone together for the first time in so long.

His gut tightened when Nylah came into view. He'd barely been able to stop staring at the woman all night. Her thick auburn hair was pulled up into a tight ponytail, and those eyes... beautiful ice-blues. God, she was gorgeous.

"Someone caught your eye?"

Liam shifted his gaze to Callum. "Maybe."

His friend grinned. "Didn't I see you talking to her earlier today while we were setting up?"

"Yeah, she bumped into my back and some glasses broke. She cut her finger." He could still feel her smooth skin beneath his fingertips as he'd lifted her hand to inspect the cut.

So damn soft.

"So you got to play doctor," Callum said, humor in his voice.

What he *got* was an excuse to touch her. An extra few minutes to talk to her. "I did. Wasn't terrible."

"What's her name?"

"Nylah."

"You should go over to her. Talk for a bit."

Liam frowned. "I said hello, and she's working."

"So, go grab a meatball. Maybe ask for her number while you're there."

"Whose number are we asking for?"

Liam turned his head at the new voice. Wyatt, from Marble Protection, came to stand beside them. He did a lot of the tech stuff for his company back in Texas and helped out Blue Halo on occasion.

"Nylah," Callum said before Liam could tell his friend to shut the hell up. "That beautiful woman with the auburn hair who's talking to your team."

Wyatt searched for her, then he nodded. "I agree. You should get her number."

"Is that what you did with Quinn?" Liam asked with a raised brow. "Just asked for her number when you didn't even know her?"

"Hell no." Wyatt laughed. "She made me work for it. She moved in across the hall, and I told myself to stay the hell away because she's the sister of a teammate. But...staying away proved to be impossible."

"I know that feeling," Callum said quietly as he watched Fiona.

Something kicked in Liam's gut. He'd never felt the need to settle down, but he'd never been opposed to it either. He dated—short relationships here and there. He'd never felt that *thing*...the connection he couldn't walk away from. Watching all the men around him not only find women they cared about but find a new kind of sanctuary...yeah, it was inspiring.

"You guys are too loved up," he finally said with a shake of his head, even though there was a voice inside him that said they were fucking right. That he *should* get her number, and if he walked out of here tonight with no way to contact her, he'd regret it.

"No such thing," Wyatt argued with a laugh.

"How's everything in Texas?" Liam asked, needing a change of subject.

"Sometimes I have to remind myself that Hylar, Carter, and all their men are really gone." Wyatt blew out a breath. "We were chasing them for so long, and now we can just..."

"Live," Liam finished for him. "It feels good, doesn't it?"

"Yeah, it does."

Hylar had been the man to lead the project and take it rogue. Carter was the leader of a SEAL team who'd basically worked as Hylar's muscle. They'd all needed to die, and that day hadn't come soon enough.

A flash of movement caught Liam's attention, and he watched Nylah exit the kitchen and beeline for the French doors.

Was she okay? Was she taking a break? There was nothing beyond the deck besides a parking lot.

Or maybe she was leaving early?

Something uncomfortable coiled his gut. If she left and he didn't have her number, he might never see her again.

He was moving before he could think better of it. "I'll be back."

There was a deep chuckle behind him, but he wasn't sure if it was from Callum or Wyatt. Liam was stopped twice on the way to the door, both times by locals. It was damn hard to be polite when all he wanted to do was chase after her.

By the time he made it to the doors, he was certain he'd missed her. But then he pushed outside to find Nylah turning his way.

Her pink lips parted, and her eyes widened. "Liam."

God, his name sounded good on her lips.

"Hey." He closed the door behind him and stepped forward. "I saw you come out here and wanted to make sure you were okay."

There was the smallest lift of the corners of her mouth. "You sound like you were watching me."

That's because he was, but no way was he going to say that out loud and come across as a damn creep. "Just checking in."

Her gaze softened. "Thank you. One of my brothers just called."

"Everything okay?"

"Oh yeah. Just Kayden being Kayden. I have five brothers, all of whom love to look out for me."

"That sounds nice."

"Most of the time." She looked past him toward the ballroom. "The party seems to be a hit."

"Aidan and Cassie are having a good time, which is what counts."

"Are *you* having a good time?"

His heart thudded. Because he liked this woman asking about him? "Yeah, Ny. I'm having a good time."

There was a flicker of emotion in those blue eyes. "Ny...that's what my family calls me."

"Is it okay if I use it, too?"

Her eyes warmed. "Yes."

He took another step closer. "How long have you been in town?"

She'd already told him she was new in town when he'd

bumped into her earlier this afternoon, but he wanted to know more. He wanted to know everything he could about the woman.

"Only a couple of days."

"What made you choose Cradle Mountain?"

"My friend had an empty condo that was available while she's away. Plus…why not? I wanted somewhere to have a fresh start, and here was as good a place as any."

He shifted beside her, almost able to feel the heat of her arm. "And what do you hope to do here?"

She sighed, gaze moving to the dark night sky. "Be independent. Watch the stars. Explore the history of a new town."

There was something so soothing about her voice. So calming. And, fuck, he wanted to hear more of it.

She looked back at him, gave him a smile that almost sucker-punched the air from his gut. "I should get back inside."

She started to step past him, but he slipped his fingers around her wrist, tugging her to a stop. "Tell me if I'm overstepping…but I'd love to get your number. Maybe I could show you around town."

What he really wanted was a date, but there was no part of him that wanted to scare this woman off. Baby steps felt safer.

That bottom lip disappeared between her teeth, and it took a fucking truck load of self-restraint to not reach up and pull it out. "I'm not sure if that's a good idea."

"Why not?"

She paused, like she was deciding whether to give him an honest answer or not. In the end, she didn't answer at all, just nodded. "Okay. I'll give you my number."

His heart thumped. The kind that told him he'd just scored a big win.

Gently, he slid her phone from her hand when she grabbed it from her pocket, not missing her small intake of breath when their fingers grazed. He typed in his number, then called himself before hanging up and passing it back. "I'll text you."

"I look forward to you showing me around town, Liam...?"

"Shore."

"I'm Nylah Walker. Have a nice night, Liam Shore."

The second she stepped through the door, he had to stop himself from tugging her back again. Because he was pretty sure he could talk to the woman out here, under the stars, all damn night.

His muscles were tense as he turned and gripped the railing, gaze moving out over the parking lot for a few quiet minutes.

He was about to turn back when something caught his attention. A white van.

He frowned. He'd seen that same van earlier today. The guys who'd been doing some electrical work in the ballroom had used it. Why were they still here?

Something in his gut told him to go check it out, and his gut had never been wrong before.

Instead of moving back inside, he climbed down the steps of the porch into the parking lot. He didn't walk directly toward the van, instead crouching so he couldn't be seen, then weaving through the vehicles. It could be nothing, but his gut had saved his ass so many times, he'd be an idiot to ignore it.

When he reached the van, he stilled and listened, hand moving to his concealed weapon.

At first, there was silence, bar the beating of one heart. It stretched out for so long, he was almost going to walk away. Then he heard something beneath the silence of the night. The hum of...a computer? A few computers?

"Two minutes, boys, then we're a go."

Liam's muscles tensed. Ready to go for what? Who the fuck *was* this?

"Get in position. Let's get these assholes."

Blood roared between Liam's ears, the air moving too damn fast in his chest. He sent a group text not just to his team but to the Marble Protection guys as well.

Liam: People have infiltrated the event center. Something's happening in less than two minutes.

The guys would be on the lookout now, at least.

The second the message sent, he swapped his phone for his Glock. Then, quietly, he wrapped his fingers around the back door handle of the van and quickly broke the lock before wrenching it open.

A guy spun away from the screens in front of him and went for a gun, but before he could lift it, Liam fired, getting the asshole in the chest.

The man dropped from the chair to the floor of the van. Liam climbed on top of him, aiming his Glock at the asshole's head. "Who are you and what are you doing here?"

The guy's breath shuddered out of him. "Fuck you!"

"Tell me before I put another bullet in your body."

When he just laughed, Liam's finger twitched on the trigger.

"You're too...late."

"Too late for what?" When the guy didn't answer, Liam pulled him up and slammed him back to the floor of the van. "Too late for *what?*"

"You're all...gonna die tonight." He coughed, blood dripping from his mouth. Then his eyes closed.

When his chest stopped moving, Liam swore and focused on the screens—just in time to see gunfire.

CHAPTER 3

*H*er number. She'd given the man her freaking number. A former special forces soldier.

Oh God.

Nylah pushed into the kitchen and grabbed another tray.

She shouldn't be surprised she'd caved, not with his big, beautiful gray eyes. Every time he touched her, she felt it everywhere.

Her breath shuddered out of her chest as she stepped back into the ballroom, tray in hand. She took a few steps toward the first group of men, a mixture of Blue Halo and Marble Protection guys—but stopped when she saw the expressions on their faces. Hard, intense. Their gazes flicked around the space like they were searching for something.

It reminded her of her brothers when they knew something was wrong. Was something wrong right now?

Some held phones in their hands, but they *all* had a hand near the waistband of their pants. Were they carrying concealed weapons?

A chill swept over her skin as she searched the room for the other men. They all looked the same. Hands hovering near their waists.

Something *was* wrong.

With shaking hands, she set the tray on the nearest table.

Bang.

Her heart stopped, gaze swinging toward the sound to see one of Liam's team members in a shooting stance, gun still aimed at a man near the kitchen door, who was dressed in server attire... and wearing a mask.

As the man dropped, so did the gun in his hand.

Screams sounded around her. The stomp of shoes and the rustle of movement as people ducked for cover.

"Everyone get down!" someone shouted.

She wasn't sure which man the words came from, but the second they were out of his mouth, more shots were fired.

She dropped, breath sawing in and out of her chest as she crawled behind the closest table. Under the sound of bullets, she heard the distinct sound of people hitting and moving on the floor. Party guests trying to find cover or safety.

With a quick breath, she shifted her head out from behind the table. It was easy to spot the shooters. Some were dressed as servers. Others were men wearing suits, possibly having infiltrated the party as guests. But *all* of them had pulled balaclavas over their heads, making them stand out. They moved with confidence and speed, like they had military or law enforcement training.

Everyone was trying to take cover behind something.

It was chaos. Pure chaos. Bullets flew everywhere, and every so often, a body hit the floor.

Oh God. Who were they? And why were they attacking the party? They only seemed to be shooting at the Blue Halo and Marble Protection guys, but maybe that was because they were the biggest threats?

At the loud thud of a body dropping behind her, she turned to find one of the masked servers had fallen to the floor just feet away.

Her breath caught. He was also wearing a balaclava, but his eyes were open, bullet wound to the forehead. She recognized those eyes. Almost black…

It was the man she'd almost bumped into on her way into work.

Oh, Jesus.

A whimper sounded from her right, and Nylah turned her head to see a woman holding a young child against her chest. The girl didn't look much older than five.

The mother was looking around the room, likely searching for an exit, except both the front and back of the room were covered, and who knew if there were more shooters in the kitchen.

Nylah scanned for the small storage room she'd accidentally stepped into earlier in the day. It was a few feet away, tucked into the corner. Inside, there was a door that led to a side exit of the building.

Maybe none of the attackers knew about it, because no one was trying to cover the storage room to prevent escape.

She shuffled toward the mother and child. When she was close, the mother raised her head.

"There's a door that leads outside in that storage closet over there," Nylah whispered. "I'll lead you over."

The mother looked at it with desperate eyes. "Thank you! I need to get Mila out of here."

Nylah nodded, her heart aching for both of them. The kid already looked terrified.

"Follow me. I'll try to cover you." Nylah turned, and as they slowly made their way to the door, she made sure to stay between them and the bullets flying across the room. As she passed the dead body, she grabbed the guy's gun and kept moving.

When they made it to the door, Nylah briefly looked around, then reached up and opened it, breathing a sigh of relief when it was unlocked.

The room was small and dark and filled with cleaning supplies. She closed the door once they were all inside, flipping on the lights before hurrying across the room to the other door. Locked. Crap!

Quickly, she pulled a bobby pin from her hair.

"What are you doing?" the woman asked.

"My twin brother showed me how to pick a lock when I was a teenager. You can only really do it with old locks like this." She stuck the bobby pin into the keyhole and worked it the way Cody had taught her. Every second that passed had another trickle of sweat beading on her forehead. When she heard the click of the lock, she finally blew out a relieved breath.

Thank you, Cody.

She tugged the door open. Before sending the mother and child out, she stuck her head outside to see that no one was around. Good. She looked back at the woman. "Go! Find safety."

The woman stepped out, then turned. "Aren't you coming?"

"No. I'm going to go back and see if there's anyone else I can help get out. Do you know how to shoot?" The woman nodded, and Nylah handed her the pistol. "Take this. Shoot anyone who looks like a threat."

The woman's brows flickered, and for a moment Nylah thought she wasn't going to take the weapon. Finally, she slipped the gun from Nylah's fingers. "Thank you."

She nodded and closed the door, taking a single step toward the ballroom when the door suddenly opened.

She wasn't sure why—maybe gut instinct, maybe because anyone could be a threat right now—but she threw herself behind a tall stack of chairs, peeking through the holes in the back.

The man who stepped in wore a crisp white shirt, black pants, gloves, and a balaclava.

Her heart jumped into her throat.

He tugged the door closed and engaged the lock.

"Everyone get the fuck out," he growled into what must've been a communications device of some kind. "We were compromised."

When he moved toward the outer door, Nylah's throat closed. She couldn't let the guy go out there so soon after the woman and child!

Desperately, she looked around, spotting some cleaning spray. Without thinking, she grabbed it and popped up—spraying the guy in the face just as he passed.

He cursed, the gun dropping from his hands as he reached for his eyes.

Nylah lunged for the weapon. She'd just wrapped her fingers around the grip when he grabbed her around the waist and threw her to the side. She didn't have time to scream before her head hit the wall, hard, her teeth clattering against each other. Her knee slammed into the floor, and pain spidered up her thigh.

She ignored the pain, gaze sweeping across the floor, searching.

Shit! Where did the gun go?

But then the man was on top of her, a thigh on either side of her body. He flipped her to her back. His fist flew toward her face, but she dodged it, immediately reaching up and going for the closest soft points—the eyes. He growled as her fingers dug into his eyes like claws, and he yanked away, his balaclava coming off in the process.

Dark brown eyes. Short brown hair with a few grays. Late thirties...and nothing like the thug she'd expected to see.

She was so busy casting every detail to memory that she didn't have time to avoid the next blow.

His big fist hit her hard and fast, causing pain to explode through her skull and darkness to hedge her vision.

His arm was lifting again when the door handle rattled.

The guy looked up, cursing, before his weight suddenly lifted off her. Then he was gone.

22

* * *

BEFORE LIAM HAD EVEN LEFT the van, he spotted two shooters exiting the kitchen door. They spun and took up positions, obviously tasked with making sure no one came out.

He fired two kill shots to the back of their heads, then crossed the distance back to the French doors off the deck and stepped inside.

Guest were on the floor, hiding. Some crawled toward exits. Both his team and the Marble Protection men were taking cover and firing. Luca shot a man in the chest by the door, while Logan put a round in the throat of another.

Fuck, how many of these assholes were there?

A man took aim at Callum from behind. Liam fired before the guy could get his shot off, getting him between the eyes.

To the right, Asher and Flynn were going hand-to-hand with a couple of men. Liam barely spared them a glance—no one stood a chance against his team when it came to close-quarters combat. When he saw a man slip into the kitchen, Liam followed, sticking close to the wall and running, Glock raised.

If the assholes thought they were getting away, they were dead wrong.

He burst through the kitchen doors to find two men in chef uniforms bleeding on the floor, while a couple of servers were hiding behind a counter. One of the servers glanced toward the large commercial fridge in fear. Liam turned toward it just as a bullet flew from behind the refrigerator, narrowly missing his head.

He dropped and rolled, using the work counter that centered the room for cover as he inched closer. He focused on listening to the guy's breaths. His heartbeats.

"Your time is limited, asshole," he yelled. "Come out and I just might let you live." At least until he had answers as to why the fuck they were being attacked.

There was a shuffling sound, and the second an arm poked out from the fridge, Liam fired, getting the asshole in the hand. The gunman screamed and dropped the gun, and Liam ran out from behind the counter before shoving the guy to the floor and pressing the muzzle of his Glock to his head.

"Who are you?"

The guy growled, his chest heaving. "Get the fuck off me!"

"If you don't talk, you're useless to me and I shoot. Who are you?"

"I'm no one. Just a guy who wants to see you and everyone like you *dead!*"

Liam's eyes narrowed. "Why?"

"Watch out!"

The shout came from one of the servers, and it gave Liam enough time to roll to the side as a man fired from the door. Liam fired back—two shots in the chest. But when he looked back to the first man, he saw that the bullet meant for Liam had hit *him.*

Fuck.

He pushed to his feet and moved to the two chefs. He didn't need to touch their pulses to know they had faint heartbeats.

Blood roared between his ears and fury pulsed through his veins as he instructed the others in the kitchen to apply pressure to the wounds before he returned to the ballroom. Guns no longer fired. In fact, there was almost no sound at all. His team slowly stepped out into the open, scanning the room and watching each other's backs as they went.

It was over. But did that mean they didn't have a single survivor? Someone who could tell them what the hell they'd been doing here tonight?

The men all moved to their women, checking on them. Checking on the guests. Liam scanned the room too. Where was Nylah?

Sirens wailed from the street. He started to cross the room

but stopped at a sound from the right corner. It was like a cross between a groan and a gasp.

He moved toward a door and tried the knob. Locked.

With a frown, he turned the knob harder, breaking the lock with a single twist—and what he saw inside made fury wash through him like a tidal wave.

Nylah, on her side on the floor, her face bleeding.

He was across the room and on his haunches in a second. She flinched, readying for an attack, but then her eyes met his.

"Liam," she breathed.

Gently, he slipped his fingers around her upper arms, helping her sit up. "What happened?"

"I helped a woman and her daughter get out. A guy came in, and when I tried to stop him from following them, he attacked me."

A woman and her daughter... Willow and Mila, Blake's wife and daughter? Mila was the only child in attendance tonight that he knew of.

When Nylah touched her face and groaned, Liam growled. "Tell me the man who did this is dead?" Because if not, Liam would find the fucker and murder him.

She opened her mouth, but before she could say anything, a paramedic burst through the open door and dropped to Nylah's side.

CHAPTER 4

Sitting in the back of an ambulance, Nylah barely suppressed a flinch as the paramedic pressed and prodded at her cheek.

"Sorry," he said softly, inspecting her face. "I'm done now. Nothing appears to be broken."

She sighed as he handed her an ice pack. "That's good." She hadn't thought anything was broken, but getting the confirmation was a relief. It meant less recovery time.

She also had an ice pack on her bruised knee, but again, the paramedic had confirmed there seemed to be no broken bones. Though he encouraged her to go to the hospital for X-rays to be certain. Right now, she just wanted to go home. She kind of felt like one big bruise.

Memories flickered in her mind...of the stranger's big body on top of hers. Of the anger in his dark eyes. She shuddered. There was no doubt in her mind that if Liam hadn't tried to open the door when he had, she wouldn't be here right now.

She'd been lucky. People had died tonight, and not just the bad people. She ached for every innocent who'd suffered. The servers. The guests.

The paramedic prodded at her knee again, but she barely registered the pain because at that moment, Liam stepped out the front door, closely followed by a few of the other guys. Immediately, he scanned the throngs of people. The police. The paramedics. His gaze passed all of them to find her. And God, he looked intense.

When he started toward her, her heart thumped, and she had to remind herself to breathe. He didn't take his eyes off her once. And the way he looked at her...like he was going to tear down the world to get to her.

He stopped beside them, his gaze moving over her face, his eyes narrowing. "Are you okay?"

"She's going to be fine," the paramedic answered before she could. "Just a bit bruised. I'll get some pain medication."

The second he disappeared, Liam stepped closer, his fingers brushing over her cheek. Surprisingly, when he brushed the pad of his thumb over her bruise, it didn't hurt. It actually almost felt better...soothing. How was that possible?

"I'm sorry you got hurt, Ny."

She forced air into her lungs. "I'm sorry people died. That they tried to kill your team."

The muscles in Liam's forearms visibly bunched. "Everyone who was a part of this is either already dead, or is *going* to die for the part they played."

Her skin pebbled. There was so much danger in his voice. It sounded like both a threat and a vow. "Did any of your team get hurt?"

"No, thank God. And all the women are safe too. Thank you for helping Willow and Mila."

Her heart hurt at the memory of that child being in there. "The girl looked terrified. I hope she's okay?"

"Willow said you wouldn't follow them out because you wanted to go back in and help more people escape." There was a small narrowing of his eyes, like he disapproved.

"Of course. There were so many people, and they needed to find safety."

He was shaking his head before she finished. "Leave that to us next time. You need to look after *you*."

She pulled back at his words. Her brothers and father had said stuff like that her entire life, and she hated it. Just because she wasn't a man, or trained to fight, didn't mean she couldn't be useful.

"If I can help others, I will."

His brows flickered. Was he irritated by her answer? He opened his mouth, but then someone called his name, and his head shot around.

"Sorry, I just need to speak to my team. Are you—"

"I'm fine," she said quickly, not wanting to keep him from whatever he had to do. "You go."

He hesitated, then wrapped his fingers around her upper arm and gently squeezed. "I'll be back."

The imprint of his fingers on her skin lingered as he walked away. Then her gaze caught on other things. Men and women in uniforms pushing stretchers with covered bodies. On one gurney, an arm had slipped out. Her belly rolled, and she looked away.

"Hi."

Nylah turned to see a uniformed officer. He had a small notepad in his hand, but he was barely looking at her. Instead, his gaze was caught on the group of men Liam stood with, like he'd rather be interviewing *them*.

"I'm Officer Pierce Carlson," he said.

"Nylah Walker."

"Miss Walker. Can you tell me your account of what happened tonight?"

She blew out a breath, then gave him her version of events. He hardly wrote anything down, just a few brief notes. And the few times he actually looked her in the eye amounted to almost nothing.

"I can give you a description of the man who attacked me, if you'd like?" she suggested when she finished.

He closed his notepad, his gaze once again moving to the group of men. "That won't be necessary, Miss Walker. A man seen fleeing the storage area was shot and killed. Do you have a ride home?"

"I have my car here."

"Great." His gaze flicked back to her before he offered a brief nod. "Thank you for your time."

He headed toward the Blue Halo guys, just as the paramedic returned with some pills. "Here you go. Take two, morning and night, until the pain recedes. You can also take the ice packs with you and keep them on for twenty minutes at a time until you go to bed."

"Thank you." She slipped the small bottle of pills from his hand and rose from the back of the ambulance, cringing at the ache to her knee. She took a step toward Liam, then stopped. The conversation looked...tense. Every man looked ready to kill. And she didn't blame them.

She changed direction. She had his number and could text him tomorrow, let him know she'd made it home okay. He'd probably forget about her anyway. With everything that had happened tonight, how could he not?

Wrapping one arm around her middle, she slowly limped to the back parking lot. Once she was inside the car with the doors locked, a shuddering breath rippled from her chest, and she finally let the stoic expression drop from her face.

Tears filled her eyes, and her breaths came too fast. She pulled her phone out to call Cody—her twin's voice had always soothed her—but paused at the blank screen. The phone was dead.

Crap. She lowered it to the passenger seat, then leaned her head back, closed her eyes, and let her tears fall.

It was probably better this way. If she called her brother, if she told him even a little of what had happened tonight, he'd tear the world apart to get to her, then he'd try to drag her home.

She took a long, steadying breath. She'd be fine. What she needed was a good night's sleep.

* * *

"I can't get in contact with Steve at the moment, but I've sent him the photos," Logan said in a low voice.

Steve was their FBI liaison, and they'd be making damn sure his team was involved in getting to the bottom of the shitstorm that had happened tonight.

All sixteen men stood outside the event center. Fifteen had eyes on their women, who also stood close by.

Callum ran a hand through his hair. "I'll also do some research tonight."

"I'll do the same," Wyatt added.

There was an undertone of fury in their voices. A couple of guys had been nicked by bullets, but other than that, both teams had come out of the chaos uninjured. People had died, though. Innocent people who'd gotten caught in the crossfire.

Liam's gut clenched.

He turned his head to search for Nylah, spotting her talking to a police officer. Something shifted in his chest. Fuck, she'd been so brave tonight. So damn strong and selfless, putting the safety of others in front of her own.

He turned back to the guys as Blake quietly said, "They could be connected to another religious group."

"*Another*?" Luca asked.

Blake's jaw clicked. "My family and I were targeted by a group of people from a church in Ketchum a few months ago. They thought we weren't 'as God intended,' so they tried to kill us and take Mila."

The air thickened as every man let his words settle.

"It's a lead we'll look into," Jason said.

Flynn glanced Liam's way. "Did either of the guys you questioned say anything before they died?"

A vein throbbed in Liam's temple. "No. Just that they wanted us dead. The van outside had a workstation with computers, but I think they've been confiscated by police. We need to talk to Steve about getting access."

Another tense beat of silence.

A uniformed officer stepped up to them, the same guy who'd been talking to Nylah. "Hi. I'm Officer Pierce Carlson. My team and I need to get each of your version of events."

Liam bit back a curse. All he wanted to do was return to Nylah and get her home safely. And all the others were no doubt thinking something similar about their women, because no one looked happy about talking to the police.

Liam let his friends go first, stepping away and turning to walk back to Nylah. The ambulance was empty.

He searched the area but didn't see her.

Fuck, where was she?

A paramedic was climbing into the vehicle. Liam jogged over and grabbed the door before it could close. "Hey. Do you know where Nylah went? The woman you were looking after?"

"Not sure. I cleared her to go home."

"You cleared her to go home? She took a hit to the head and has a bruised knee. Is she even okay to drive?" The words came out too damn harshly, but fuck, he couldn't control his emotions right now. Even if she hadn't been hurt, after what happened tonight, she shouldn't be alone.

The guy frowned. "I thought she was with you, or part of your team, and assumed someone would take her home."

Goddammit.

He let go of the door and jogged around to the employee parking lot. He didn't even know what kind of car she drove.

When he didn't spot her, he pulled out his phone and searched for the new name in his contacts. The second he called it, it went to voicemail.

"This is Nylah. Leave a message. Unless it's Cody. Cody, stop bugging me."

Was her phone turned off?

Instead of leaving a message, he hung up and sent a text.

Liam: Hey. It's Liam. I wanted to drive you home, but I can't find you. Are you okay?

God, he was an asshole. He should have stayed with her. She'd already told him she was new in town and had no family here. After getting caught up in a fucking gunfight, getting hurt and a hit to the head, she shouldn't be alone.

He waited for a minute, but when no response came through, he cursed and shoved his phone into his pocket as he made his way back to the team.

CHAPTER 5

*N*ylah cringed as she looked at her reflection in the bathroom mirror. God, the black eye looked even worse this morning. To be fair, her sleep had been rocky as hell, so the deep bags under her eyes probably weren't helping, but still...

She prodded at the bruise, flinching at the shot of pain that coursed through her face.

Argh. That was going to take a while to heal.

When memories started slipping back in of being in that room with the man, of the fear that she couldn't protect herself, panic pressed at her chest. She closed her eyes and took a moment to breathe. To allow the air to flow in and out of her lungs without it becoming stuck.

When the memory no longer sat on her chest like a million rocks, she opened her eyes, forcing her gaze away from her reflection.

After peeling off the tank top and shorts she'd slept in, she limped over to the shower. Her knee was killing her. It was worse when she walked, but even while in bed, the second the pain medication had worn off, the deep ache had woken her from a fitful sleep.

She stepped under the stream of water, letting the warmth wash over her cool skin.

Earning money was priority number one. There was no way she'd be able to return to the job at the event center. The mere thought of stepping foot inside that place again made her break out in a cold sweat.

Today she'd search for a new job...if her knee allowed it and she could layer on enough makeup that she didn't look like such a mess, that was.

She closed her eyes as the warm water hit her shoulders.

She still hadn't charged her phone. The second she'd returned to the condo, all she wanted to do was scrub her skin clean, slide into bed, and wish the horrible night away.

Well, not completely horrible. There had been one part of last night that was worth remembering.

Those beautiful, intense gray eyes.

She absently touched her cheek again, right where he'd grazed the skin. His fingers had been so gentle. Feather-soft.

She hoped he and his team figured out who was behind last night, not only so they stayed safe but so their families did, too. So that little girl, Mila, was safe.

Her attacker's dark eyes flashed in her head for what had to be the hundredth time since last night, making her shudder. The only thing that kept her calm was Officer Carlson's assurance that he was dead. She'd never see him again.

When she'd pulled off the balaclava, she'd expected someone different. A man with scars and tattoos down his neck. Someone who looked rough and dangerous. The typical stereotype of every movie bad guy. He'd looked neither rough nor dangerous, apart from the rage in his eyes. He'd just appeared... normal. A man she wouldn't look twice at if she passed him in the street.

Nylah spent so long under the water that her skin began to wrinkle, and her knee throbbed from being on her feet.

When she finally stepped out, she dried off and pulled on some leggings and a sweatshirt. Then she sat on the side of her bed, trying to massage some of the pain from her knee. Maybe job hunting wasn't the best thing for her today.

With a long sigh, she grabbed her phone and plugged it into the charger. The second the screen lit up, notifications dinged.

Her brows tugged together at the two messages.

Liam: Hey. It's Liam. I wanted to drive you home, but I can't find you. Are you okay?

Liam: Can I come see you this morning? I'd like to check that you're okay. I'm worried.

Crap. Maybe she should have made more of an effort to say goodbye to him last night.

Her gaze ran over the words again. *I'm worried.* She nibbled her lower lip, guilt but also something else settling in her chest. Something that felt hot and comforting...because she liked that he cared.

She was about to respond when Paisley's name popped up on the screen. Her finger hovered over the cancel key. Usually, they told each other everything, but her best friend would worry if she told her about last night.

But if she *didn't* answer...

Dammit. She hit the answer key. "Hey, Pais."

"Hey. How was your first event last night? Engagement party, right?"

Despite everything, a smile she couldn't stop spread across her lips at the sound of her childhood best friend's voice—so familiar, she wanted to reach through the phone and hug her.

"I met some of those Project Arma guys," she said, not really answering the question.

"Really? That's kind of like meeting famous people. How were they?"

"Different from what I expected. Down to earth. Friendly. At least from what I gathered, the little I spoke to them."

"That's awesome. They're all cute, too, so that's an added bonus."

Oh, they were more than cute. They were gorgeous. All sixteen of them.

She went to pull her legs up to cross them but gasped at the ache in her knee. *Shit.* For a second, she'd actually forgotten.

"What was that?"

Nylah wrinkled her nose and tried to feign innocence, knowing full well it wouldn't work. "What's what?"

"Don't *what* me. You sound like you're in pain. What happened?"

She scrunched her eyes, taking a moment before responding. "Something kind of happened last night."

The pause was long, and when Paisley finally spoke again, her voice was low. "What?"

"I'll tell you, but you have to swear you won't tell my brothers. Not even Cody when he gets all sweet and caring, saying he just wants to make sure I'm safe."

"I would never—"

"You *did*. Eleventh grade? I broke up with Joel Tucker, so he shoved me against the locker? I told you not to say anything, but two seconds of pressure from Cody and you cracked."

"I was seventeen, and your brother's hot and intense. Of *course* I cracked. This is different. I'm a fully grown woman, and I live far away from him. I won't say anything. Just tell me what happened."

She ran her finger along a crease in the sheet. "There was a shootout at the engagement party."

"*What?*"

Nylah pulled the phone from her ear in an attempt to save her eardrum. God, when Paisley got loud, she reached whole new decibels.

"I'm okay. The Blue Halo and Marble Protection teams killed the bad guys."

"But you got hurt?"

She swallowed. "Just a bruised knee."

"Nylah..."

"Okay. And a black eye."

This time, her friend gasped. "Jesus, Ny! Are you okay? I know physically you said yes, but in every other way? Do you need me to come home?"

"*No.* I'm fine." She wasn't sure how true that was, but this trip to Bali was big for Paisley. No way was she forcing her friend to cut it short.

"You should tell your brothers," Paisley said quietly.

"No. Absolutely not. They'll force me to come home, and I'm not ready for that."

"But Ny...being around those guys, or even in that town, can be dangerous. This isn't the first time danger has found them since they got out of Project Arma. Hell, a few months before I left, a woman was held at gunpoint in a bar."

She swallowed. "There could be danger in any town I go to. I need to do this. This is about..."

"Your freedom," Paisley finished when Nylah couldn't.

"Yeah."

Paisley blew out a long breath. "Okay. But if there's any more trouble, you tell me. Okay?"

"Of course." Even if she didn't want to, her friend would probably squeeze it out of her.

"Are you *really* all right?"

The sudden softness in Paisley's voice was so swift, it made Nylah's breath catch. She absently touched the bruising on her cheek, the man's eyes flashing in her head again.

"I don't know," she finally admitted.

Her phone dinged with a text, but she ignored it.

"Oh, Ny. I can come home for a few nights at least?"

She closed her eyes and shook her head. "No. I'm okay. Last night was just a lot, and I need some time to move past it."

"Of course you do. But if that changes, call. Because you know I'll be there within a second's notice."

"I know, Paisley. That's why I love you." It was one of the *many* reasons she loved her best friend.

"I love you too, Ny. You *will* call if you need me, right?"

"Yes. I promise."

When she ended the call, Nylah lay back on her pillow, ignoring a buzz from her phone. Probably one of her brothers —*again*.

She was working on blocking out the memories from last night when a knock came at the door.

She frowned. Who could that be?

* * *

LIAM'S FOOT tapped against the carpeted floor beneath the table. He'd been in this meeting for over a goddamn hour, and they'd discovered nothing.

"How can *none* of the shooters be connected to one another beyond the fact they have a military background?" Liam growled, his gaze moving around the photos scattered across the conference room table. Photos of the men who'd been shot and killed last night. They were from all over the US and every branch of the military. But none of them had served together. There was seemingly no damn connection.

Half the Cradle Mountain and half the Marble Falls teams were at the office, while Steve came through the speaker in the center of the table. Everyone wanted goddamn answers.

"I don't know," Steve said, sounding just as frustrated. "But we'll find out. We're going to interview every family and seize all technology. I'm putting my best tech guys on it."

It didn't feel like enough, but then, nothing would. Because while the FBI searched for information, there could be more of those assholes watching them, plotting another attack.

Fuck, they didn't even have a motive.

As the team talked security measures, Liam's gaze moved to his phone. Nylah still hadn't called him back or returned his texts. Every minute that passed had the dread in his gut tangling tighter. Had she gotten home safely last night? Was she okay? How bad was the pain from her injuries?

He wanted to text again. Hell, he wanted to call until she damn well picked up.

Callum inched a piece of paper toward him on the table.

Liam frowned. "What's that?"

"The information you asked me about this morning." He kept his voice low, as the other men continued to talk around him. "I had to dig a bit. Hack into places I had no business hacking. I found her name on the employment list at the event center. This was the address she gave."

Liam unfolded the note, his gaze skimming over the location.

"We're gonna head back to Texas," Luca said, pulling Liam's attention back to the group. "There's more security in our houses there than in our hotel rooms here. And if there are more people targeting us, being in separate places will make it harder for them."

He was right. They had to assume that, somehow, these assholes had found out all sixteen men would be in the same place at the same time.

Another task—working out who'd leaked that information. It must have been leaked in advance, because that attack had taken time to plan.

Once the meeting was finished, Liam rose and left the conference room. He didn't go back to his office, instead passing through reception, dipping his head toward Cassie behind the desk before taking the stairs down to his car.

He didn't care that he barely knew this woman, he drove straight to her condo. Before climbing out, he sent another text.

Liam: Hey. I'm at your apartment to see you. Can I come in?

He waited. Every second that ticked by had his fingers clutching the phone tighter. Long minutes passed, and every one of them felt like a damn lifetime.

Fuck it.

He climbed out of his car and moved to her door. The second he knocked, he heard the rustle of movement from the other side. The groan of a mattress, followed by the soft pad of footsteps. The door opened, and Liam felt like he'd been kicked in the gut.

God, she was beautiful. The plump pink of her lips. The soft fall of her hair as it flowed around her shoulders. And those eyes…so pale blue, he thought he'd drown in them.

Her mouth opened and closed a couple times. "Liam. What are you… How did you know I was here?"

"You weren't answering my texts, and I was worried, so I had one of the guys look into it."

A bruise had bloomed across her cheek, and he couldn't stop the growl that reverberated from his chest.

She swallowed. "Do you want to come in?"

When she stepped back, she winced in pain. His gaze shot down to her knee, his muscles tightening. He wished he could go back to the previous night and personally murder the fucker who'd hurt her.

Without hesitation, he stepped inside and lifted her off her feet.

She gasped. "Liam! What are you doing?"

Instead of answering, he kicked the door shut and moved into the living area before gently setting her on the couch. Then he lowered to his haunches.

"Where are your pain meds?" The words came out strained, but he couldn't help it. He was angry that this beautiful woman had gotten tangled in this mess.

"In the kitchen."

He found the small bottle and filled a glass with water. When he returned, he lowered in front of her once again and touched a pill to her mouth, feeling the softness of her lips as she opened. Then he followed it up with the glass.

"Thank you," she said quietly.

"Are you okay?" he asked, some tendrils of calm finally slipping into his voice.

An emotion slipped over her face, coming and going so quickly that he almost missed it. She *wasn't* okay.

"I'm lucky I got to walk out of there last night."

His jaw clicked. He hadn't asked if she was *lucky*, he'd asked if she was okay. And by her non-answer, she confirmed she wasn't. "You shouldn't have gotten hurt. I'm sorry."

"The injuries will heal."

But what about the rest of her? The emotional side? She could never go back, erase what she'd been through.

He lifted a hand and grazed the bruise beside her eye. He did it lightly, so as not to hurt her. She didn't flinch or move away, but her breath did hitch and he easily heard her pulse pick up. "Why didn't you wait for me last night?"

She stared at him for a moment. "You were busy with your friends, and I didn't want to disturb you."

"It wouldn't have been disturbing, Ny. I needed to know you were okay." Fuck, he'd barely slept last night, this woman's blue eyes tormenting his dreams.

"Did you figure out why they were there?"

Anger spiraled through his veins. "No. But we're working with the FBI to get to the bottom of this." And they would. Soon.

She nodded slowly. "I'm sorry."

She was saying sorry? "What can I do to help?"

Her lips stretched into a small smile, but it didn't reach her eyes. "I don't need anything."

He didn't believe that. The woman could barely walk. "What are you doing today?"

"I'm thinking of dropping off my resume at a couple of businesses."

His brows rose. "You need a job?"

"Yeah. The event center shifts aren't exactly steady, and I'm not really excited to return there for a while."

Guilt cut across his skin like a knife. What happened last night wasn't his fault, but it was his team that had been targeted.

Another swipe of her cheek. "Jason's partner owns a coffee shop here in town. I could ask her if she needs help?"

She was shaking her head before he finished talking. "No, I couldn't ask you to do that."

"You're not asking. And I don't think you should be on your feet today regardless. Rest. Let me talk to her."

She nibbled her bottom lip, and just like last night, he got the strong urge to tug it out. "Are you sure?"

"Absolutely." Then, because he couldn't stop himself, he said, "Now, tell me how you're *really* feeling."

A sheen of tears coated her eyes. "I keep seeing his eyes in my head."

Fuck.

He rose and took a seat beside her before gently pulling the woman onto his lap and holding her. They barely knew each other, but Nylah leaned into him like she'd known him for years. Like he was her safety net. She nestled her face into his shoulder, letting the silent tears fall. And his chest cracked wide open for her.

He made a vow right then and there that he would protect this woman with his life.

CHAPTER 6

The smell of roasted beans in the warm coffee shop was so heavenly that it almost had Nylah stopping in her tracks. God, she hadn't realized how deprived she'd been of good coffee these last few days until this moment.

Tables lined the middle of the café, with a few booths by the windows. The place wasn't big, but it wasn't small either. And it was busy.

Carefully, she weaved between the tables and customers, making her way to the front counter.

A couple of days had passed since the attack. She'd gotten a lot more sleep last night than the previous two and finally felt like she could function again. Although, part of that was likely due to Liam. The man had stayed for hours the day after the shooting. Massaging her knee. Making her food. And even though she hadn't seen him yesterday, he'd messaged a lot.

She would have been embarrassed about the way she'd cried on his shoulder, except he made her feel the opposite. He made her fear and worry feel validated.

With a sigh, she stopped at the counter. A woman with light

brown hair served on the floor while two blondes stood behind the counter, one with two green streaks in her hair.

When the lady with the streaks finished serving her customer, she stepped in front of Nylah. "Hi. I'm Courtney. What can I get for you?"

The woman had the most beautiful eyes—one green and the other a pale brown. She'd never met a person with different eye colors before, and she couldn't look away.

"Hi, Courtney. I'm Nylah Walker. Liam told me you might have a job vacancy?"

The woman's eyes lit up. "Nylah! You're the woman who got Willow and Mila out during the shooting!"

She frowned. Had Liam told her that? "It was nothing."

"It wasn't *nothing*. Willow was terrified for Mila. Damn straight, I'll hire you."

"Are you sure? I only have experience working in a bar—"

"Then you're experienced in the hard part—customer service. The coffee machine's easy to learn. But if you find it difficult, I'll do the coffee and you serve the drinks. Or we'll get El or Vi to do the coffees."

The other blonde woman stopped behind Courtney. "Hi, I'm Eleanor, and I'm a whiz at coffees, so that's no problem."

Nylah smiled, her chest decompressing. She hadn't realized how worried she'd been about finding more consistent work until this very moment. "Thank you."

"You're welcome," Courtney said. "I can offer you about thirty hours a week. How does that sound?"

"Amazing."

"Great! If you like, I can give you a quick run-through today, and you can start this weekend. If that works for you? I heard you hurt your knee?"

"Oh, it's fine now. Just a little bruised." And fortunately, she wasn't limping anymore.

"Glad to hear it. Well, pop on around the counter, and I'll take you through everything."

Courtney led her into the back room first.

"This is the kitchen where a lot of food is stocked and prepped. We also have an industrial fridge and freezer over here. We keep the back door dead-bolted and only take the trash out at the end of the day."

Nylah's lips twitched. That sounded like something her father or brothers would implement. "For safety?"

"Yep. You get attacked a couple of times through the back door, and suddenly your boyfriend wants to brick it up. I joke, but...not really."

Nylah frowned. "You were attacked more than once?"

Hell, even once was too much.

"Oh yeah. That happens a lot in this town. Not because it's unsafe, but because trouble seems to find a lot of us." Her features darkened. "None of us were expecting what happened at Cassie and Aidan's engagement party, though. I'm sorry you got caught up in it."

"You don't need to apologize. Everyone suffered. I just hope they make sure anyone who was involved and not there that night is arrested."

"Me too. I'm a bit nervous because the attack was very well organized...and the group could be a lot larger than we think."

Dread churned in her belly at the idea of Liam still being in danger. "The Blue Halo guys can take care of themselves though, right?" It was like she needed the confirmation. She knew they were badass, but they weren't bulletproof.

"Of course."

But even as Courtney said it, there was a flicker of worry in the woman's eyes.

Courtney clapped her hands. "Okay, next."

Nylah followed her around the shop as she explained how everything worked. She showed Nylah how to use the coffee machine, something she'd definitely need a refresher on once or twice. She also introduced her to the brunette waitress, Violet, who seemed lovely.

Courtney made her a coffee, which tasted as good as it smelled, and also let her taste test a couple of the foods.

When they were done, Courtney asked, "So, what do you think? Have I scared you off?"

"Nope. You've just made me want to start sooner."

Courtney laughed. "Trust me, I'd have you start today if it weren't for your knee."

Nylah opened her mouth to say that she was fine, but Courtney cut her off.

"Nope. Don't tell me you're fine. I want you to put your leg up and rest, then we can start working together this weekend and become best friends."

Nylah's smile softened. "That sounds wonderful." Especially the 'friends' part. Without Paisley here, her friend list was literally one person—Liam. And technically, he wasn't even a friend.

"Great." Courtney turned her attention toward the door as it opened, the smile across her face widening.

Nylah followed her gaze to see two of the Blue Halo men stepping inside. Courtney rounded the counter and stepped right into one of the men's arms. The embrace was intimate and protective. Loving. And it made Nylah want to sigh.

The second guy frowned as he glanced at her. "Nylah, right?"

She nodded, not sure how the man knew her name.

His eyes darkened, a new intensity seeping into his features. "You got my family out of that party the other night."

Her brows rose. "Mila is—"

"My daughter. And Willow's my wife. Thank you. It's a debt I'll owe forever."

She shook her head. "No, anyone in my position would have done the same thing."

"Not true. A lot of people would have covered their own asses and gotten themselves out of there."

She swallowed, the depth of emotion in the man's eyes swirling inside her like a storm. "I'm glad they're okay."

His dipped his chin.

Courtney cleared her throat. "Jason, have you met my newest employee?"

Nylah swung her attention toward the other tall guy.

Jason grinned. "Nylah! Liam's woman, right?"

Wait, what? "No. I'm not his." Although, she blushed furiously, and the fine hairs on her arms stood on end at being described that way.

One side of Jason's mouth lifted, like he knew something she didn't. "It's nice to meet you."

"You too." She turned to Courtney. "Thank you so much for the job, and I'll see you this Saturday. Or earlier if I stop in for coffee."

"Really looking forward to having you work here, Nylah."

When she stepped onto the street, Nylah wanted to fist pump the air. Yes! A new job already. God, she was actually doing it—living on her own terms in a new place. And it felt good.

She tugged out her phone as she walked toward her car.

Nylah: Guess who got a job with consistent hours?

Paisley: Oh my God...tell me everything.

Nylah: It's just serving coffee at the local café, but I'm excited.

Paisley: You should be. That's amazing, Ny!!

Yeah, it was. She was typing a response when another message came through. The name had her foot catching on the pavement. She barely caught herself.

Liam: Hey, beautiful. How'd it go with Courtney?

Okay, not just seeing Liam's name. The endearment. The way he checked up on her.

Her belly tingled.

Nylah: Good. I start this weekend.

Liam: Will your knee be good enough by then?

Nylah: Yes. It's almost feeling okay today, actually.

The three dots came up, then disappeared.

What were you about to write, Liam?

She was sliding into the car when someone across the parking lot caught her attention. A man who was staring straight at her.

The second her gaze collided with his, he turned away and got into a Honda.

Had he been watching her?

Her phone pinged again.

Liam: If you need to start a bit later, I'm sure she won't mind.

Nylah: You worry too much.

Liam: No such thing.

As she started the car, her phone rang. Her heart skittered in her chest. He was calling her now? "Hey."

"It's good to hear your voice, Ny."

A shudder rolled down her spine at Liam's deep, raspy tone.

"So, I was wondering," he started slowly, "if you'd let me take you out tonight?"

Her breath caught in her throat. That sounded like a date. And yes, she liked him, and she wasn't opposed to dating. But Liam was...

Well, he was everything she'd left behind in Misty Peak. Every bit as protective as her brothers.

"I'm not sure," she finally said honestly. She opened her mouth to give him a reason but stopped. What could she say? Sorry, you're too protective? Would she give him her entire life story about being the only girl in a military family? Explain her deep desire to live on her own terms for the first time in her life, without anyone watching over her shoulder?

"I see," he finally said.

There was another small pause, and she wanted to squirm.

"What if I said it was just as friends? Me showing you around Cradle Mountain?"

Her fingers clutched the steering wheel. "Just as friends?"

"Yep."

She wet her lips. She should say no. Heck, a voice in her head screamed the word at her. She wasn't at all sure she could be "just friends" with this man. But...a night with someone who'd been so kind? Who made her skin tingle with a single touch?

"Okay."

"Great. I'll pick you up at six?"

"Sounds good."

The second she hung up, she touched her forehead to the wheel in disbelief that she'd actually said yes. But was there *any* woman who would have been able to say no to a man like Liam? He was all power and sex.

With a groan, she pulled the car onto the road. Even though she was shocked, she was also excited. So unbelievably excited.

Nerves were still skittering down her spine when she stopped at the light and glanced in the rearview mirror.

She frowned at the car behind her. A Honda.

It was the guy who'd been looking at her in the parking lot.

It was probably nothing...but then why did something hard and uncomfortable lodge in her stomach?

When the light turned green, she moved forward, but instead of continuing to her condo, she took the first left. Her heart rate picked up when the car followed.

It was a good distance behind her. Was he actually following, or just heading in a similar direction?

She took the next right, her gaze barely on the road in front of her, panic surging in her chest. When the car didn't show up in her rearview, she blew out a long breath, muscles relaxing.

Jesus Christ. What was wrong with her? Of *course* they weren't following her. One night caught in the middle of a shootout, and suddenly she thought every man who looked in her direction was out to get her.

When she finally pulled into the condo's parking lot, she inspected the area, and nope—no car had followed. She ran her hands over her face. It was official. She was losing her mind.

CHAPTER 7

*L*iam knocked on the door of the condo. His gaze moved up and down the building exterior, hating that she was on the bottom floor. From a safety perspective, it wasn't ideal.

Shuffling noises sounded from inside the apartment, then the door opened.

His chest constricted. Nylah's hair was down again, flowing over her shoulders like a river in what was his new favorite style. She wore a high-waisted floral skirt with a long-sleeved black top, the fabric pulling tight against her ample chest.

Beautiful. So damn beautiful, he wondered how he was supposed to take his eyes off her.

He stepped forward, needing to be closer. Needing to touch her. "You look gorgeous."

The smile that stretched across her lips was soft and slow. "You look good too." Her gaze brushed over his chest. He loved the woman's eyes on him. "I like a man in white."

He touched a hand to her waist, then lowered his mouth to hover over her cheek. "Then I'll wear white every damn day."

Softly, he kissed her cheek, feeling the warmth of her flesh beneath his lips. Every part of him wanted to tug her close, see if she tasted as good as she looked and felt. But fuck, it was too soon for that. Especially when she was so reluctant to the idea of a date.

Plus, he had a feeling that one taste of this woman wouldn't be enough.

"Ready to go?" he asked in a voice that was too gruff.

She wet her lips. "Yes. I'll just get my purse and jacket."

As she disappeared into the bedroom, he stepped inside, checking out the living and kitchen area to the right. The space was small but well designed, giving it the feeling of being bigger.

Memories of his time here the other day came back to him. Of sitting on the couch with her and talking about nothing all afternoon. Hearing her laugh. Watching her smile. The smallest things about this woman seemed to make him giddy.

"You said your friend owns the place?" he asked, calling to her.

"Yep," she shouted from the other room. "She bought it about six months ago. She was going to open a Pilates and yoga studio but then got offered a position at a Bali retreat and couldn't turn it down."

"Sounds exciting."

"Oh, I was super jealous. Especially because I've barely been anywhere in my life." She returned to the living room with a smile. "Ready."

He placed a hand on the small of her back as they stepped outside.

"So," she started, "where are you taking me?"

"There are two parts to this—" The word date was on the tip of his tongue, almost slipping out into the air. He just stopped it. "Two parts to tonight. The first involves a short drive."

"Mysterious. I like it."

He helped her into the car, then moved around to the other side.

"What did you do today?" she asked as they drove.

His jaw tightened with frustration. "I was at the office. Our FBI liaison is trying to get us access to the laptops from the white van at the shooting so Callum can analyze them, but that hasn't gone well so far. We're not sure why there's a holdup. He normally has access to just about anything."

It was pissing Liam off. Steve had been less than forthcoming about why he was having trouble gaining access. He knew Callum was damn good with technology. If there was information on those computers that could tell them more about the people involved and their objective, he'd be able to find it.

"I'm sorry."

He forced the strain from his face as he looked at her. "Steve will get us what we need eventually. He always does."

When he reached the first stop of their non-date that he was totally considering a date, he pulled into a parking spot on the street.

Nylah leaned forward, her brows drawing together. "The Cradle Mountain Museum?"

"It's small, but there's a bit of history for you to explore here."

Her attention shot to him, her voice quiet. "You remembered."

"Of course." The woman wanted to learn the history of a new town. This was where she'd find it. He felt like everything she'd said in the few days he'd known her was ingrained in his head.

He led her toward the door, not surprised to see Ned, the manager, waiting for them.

Ned dipped his head. "Evening. Welcome to the museum. I hope you both have a great night." He handed Liam the key before smiling and pushing through the door.

Nylah watched him go before turning toward Liam. "Who was that?"

"He runs the museum. They're actually closed, but Ned's a friend. We've helped him out with a couple of security issues, so tonight he's doing me a favor."

Her smile grew. "Are you telling me we have this entire place to ourselves?"

"Yep."

She shook her head. "You just keep surprising me, Liam Shore."

"Good surprises, I hope."

"The best."

When they entered the first gallery, Nylah's eyes lit up and she moved toward the wall, reading over the historical details of Cradle Mountain before focusing on a series of small artifacts. She didn't touch them but got really close, inspecting each carefully.

"Have you always had a love of history?" he asked quietly, eyes forever on her, loving the way she seemed so captivated by the display.

"Yeah. I find it fascinating. Everything from our settlement in this country to ancient history around the world. I love it all."

She moved to the next exhibit, and he followed. "Have you ever considered studying the subject?"

He regretted the question immediately. Her lips lost a bit of their curve, and her eyes a bit of their brightness. "I completed my first semester at Columbia after I graduated from high school."

His brows flickered. "But you didn't continue?"

She shook her head, her gaze running over the next exhibit. "My dad got sick. He ran a bar that *his* father had left him. Selling it would have killed him, and my brothers were all either already in the military or destined to be in the military, so I..."

"Gave up your dream so they could have theirs."

She lifted a shoulder. "Dad and I were close, and I wanted to be with him. I would have gone home anyway. I ended up taking over the bar. My brothers offered to do the same, but I wouldn't let them. It was always my plan to go back to school at some point."

"But you didn't?"

She tilted her head. "Not yet."

They moved into the next gallery, her eyes never leaving the exhibitions. Liam had never been a museum kind of guy. Definitely not a history guy. But as she walked, she spoke about each historical fact she read with such excitement that he *wanted* to be a history guy.

When they reached another room, she smiled. "This is cool!"

The large space held an old train. A lot of people in the community loved that this was here. It was just the engine car, where the driver would sit. But still, it was a big draw for the museum.

He inched closer. "Ned tells me it was the first to run in Cradle Mountain. It was used to transport food."

She ran her hand over the railing. "Can you imagine being transported back to that time? Even for a day, to just live how they lived. Wear those clothes. Be submerged in that culture." She leaned over the railing to look inside.

"I wouldn't like it."

Her head swung back to him. "What? Why?"

He leaned in, his mouth touching her ear. "Because you wouldn't be there."

Her lips parted, air audibly whipping past her lips. "You say pretty sweet things for someone who's out with a friend."

"Guess I'm a sweet friend."

It was a damn lie. He didn't see this woman as a friend any more than she saw him as one. But she obviously needed to go slow, so he'd give her that.

She swallowed. "Tell me about your team."

"They're the brothers I never knew I needed. We went through the hell of Project Arma together, and that bonded us like nothing else could."

Her eyes softened as she moved around the train. "I'm sorry about the project. What happened to you was…awful."

He could think of a lot stronger words. "Fortunately, Hylar, the person responsible, is dead. And so are his followers."

"Did he have many followers? Surely not."

"A few, the main being another SEAL team that was led by a man named Carter. He outlived Hylar and the rest of his team. He was evil to the core. A monster. And not a day goes by where I'm not glad he's dead."

Her expression turned sad for him.

Fuck, what was he doing, talking about that stuff tonight? He wanted to kick his own ass. "Sorry, that's not really a first-date discussion."

A ghost of a smile played at her lips. "I thought this wasn't a date?"

He shook his head, smiling. "Come on, you. I want to show you the next gallery." He escorted her through the next doorway.

When they were finished at the museum, they locked up and walked back to the car.

"What's part two?" she asked when they were driving again.

"You'll have to wait and see."

As he turned into her condo's parking lot again, she frowned. "Um...is an early night part two?"

"No. Wanna go for a walk with me?"

"Sure."

They slipped from the car and immediately, he reached for her hand. A part of him wondered if she'd pull away, what with this not being a *date* and all.

She didn't.

Instead of moving toward the condo, he headed into the wooded area beside the building. "It's not far, but tell me if your knee hurts."

"It's fine."

Nylah said that a lot. And he almost never believed her.

"Where are you leading me?" she asked softly when they were deeper into the woods.

A couple hundred yards in, he slowed as the clearing came into view. "You wanted to learn about the history of Cradle Mountain. You also wanted to see the stars. So for part two, I'm taking you to the stars."

Her mouth opened at the sight of the blanket and picnic basket. "Liam…"

"By the time we finish eating, I promise you, there'll be a perfect view of the night sky."

She was silent, and for once he couldn't quite read her expression. "Are you okay?"

"I'm just thinking how easy you'd be to fall for."

That was so much more honesty than he'd been expecting. "I wouldn't have a problem with that."

She swallowed and didn't respond. He knew she was keeping a part of herself locked away. Why did falling for him scare her so much? Because he'd heard the fear woven through her tone, even though she'd tried to mask it.

They lowered to the ground and together took out the food.

"When did you set this up?" she asked.

"Actually, I cheated. Callum and Fiona brought it out here for us. But I *did* pack it all. Do I lose points?"

"Depends on what you packed."

He pulled out a bottle of wine.

"Oh, you definitely get points for this." She took the wine from his hand, inspecting the label. "How is any other *friend* supposed to match tonight, Liam?"

"They're not."

Her gaze flicked up, eyes darkening. She sighed, shaking her head as she pulled out the Key lime pie and groaned. "Oh my God, you might just need to carry me home after this."

One side of his mouth lifted. Hold this woman in his arms? Hell yes.

When all the food was out, they each loaded a plate.

While they ate, he was reminded once again of how he

could listen to Nylah talk all night. Her voice was soft and soothing, and when she laughed, every part of her face lit up.

They were just finishing their food when she gasped.

He straightened and scanned the area, looking for a threat. When there was nothing, he turned back to find Nylah staring at the sky.

"The first star of the night," she whispered.

He looked up, and sure enough, there it was.

"Aren't they magical?" she whispered.

He faced her, fixated on the softness in her eyes. The awe. "Yeah, I can definitely see some magic."

But he wasn't talking about the stars.

* * *

"Tell me about your family."

The fork paused midway to Nylah's mouth at Liam's statement. He'd stopped eating about ten minutes ago and was leaning back against his hands. She'd been shoving pie into her mouth to take her mind off how sexy he looked, lying like that with his thick arm muscles on display.

She swallowed. "I have five brothers. One of them is a twin, and we're the third born in the family, so I have two older and two younger brothers. One of them has a daughter but is separated from the mother."

"Five brothers. Wow. You and your mom were a bit outnumbered."

She prodded the pie with her fork. "My mom died when I was eight. Breast cancer."

His brows slashed together. "I'm sorry."

"Thank you. It was a hard time, and after that, my dad and brothers became a whole new level of overprotective, I guess because I was the only girl in the family. Getting away to study at college was like a breath of fresh air, even if it was just for a semester."

"Is this your new breath of fresh air?"

"Yep. My time for me."

He nodded, looking at her like he really did understand. "Are you gonna go back to college?"

It was definitely something that had been playing over in her mind. "Maybe."

"You should."

The certainty in his expression and tone—like it was all that she *should* be doing—made her belly clench.

At this point, she'd probably agree if the man told her to get on a spaceship to the moon.

She looked back at the sky. She hadn't been lying when she'd said the stars were magical. Sometimes when she looked at them, the rest of the world melted away.

"What about you?" she asked, turning back to face him. "Family?"

There was a slight tightening of his jaw. It was so brief that she almost missed it.

"I was raised by my mom. But when I was twelve, she was killed in a home invasion."

The gasp of air that pulled into Nylah's chest was so sharp, it bordered on painful. "Oh my gosh, I'm so sorry. Were you home?"

He shook his head and tugged at a string in the seam of his pants. "I was at a friend's house. And I've always hated that I wasn't there to protect her."

Guilt riddled his voice. And pain. So much that she could hear it clearly.

She lowered her fork and shuffled closer, touching his arm. "Hey. You were a kid. I doubt there was anything you would have been able to do. And your mother was probably *glad* you weren't there."

Had he lived with this guilt his entire life? God, her heart ached for him.

When his gaze fell on hers, the pain was still there. And a dozen other emotions she couldn't place.

Every part of her wanted to draw him out of that dark place. She cupped his cheek. "Liam. I'm so sorry. But you wouldn't have been able to stop what happened." Her thumb grazed his cheek.

His eyes shifted between hers, like they were searching for something. Answers? Peace?

"Is that why you joined the military?" she asked softly, trying to understand this man. "To save people because you couldn't save her?"

"Yes. But that hole in my chest never fully pulled together."

Of course not. That kind of pain changed a person.

She lowered her voice, emotion clogging her words. "She would have been so proud of the man you've become." She'd known him less than a week, and she already knew that.

His eyes darkened, his gaze shifting down to her lips. Time slowed as his head began to shift closer to hers. A part of her knew she should pull away. That after she'd felt this man's lips on hers, that would be it. She'd be his.

But in the end, she didn't have to make that decision, because the trill of her ringing phone cut through the evening quiet, pulling them apart.

She sucked in a quick breath and straightened. Liam shifted away from her, and the loss felt like a blast of cold over her skin.

When she lifted her phone to look at the screen, she was somewhere between laughing and crying. Cody. Of course her twin brother chose that exact moment to call. How many times had he scared men out of her life? It was only fitting his call broke their possible kiss.

She canceled the call.

When a small shudder raced down her spine, Liam's brows pulled together. "Cold?"

"A little."

"Come on. I'll get you home."

The protector...it was a part of him. And now that she knew what had happened to his mother, she knew how deeply ingrained in his personality it really was.

The walk back was a lot quieter than the walk there. Liam carried the basket and blanket in one hand, while holding her hand with the other. It was dark, but fortunately the moon cast a dim glow over the path in front of them.

Romantic. That's what it was. And the silence wasn't uncomfortable. In fact, it felt good. Peaceful. When they reached the condo building, she was almost sad the night was over.

She was just about to round the corner to the front of her apartment when Liam suddenly pulled her back.

She opened her mouth to ask what he was doing, but his hand covered her mouth and his body pressed into hers, giving her no space to move.

Then his mouth was at her ear, his voice a whisper as he said, "There are men inside your apartment. There could be more in the parking lot."

CHAPTER 8

*L*iam fought every fucking instinct demanding he leave the shelter of darkness at the side of the condo. He wanted to attack the assholes—hurt them for breaking into her place and demand to know who they were.

He could hear two distinct heartbeats inside the apartment, another outside, near the door, and like he'd told Nylah, there could be more in the parking lot. Accomplices in cars, ready to shoot.

There was no way he was leaving her alone.

When she trembled, he quietly set down the blanket and basket to smooth his hand down her arm. He lowered his head and whispered, "You're safe with me, Ny. I'm gonna take my hand away from your mouth, but I need you to not make a sound, okay?"

She nodded, and he slowly removed his hand but didn't move back an inch. His entire front pressed her against the wall, covering her. If someone saw them, if someone fired a bullet, he wanted her protected.

Quickly, he slipped his hand into his pocket and pulled out his phone. He sent a text to his team, alerting them to what was happening. They'd be here within minutes. Then he heard more movement from the door of the condo.

"No one's fucking here," a man growled.

"It doesn't make sense. The car's in the lot."

Then a third voice. "Let's go before the others get tired of waiting and leave without us."

Others…there *were* more. Thank fuck he hadn't left her side.

Liam listened as the last two men stepped outside and closed the door. When they started moving across the lot, his legs once again twitched to go. Give chase and capture the fuckers. He needed to know who they were, why they were here. But if he left Nylah and she was attacked, he'd never forgive himself.

Everything in Liam told him that protecting this woman was his main priority.

He and Nylah watched as two cars left the parking lot. The interior light flicked on in the second vehicle, and he could just see the driver. Dark hair and eyes. That was as good as the description got.

But the plate was clearly lit as the car passed. He committed those numbers to memory.

They stayed exactly where they were for another few minutes. Then, slowly, he pushed back from the wall, still watching the lot.

"Are they all gone?" she whispered.

"Yeah."

She wet her lips and went to step away, but he grabbed her arm and tucked her into his side. He wanted her as close as possible. Fortunately, she sank against him. They headed toward her condo.

Callum's car pulled into the parking lot before they reached the door. He climbed out and unholstered his weapon. "You guys okay?"

Liam nodded, tipping his head toward the apartment. Callum understood. His friend moved into the condo, gun raised. Liam couldn't hear anyone in there, but then, they could have left something. He needed confirmation that it was safe before she stepped inside.

A couple minutes later, Callum returned. "Clear. The place is trashed, but other than that, looks safe."

Nylah's lips turned down. "I hope nothing of Paisley's is broken."

Liam touched a hand to the small of her back. "Let's have a look. But be careful not to touch anything. Police will dust for prints."

She nodded, and they stepped inside. Liam's chest constricted at the sight of her couch tipped over, the cupboard doors open, and things pulled out and broken.

It was the bedroom, though, that had the worst of the damage. Every drawer was open. Clothes lay on the floor.

Liam's hands fisted. He wanted to fucking catch those assholes. When they hadn't found anyone here, had they tried to stage it to look like a break-in, to cover the fact the lock was broken?

By the time they went back outside, Logan, Jason, and the police were all pulling up.

"I called them," Callum said under his breath, as two officers climbed out. Liam recognized them from the night of the shooting.

They'd call the FBI too, because he was certain those assholes tonight were connected to the attack on the engagement party.

Gently, he curved an arm around Nylah's waist and once again tugged her into his side. She'd been quiet the entire apartment walk-through.

Logan's gaze ran across the parking lot before falling on Nylah. "You guys okay?"

"Yes." Liam turned to Callum. "I have a plate for you to run."

"Give it to me."

He quickly rattled it off as Callum put it in his phone.

"What happened?" Officer Carlson asked as he came to a stop in front of them, his partner close behind.

"Three men broke into Nylah's condo," Liam said, his voice a hard thread of anger. "A couple more were waiting in cars in the lot."

The officer turned his attention to Nylah. "Do you own this place?"

"No. My friend Paisley does. I'm just staying here while she's away."

Carlson nodded, the guy behind him taking notes as he said, "We'll need her full name."

"Paisley Archer."

"Was anything stolen?"

She shook her head, wrapping her arms around her waist. "No. Not that I can see, but I only moved in a week ago. I don't know everything that was here."

At her slight tremble, Liam grazed his hand down her arm, trying to offer the comfort she needed.

"Where were you two when this happened?" the officer asked.

"Around the corner," Liam said, nodding toward the side of the building.

Carlson looked that way, then back at Liam. "Did you hear them say anything?"

"They were angry that no one was here. Mentioned that the car was in the lot."

"Were *both* your cars in the lot?"

He was clearly on the same thought train as Liam. "Yes."

Nylah's gaze shifted between them. "Wait...you think they were after Liam?"

"It would make sense," Liam said quietly. "Someone failed to take us out at the party. So...target us while we're in places with less security. I didn't think I was being tailed, but I may have missed something."

He'd been so damn distracted by Nylah, he'd barely checked for a tail. Damn, he wanted to kick his own ass.

"Did you get a look at them?" Carlson asked.

"I saw a glimpse of the guy behind the wheel of one car. Dark hair and eyes. That's it. But I did get a license plate." As he recited the plate numbers for a second time, the officer behind Carlson scribbled them down.

"We'll look into it. We'll also ask neighbors if they saw anything." Carlson shifted his attention to Nylah. "Do you have somewhere to stay until the lock's repaired?"

"With me." Liam's words were out before she had a chance to respond.

She shifted her attention to him. "What? No. I can't do that."

"You can and you will."

He regretted his words immediately. They were too hard. Too demanding.

Her brows flickered. "I *will*?"

Fuck. "Nylah, I didn't mean it like that. I just want you safe."

"If they were after you, then I can stay in a motel and be safe."

Every muscle in his body pulled too fucking tightly at the idea. No part of him wanted this woman out of his sight after hearing those assholes in her place tonight.

Callum cleared his throat and talked with the officers, turning the focus away from them.

Liam took a small step closer, lowering his voice. "Ny...please let me protect you. Without knowing exactly why they were here, we can't assume the men *weren't* looking for you."

She nibbled her bottom lip, glancing at her condo and then back at his chest.

He cupped her cheek, tilting her face up to his. Independence was important to her. He could see that. But he needed her safe. "Please."

He wasn't too proud to beg if he had to.

"Just until the lock on the door is fixed," she said quietly.

His chest tightened. It wasn't enough. But by the set look in her eyes, it was all she was offering for now.

"Just until it's fixed," he agreed, the words tasting like acid in his mouth.

* * *

NYLAH STEPPED inside Liam's house with her mouth slightly agape. The ceilings were high—so high she was sure there'd be an echo if she spoke. There were intricate details on the wooden railing of the stairs, which she twitched to run her fingers over. And those cornices...they looked original.

"When was this house built?" she asked quietly, captivated by the wooden floorboards.

"Eighteen eighty-nine, but it was remodeled about ten years before I bought it."

Gorgeous.

The marbleized slate mantel with the cast iron firebox underneath probably kept the house toasty warm in the winter. She moved farther into the house, seeking more of the house's personality. It was modern and new, but with small original details. A cozy breakfast nook. An old iron fire back.

"I didn't picture you living in a house like this," she said quietly, her feet itching to step into that kitchen and touch every fine detail.

"What kind of house *did* you picture me living in?"

His voice was close. When she turned, he was right there. Heat radiated off his skin. "Something with sleek, modern lines and dark, masculine tones."

"I guess looks can be deceiving." He slipped his fingers though hers, causing a shudder to run down her spine. "Come on, I'll show you to the spare room."

She trailed up the stairs after him. Why did this man touching her feel so right? Why did she want to pull him closer? Hold him longer?

With a quiet sigh, she followed him into a large room. A bed with a beautiful mahogany headboard centered the space. An open door to the right led to a connecting bathroom.

"Are you sure you don't mind me staying here?" she asked, turning back to him.

"You can stay for as long as you need."

She swallowed, the familiar panic of losing her freedom crawling around her chest, squeezing at her heart. "Just until the lock's fixed."

His eyes narrowed. The action was subtle, but she caught it. She moved to step past him, but his fingers slid around her wrist, stopping her. That simple touch spiraled up her arms.

He stepped closer. "Even if those men were after me, they obviously know you're *connected* to me."

"Liam, I'm just…concerned. About what this means for us."

"It means I'm keeping you safe. I'm watching out for you."

She gave him a small smile. "People have been keeping me safe and watching out for me my entire life."

"This is different. This time, dangerous people know where you live." He tilted his head. "It would just be for a short amount of time."

Her need for freedom battled with her need for safety. Clearly, he was right. But God, she craved independence. And staying here, with a man who was every bit the protector her brothers were…

"If you want me to stay somewhere else—" she started.

He tugged her into him, her chest hitting his.

"No." His breath brushed over her face, causing the fine hairs on her arms to stand on end. Then his head lowered, his mouth so close, she could almost feel his lips against hers.

"I want," he whispered, "to wake up knowing you're okay. In the few days I've known you, that's become important to me."

She swallowed. "It's important to me that you're safe too." Which was crazy. A week ago, they'd been strangers.

"I can take care of myself."

And she couldn't...wasn't that what he really meant?

As if he heard her thoughts, he shook his head. "Nylah—"

"No one has ever thought I can take care of myself, Liam."

His fingers slid down her cheek. "I'm sorry. I didn't mean you can't protect yourself. I just... Protecting people is what I do, Ny."

"How about we make a deal."

His brows rose, humor dancing in his eyes. "A deal?"

"One week. I'll stay here for one week. If no danger pops up, then I return to the condo."

His head lowered, a light kiss brushing over her cheek. "Is that the best I'm gonna get?"

Her heart beat faster as he kissed her again, this time closer to her mouth. She nodded, not sure she could manage words.

"Then I'll take it." He lifted his head, but only for a second, before he took her mouth with his own.

For a moment, she didn't move, his kiss shocking her into stillness. Then his lips moved across hers, teasing, and the sensation caused her heart to thump and her belly to quiver.

Like her body had a mind of its own, her limbs softened, her hand went to his chest, feeling the heavy beat of his heart beneath her palm. It was like those beats pulsed into her, aligning with her own heart.

Her lips parted, only a fraction, but that was all he needed to slip inside and deepen the kiss.

She groaned at the taste of him. At the feel of his hands on her. It was like her body knew him. Or maybe it had just been waiting...waiting for him to step into her life. Every kiss that had come before was so ordinary. So far from the fire that erupted from this one.

Liam turned them slowly, gently pushing her against the wall.

She curved a leg around his waist, tugging him into her like she was trying to mesh them together.

When he finally came up for air, she wanted to protest. To pull him back and lose herself again.

He lowered his forehead to hers. "How is it possible that I feel like I've known you so much longer than I have?"

"I don't know." She felt it too. The yearning to be with him. The tug of rightness.

But how could he be right, when he was everything she'd been distancing herself from?

CHAPTER 9

"*D*id they all have the same tattoo?" Liam asked from the passenger seat as he zoomed in on the image on his phone screen.

The tattoo was of an angel wielding a dagger.

Callum took a left. "Yep. Exact same place, on their left lower back."

Jesus. He clicked out of the image and leaned his head back. "And someone trailed Blake last night?"

Callum's knuckles whitened on the wheel. "Yeah. He gave chase, too. Blake couldn't do anything because Willow and Mila were in the car and he needed to get them to safety, so he just lost the assholes."

"We need to get to the bottom of this shit before someone gets hurt."

Blake hadn't gotten plate numbers due to the asshole blasting his high beams. But it may not have mattered—the plate number Liam had gotten off the car leaving Nylah's condo turned out to be stolen.

"I know we do," Callum said quietly, barely concealed rage

coating his voice. "I hate these assholes being around when we only just ended the danger surrounding Fiona."

Callum's relationship with the local librarian hadn't been without its challenges. Fiona had almost been killed because she'd been mistaken for someone else. If Callum and his team had been a few seconds later, she wouldn't be here right now.

"She doing okay after everything?" Liam asked.

"The stuff with her family is complicated and messed up, but she's strong and doing well, considering."

Even though Callum's relationship had its challenges, Liam had never seen his friend so happy.

"How are things with Nylah?"

His blood ran hotter at the mere mention of her name. At the memory of their kiss the previous night. "I want her to stay with me, where I know she'll be safe."

"She didn't seem happy about the idea last night."

His jaw tightened. "She's from a family of five brothers, all either military or former military. She came here to get a bit of freedom."

"Ah. And staying with you is the opposite of that."

"It's for her safety, though." Fuck, his chest got damn tight just thinking about her being out there on her own. "They went to her damn condo. They know she's connected to us and where she lives."

"So how long's she staying with you?"

"A week." He had six more days to convince the woman that his house was exactly where she needed to be. If it was up to him, she'd be there a lot longer. But hell, she even seemed hesitant about having a relationship with him, probably for the same reason she didn't want to live in his house.

He hadn't been lying last night. He *was* a protector. It was firmly ingrained in his DNA. But once the threat was gone, he'd be more than happy to respect her boundaries.

"Maybe she doesn't see it as your job to protect her," Callum said quietly.

The woman had said something similar last night.

"It is." The words were out before he could stop them. But they felt right. She felt like *his*, and he didn't give a shit that they hadn't known each other long.

There was a heavy pause before Callum spoke. "I know what happened to your mom affected you. Maybe a bit of this is that you don't want to lose someone else, when you feel you can save them."

His heart thumped. How did his friend see so much? What happened to his mother when he was young had changed him completely, turning him into the person he was today. "You're right. The fear is there, and it's gut wrenching. I don't want to lose her before we've even begun."

Callum pulled up outside a weathered brown house. Neither of them moved to get out. Instead, his friend turned toward him. "My advice, and ignore it if you want—push her too hard and you'll lose her anyway. Yes, let her know you're there for her. That you want to make sure she's okay. So if she needs you, she knows she has you."

Liam scrubbed a hand over his face. Callum was right. Of course he was. Be the nice guy without pushing so hard that she walked away.

One side of Liam's mouth lifted. "You a relationship guru now?"

"Nah, I'm just wise as hell."

Liam laughed as he climbed out of the car. The smile slipped when he reached the front door of the house and knocked.

So far, Steve hadn't been able to get them clearance to question the families of any of the deceased. *Why* he couldn't do so, Liam had no fucking idea. So Callum had found this address on his own. They weren't supposed to be here, but they were past caring. No one had been able to find anything of interest, and if his team didn't act, they were sitting ducks.

A shuffling noise sounded from inside. When a beat passed and no one came to the door, Liam knocked again, this time louder.

There was a huff, then the click of shoes against floorboards before a middle-aged redheaded woman opened the door. "Who are you?"

"Hello, ma'am. I'm Callum Thomas and this is Liam Shore. We're here to ask you a few questions about your husband, Murphy Reynolds."

"I've already spoken to the police, so fuck off."

She tried to close the door, but Liam shoved his foot in front of the wood. It was an effort to keep his voice calm. "We're here under instructions from the FBI." Not true at all, but if lying got them in, they'd tell this woman whatever she needed to hear. "And we're not leaving until you speak to us."

The woman's lips pursed, then she rolled her eyes and stepped back. "Fine, but you'd better be the last."

She moved into the shabby living area, grabbed a bottle of vodka, and added a slug to whatever was already in her mug. "Well, come on. Ask. The sooner you start, the sooner you leave."

Liam closed the door behind them, while Callum stepped forward and asked, "Do you know why your husband was at the events center last week?"

"Yeah. To kill *you* guys. But I only know that because the police told me. That lazy idiot didn't tell me shit."

Liam took note of her breathing and her heart rate, watching for any signs of a lie. She was telling the truth. She didn't know anything.

"Your husband retired from the Army a few years ago. Is that right?" Liam asked.

"Yep. Then he spent all day, every day in that goddamn office of his. I barely saw him." She took a big drink. "Go have a look if it will get you out of here faster. They took his computer but left everything else."

Liam frowned. Everything else?

The woman started moving before they answered. Callum and Liam followed. The place was a mess. There was trash everywhere—particularly bottles of alcohol, some empty, some full.

She stopped at a door but before opening it, turned to face them. "I never went in here because he kept it locked. I didn't really care what that no-good husband of mine was up to. I only saw the room when the police broke the lock. Happy exploring." She turned and walked away.

Liam stepped in first and narrowed his eyes. The room was dark, but his enhanced vision allowed him to see every goddamn thing.

There was an empty desk against the back wall, but that wasn't what had Liam's muscles tightening. Photos were plastered on the wall behind the desk. Photos of his team. Walking down the streets in Cradle Mountain. In the coffee shop. There were also photos of the Marble Protection men in Texas.

What the fuck? How long had these assholes been watching them?

He stepped forward, skimming the newspaper articles that were also pinned to the wall. Articles that had come out when the world first learned about the project. It was like this guy had collected every goddamn story that had ever been written about them. He'd even gone so far as to highlight and underline information.

Unparalleled speed.

Night vision.

Unbelievable strength.

The ultimate soldier.

"Jesus," Callum cursed. "All this time, these people have been watching us."

"Not just watching. Studying." Liam cataloged every detail of the room—until he stopped on a small scrap of paper sticking out from under the desk. He lowered to his haunches and pulled it out. A date, time, and location…all for the night of the engagement party. "And planning to end us."

Callum's eyes narrowed as he read the notes over Liam's shoulder. "Hawk."

Yeah, Liam had seen that too. One sentence at the bottom of the scrap of paper.

Hawk to provide details.

Callum met Liam's gaze. "So, who's Hawk?"

That was a damn good question.

* * *

NYLAH LOOKED around the condo parking lot. Two men were replacing the lock on the apartment door, and while they were at it, she was getting new locks placed on the windows too. Liam's recommendation, of course.

She stepped closer to the guy working on the front door. "Do you know how much longer you'll be?"

"Only a few minutes."

She nodded. A part of her couldn't help but feel uncomfortable about being out in the open. Even though she'd fought with Liam last night about her freedom, a lot of what he'd said was true. They did know where she lived.

God, her head was a mess.

The second she'd agreed to stay the week, she'd felt both relief and trepidation. And also something else. Something related to the fact that every time he touched her, she melted. Every time he looked at her and told her he needed her safe, something inside her chest cracked open for him.

Then that kiss…

Argh, it had been amazing. Her fingers twitched to brush over her lips, like she could still feel him there, against her. And the way his hands had roamed her body... God, she'd wanted to give up everything and just be his.

Why did she fall for men she absolutely should not be falling for?

Her phone rang, pulling her out of her thoughts. She tugged it out to see it was Paisley. Crap. She'd been too chicken to call her best friend earlier, so she'd texted her, which, yes, was the coward's way out. A quick, *Just letting you know someone broke into your condo, so I'm changing the locks to all entry points today.*

With scrunched eyes, she placed the phone to her ear. "Hey, Pais."

"Someone broke into the condo? Were you home? Are you okay? And why the hell did you tell me in a *text*? I need the whole story, Ny, *now*."

Her friend was as worked up as she'd expected her to be. The fear of calling her had been warranted. "I wasn't home...kind of. Liam, one of the Blue Halo guys, was walking me back to the apartment. He realized someone was in the condo, so he tugged me to the side of the building. They didn't see me, and we're ninety percent sure the people who broke in were looking for Liam. And I didn't text you because I was scared."

"*Ninety* percent sure they were after Liam?"

"Well, the guys drove off, so we don't know the actual reason. But they didn't take anything from the condo."

"*Guys? Plural?*" The shriek almost had Nylah pulling the phone from her ear. "And they're still out there?"

She swallowed. "Yeah, they are."

"Jesus Christ, Nylah! First the shooting at the event center, and now this! Both times while you're around those guys. This Liam is clearly a wanted man, and you're...what? Dating him?"

"No. Not dating." Kind of not dating. Their evening out had been as friends. And their kiss...well, that had been a small slip.

"Where are you staying?"

She scrunched her eyes. "With Liam."

"Oh my God…"

Okay. It sounded bad when all the information was put together. "His home has a lot of security. Plus, he's as badass as they come. I'll be fine."

Truth be told, she felt safer there and around him than anywhere else. But that was something she absolutely would not be sharing with Liam.

"So, you're just living with this guy now?"

"I agreed to stay with him for a week, but if nothing happens in that week, I'm returning to the condo—"

"That's it. You've lost your mind. I'm calling Cody."

"Paisley—"

"No. I'm calling *Kayden*. He'll yell some sense into you."

Yeah, he would. As the oldest brother, he was good at pulling rank and bossing people around. "Paisley. You're not calling anyone. I'm fine."

"You are *not* fine. You are either in danger or putting yourself in danger by staying with this guy."

God, everyone in her life was trying to make decisions for her. She just needed space to breathe. "Paisley, I know you mean well, and I know you love me, but I need you to let me handle this."

"But if something happens to you—"

"Nothing's going to happen. I told you, I'm living with Liam for a week, where I'm incredibly safe. And if nothing happens, I move back into the condo."

Paisley's silence stretched for long, heavy seconds, before her voice softened. "Are you sure? I *do* love you, and I need you to be safe."

"Yes, I'm sure. And I love you back."

"Promise you'll *call*, not text, if anything else happens?"

"I promise." If she was brave enough, that was.

The guy working on the door stepped toward her. "We're done, ma'am."

The men who'd been working inside began filtering out of the apartment, while the one who was in charge waited for her by the front door.

"I've got to go, Pais. Talk soon." She made her way back to her door and took the new keys from the man's outstretched hand. "Thank you."

"Would you like me to show you how they work?"

She shook her head. "I think I can figure it out. But thank you."

"You're welcome."

"Will you send me the bill?"

He shook his head. "Already taken care of. Have a good night, ma'am."

She frowned, wanting to ask the guy what he meant, but he was walking away. Plus, she already knew. If someone had taken care of the bill, it was Liam. He'd organized these guys to come change the locks, after all.

A text suddenly came through on her phone.

Liam: Hey. Are you okay? You're not home.

She sucked in a breath. Most women would love the checking in. And yes, it was sweet. But it also reminded her of the texts she used to get from her dad when she was five minutes late to the bar. The messages she'd get from Cody when she went out and he didn't know where she was. Or Kayden when she missed two calls in a row.

Nylah: I'm just heading to yours now.

CHAPTER 10

"**M**an, you look like you've been working in this café your whole life."

Nylah glanced up from where she was lifting chairs on top of tables to smile at Eleanor. It was closing time, and she was on with both El and Vi. Courtney had worked the early shift and left a while ago.

The last week of living with Liam had gone by quickly. It felt like she'd blinked, and the days had just run into one another and disappeared.

She'd only been working at the café since Saturday, but so far it was easy. It was the other stuff that was hard. Living with Liam while resisting his charm. Waking up to him making her coffee. Him looking at her like she was the only woman in the world.

They'd watched a movie on the couch last night, and not only had she fallen asleep on his shoulder but she'd woken this morning in her bed—meaning, the man had carried her there.

She forced herself to push those thoughts down. "Thank you. All that bar experience is transferring to this coffee shop."

"I can see that," Violet said as she cleaned the coffee machine.

"You have a natural ease with customers. Did you always want to work in customer service?"

"No. I actually love history and wanted to study that. And I did start college, but then my dad got sick and, well, family's priority. I don't regret it. We grew really close in that time."

Eleanor stopped mid-swipe of the counter. "Is he okay?"

"He passed away about six months ago. He fought the lymphoma hard, though, so we got a lot longer with him than we thought we would."

Violet pressed a hand to her chest. "I'm so sorry."

"Thank you. My twin brother, Cody, left the special forces a few months before that and started working at the bar to help. He's similar to our dad in personality and just loves the work."

Not only that, but the customers loved him too. He was a people person.

"Well, I think a certain someone is very happy you're here," Eleanor said, rinsing out her cloth in the sink.

Nylah swallowed, knowing exactly who she was talking about. Liam had been in the shop a lot over the last week—ordering coffee, having lunch. She was pretty sure it was his inadvertent way of watching out for her. But nothing had happened over the last week. Which meant tonight, she was officially back at her condo.

"Is tonight your first night back at your place?" Violet asked, reading her thoughts.

Nylah's heart thumped, and she had to remind herself that this was what she wanted. This was her choice. "Yeah, it is. It'll be nice to be back in the condo."

Lie. Big...fat...lie.

But she'd only been working with these women for a few days. She couldn't explain her lifelong struggle with independence and how important it was to her.

"You know Liam will be there, like, all the time though, don't you?" Eleanor said with a grin.

The idea made her heart race. God, her body was betraying her constantly lately. "Maybe." She needed a change of subject, fast. She cleared her throat. "Are either of you guys dating anyone?"

"I'm a lone wolf," Violet said before her gaze shifted to Eleanor. "El, on the other hand, has had...what is it, two dates with this new guy?"

Nylah's brows lifted. "New guy?"

Eleanor's features softened, a dreamy look coming over her face. "Yes. And he's beautiful. Intense, but beautiful."

Sounded a bit like Liam. "Tell me about him."

"You'll actually meet him tonight. He's picking me up. Should be here any minute."

Vi shook her head. "At the picking-up-from-work stage already. Sigh. I need one of those."

"Here he is," Eleanor said, gaze shifting to the window.

Nylah followed her gaze, her eyes immediately widening. "Wait, that's..."

"Officer Carlson to most, but Pierce to me. God, I love dating a man in uniform."

The door opened and the officer walked in. Unlike the last two times she'd seen him, he wasn't wearing his police uniform tonight, instead just jeans and a pale blue shirt. He walked straight over to Eleanor, slipped an arm around her waist, and kissed her.

Nylah swallowed and looked away because, well, that kiss was far too intimate for spectators. And it certainly didn't look like a two-date kiss.

Violet, however, stared at the couple like she was watching a play, her eyes lighting up with excitement. She looked happy for El, which wasn't surprising. Nylah had learned that the two women had moved to Cradle Mountain around the same time and become instant best friends when Violet had responded to a roommate request from Eleanor.

When the couple separated, Eleanor cleared her throat. "Pierce, you know Nylah, right?"

She looked up, sure her cheeks were beet red. "Hi, Officer Carlson."

"Hey, Nylah. Just Pierce here. How've you been since the break-in?"

"Great. Everything's been quiet."

He dipped his head. "That's good to hear."

"You guys are so cute," Violet said under her breath, but everyone heard.

Pierce smiled. "Good to see you too, Vi." When he looked at Eleanor again, his eyes heated. "You ready to go and grab something to eat?"

Okay, not only did they not kiss like a two-date couple but the man didn't look at her like they were new, either. He looked...devoted.

"I just need to clean—"

"Get out of here," Violet said, moving around the counter and just about shooing them out with her hands. "Nylah and I can take care of it, can't we?"

Nylah nodded. "Definitely. You two go."

Eleanor grinned. "If you're sure?"

At their nods, she went into the back, grabbed her stuff, and waved as she left.

Violet sighed. "I'm so glad she's happy. She deserves it." She grinned at Nylah. "Where can *I* find a guy like that?"

Nylah lifted a shoulder.

"Oh, don't pretend you don't know. You have your own man walking in right now."

Nylah looked back at the door, and sure enough, Liam was crossing the dark parking lot, moving toward the shop.

* * *

LIAM PULLED up outside the coffee shop. There was a pit in his gut, one he hadn't been able to shake all day. Because tonight, Nylah was leaving his place and returning to hers. The week had gone too damn quickly, and suddenly he regretted ever agreeing to the deal. Not that he'd had much of a choice.

He wanted her with him because he wanted her safe, but also because of the undeniable attraction that was building between them.

She felt it too. He saw it in the flickers of heat in her eyes. The acceleration of her heart when they touched. But she was fighting it—hard.

With tight muscles, he crossed the lot. The second he was inside the café, his gaze found hers. She was looking right at him, her chest immediately rising, like she was sucking in a deep breath.

He couldn't stop his smile. "Hey, beautiful."

"Hey."

That soft voice flooded his chest, heating his blood.

"Well, well...Liam. *Another* perfect man. Nice to see you tonight."

He smiled at Violet, not sure what she meant by that, but quickly turned back to Nylah at her question.

"What are you doing here?"

He took a small step forward. "I thought I could follow you back to your condo. If you'll let me, that is."

A ghost of a smile played at her lips, but it was Violet who answered. "If she'll *let* you? Who the heck would say no to you?"

Oh, Nylah could definitely say no. But on this occasion, he was hoping she'd take pity on him.

He shrugged. "I don't want to push. But I *will* be disappointed if she says no."

Violet raised her brows and glanced at Nylah. "Are you actually going to send this guy away?"

Nylah wet her lips, drawing his focus to her mouth. Not kissing her again this week...fuck, it had been hard.

"You can follow me home," she finally said. "I just need to—"

"Go," Violet interrupted, crossing the room and pushing her toward the back, much like she had with Eleanor. "I've got this."

Nylah shook her head. "No. We still have—"

"I've got it handled. This gorgeous man wants to make sure you get home safely, and my heart can't take it if you don't let him do that right now."

Nylah laughed before disappearing to the back to grab her bag. When she returned, she gave the other woman a hug before moving over to Liam. He leaned in and pressed a soft kiss to her cheek. Fuck, he lived for those kisses, platonic as they were. For every touch and graze.

As they headed out to the lot, Liam kept a hand on the small of her back, like the very idea of losing contact was inconceivable.

"I'll see you at your condo," he said before he shut her car door.

The entire drive to her place, he wanted to turn them both the hell around. Yes, she had new locks, but they would only do so much if someone was determined to get in.

The lack of trouble over the last week had done nothing to settle his nerves. Sometimes the quiet almost felt worse than noise, because it was the sound of his enemies planning something. And whatever that something was, he and his team were blind to it.

They were still fighting like hell to get access to the computers from the van—or tech from *any* of the deceased—but Steve didn't seem to have the pull on this case that he usually did.

Liam didn't understand it. Very few people outranked the FBI, basically just the US Attorney General and the President, neither of whom would involve themselves in this. So...did Steve not *want* them to have access to the computers? Or could someone else in the FBI be blocking *his* access?

That was something they had to get to the bottom of. In the meantime, nothing was getting done. It felt like no one cared about solving this case other than his team and the men from Marble Protection, which was insane, given the scope of their attack. Some asshole in the FBI even had the balls to suggest the danger was over. That all men involved were dead and the break-in at Nylah's apartment was unrelated.

He ran a frustrated hand through his hair.

When Nylah parked outside her condo, he took the spot beside hers. He inspected the lot as he climbed from his car, almost expecting a gunman to jump out. He moved to the passenger side and grabbed the takeout he'd picked up on the way to The Grind.

Nylah held the bag she'd taken to his house, but he eased it from her fingers and swung it over his shoulder.

Her eyes lit up when she noticed the takeout sack. "What's that?"

"Burgers and fries."

She slipped her hand into his as a sexy-as-fuck groan escaped her mouth. "Tonight, Liam Shore, you are my hero."

"Just tonight?"

She lifted a shoulder. "Depends what you bring me tomorrow."

He'd bring this woman the fucking stars if she asked.

She unlocked the door and stepped inside, then toed off her shoes. "I'll just get changed."

When she disappeared into the bedroom, he placed the food on the coffee table and searched the kitchen for plates. A muscle ticked in his jaw at the memory of what this kitchen had looked like a week ago—the open drawers and cabinets, the broken plates.

He shut the door a bit too firmly, then took the plates to the coffee table. But instead of sitting down, he circled the living room and kitchen, checking the locks on the windows and doors.

He was just returning to the couch when the soft shuffle of Nylah's feet sounded. "Dinner on the couch. I like your style."

She'd changed into leggings that hugged her thighs and an off-the-shoulder top, which made him want to cross the damn room and push the other shoulder down.

He stepped toward her. "How can I convince you to come back to my place with me?"

An emotion he couldn't read flashed over her face. He knew he'd done a lot of pushing over the last week, but fuck, he couldn't stop himself.

"You can't," she said quietly.

He took more steps. Slow, controlled movements, eliminating the distance between them.

"Are you sure?" When he finally reached her, he slid an arm around her waist and lowered his head so that his mouth almost touched her ear. "I can be very persuasive."

A shudder rolled down her spine.

He pressed a light kiss to her exposed shoulder, his lips barely brushing the skin. The gasp of air slipping from her lips was loud. Then he kissed her again, this time on the neck.

"Liam..." His name was so quiet it was barely a whisper.

He dropped three more kisses onto her skin, exploring her. Familiarizing himself. She tilted her head to give him more access. As he trailed his mouth toward her lips, she didn't speak. In fact, he was almost sure she wasn't breathing.

He kissed the corner of her mouth. "I'll worry about you all night."

"You don't need to worry about me."

He wasn't sure this woman understood *what* he needed.

He lifted his head, just a fraction, to see her eyes darken.

Then she quickly lifted to her toes and crashed her lips to his in an explosive kiss.

He grabbed her hips, tugging her against him, and she melted. Her limbs softening. Her fingers sliding to the back of his head and sweeping through his hair.

When her lips parted, he took advantage, slipping his tongue between them and tasting her. She groaned, and that noise sliced through the quiet, tangling itself inside him.

In one swift move, he lifted her into his arms, turned, and pressed her against the wall. The feel of their bodies flush together, the contrast of her soft to his hard, was intoxicating. Made him feel like he was drunk on her.

He gripped her hips, then shifted a hand up slowly, lifting her shirt as he went. Her heart took off in a gallop. He eased his hand a little farther, cupping her breast. Her whimper had his cock hardening. Her nipple pushed into his palm, causing blood to roar between his ears.

She groaned and arched, pressing herself into him. He squeezed her soft mound, swallowing every little moan.

He found her nipple, rolling it between his thumb and forefinger.

Nylah pulled her mouth from his and threw her head back, a cry falling from her lips. He lowered his head and wrapped his lips around her nipple through the thin bra.

She grabbed the back of his head, pulling at the strands of his hair as his tongue swirled over the hard bud.

He was just shifting to her other side when a bang sounded outside.

Immediately, he wrenched his head up. He would have moved back, but she cupped his cheek, tightening her thighs around him.

"It's just the neighbor above me. His engine makes a loud backfiring noise when he turns the car off." She swallowed, collecting herself. "But we should stop before…"

Before they got so lost in each other they couldn't find their way out. She didn't need to finish that sentence for both of them

87

to know.

She tugged her top down, then touched her forehead to his, her words quiet. "I promise you, if something happens, I'll call. I just need some time to be on my own. To date you without us being in each other's space."

"Date me?"

She swallowed, her gaze shifting between his eyes. "Well, it appears I can't stop kissing you, so I think we're past friends."

Oh, they'd skipped friends altogether. "You call at any small noise. Okay? And I'll be here within minutes."

"I know you will."

CHAPTER 11

"One steaming cup of coffee," Nylah said, pushing a mug across the counter.

The man wrapped his fingers around the cup and breathed in the aroma. "Ah, the best part of my day. Thank you, Nylah." He looked down the counter and yelled to Courtney. "You got a good one here, Court."

"Don't I know it," she called back.

Nylah grinned. "You guys are too kind to me."

Violet came up beside her, lowering her voice for Tex, one of their regulars. "Don't tell anyone else, or another business owner will try to poach her away."

Nylah laughed. "Not sure that will be happening, but glad people appreciate me."

She moved down the counter, serving her next customer. Even though she was still fairly new to working at the coffee shop, she'd already started to recognize several of the regulars. It felt good. Familiar.

Her shift was almost over, and even though the morning had been busy, it was now midafternoon, and everything was dying off. It was the opposite of what she was used to. In bars, midafternoon was when things began to pick up.

She'd just slid a piece of pie over the counter when Courtney came up beside her.

"Hey, is your knee okay?"

She swallowed. Was it that obvious? "It's a little agitated today." Probably because she'd been doing daily shifts and not resting it nearly enough.

"You should have said something," Courtney admonished quietly. "You finish up now."

"No, I've still got"—Nylah looked up at the clock—"another half hour of my shift."

"It's not busy. We can manage fine, and I want you to rest."

She nibbled her bottom lip. It wasn't in her personality to leave a shift unfinished, but Courtney was right, it wasn't busy. "Okay. If you're sure?"

"Go." Courtney gave her a light shove.

Nylah laughed and stepped into the back room to grab her phone and push it into her pocket. Then she waved goodbye to everyone and stepped outside. It was crazy to her that she could be so new to a town, yet it felt like home already. Maybe it was a small-town thing. Misty Peak was also a small town, and everyone who visited always commented it was homey, too.

Instead of walking to her car, she pivoted toward the street, heading to Blue Halo. As she walked, she pulled out her phone, smiling as she pressed a name in her contacts.

Liam answered on the second ring. "Well, this is a nice surprise...you calling me for a change."

"Hey! I call you."

"When?"

She nibbled her bottom lip, a grin on her face. "I can't think of a time right now, but I definitely do."

"Nylah, you're a texter through and through."

Dammit. He was right. But she'd been craving the sound of

his voice. "Fine. I'm calling now because Courtney let me off half an hour early, so I thought I'd pop into your office and say hello."

She scrunched her eyes. It sounded silly when she said it out loud. So silly, she almost took her words back and turned around to go to her car. The man was working. He wouldn't have time to see her.

"Are you okay walking by yourself?"

The corners of her lips twitched. "You're just down the road, Liam. I'm fine. But if you don't have time—"

"Honey...if I didn't have time, I'd make it. Come. Let me show you my office."

Her fingers relaxed around the cell, and she walked a bit faster.

A guy crossing to her side of the street caught her attention. His gaze flashed to hers, only for a second, then flicked back to the street.

There was nothing that made him stand out—average height, dark hair, jeans and a button-up shirt—yet something about his brief glance at Nylah made her belly turn.

"Nylah?"

Liam's voice pulled her out of her thoughts just as the guy turned down an alley up ahead, to the right.

Crap. She'd completely missed everything Liam said. "Sorry, Liam. I missed that."

"That's all right." His words were slow, and there was a short pause. "Is everything okay?"

"Yeah, I just saw..." She shook her head. "Nothing."

"It wasn't nothing. Nylah, what was it?"

She swallowed. "I saw a guy, and I thought I recognized him from somewhere. He made me feel uneasy. But he was probably just a customer from the coffee shop. Maybe he was rude or something..." She hadn't had many of those, but there were a few everywhere.

"Turn around."

She frowned. "What?"

"The guy affected you, I can hear it in your voice. Turn around, go back to The Grind."

She started to step past the alley. "Liam—"

Suddenly, she was grabbed around the middle, pulled off the street, and shoved against a brick wall. The phone fell from her fingers, and her breath cut off with a gasp.

The man threw a fist toward her face. She ducked just in time. He howled when his knuckles hit the wall.

When he lifted his untucked shirt and went for a concealed gun, Nylah quickly swung a knee into his balls. He managed to pull the weapon before doubling over in pain, and she kicked at his hand—hard—the gun flying down the alley.

Then Nylah threw a punch of her own, landing it right in his left eye.

The guy cursed, grabbing his eye even as she lunged for the gun. Lifting it, she aimed at the asshole's chest. "Sorry, buddy, but my brothers taught me how to protect myself. *And* how to shoot." The second he straightened, she realized where she'd seen him. She gasped. "You were one of the guys who broke into my condo!"

The man scowled, rage transforming his features. "Fuck you."

If he was scared of getting shot, he didn't show it. "*I'm* holding the gun, and I *will* shoot. Tell me why you broke into my place."

She wasn't sure how accurate that statement was. She liked to *think* she would shoot, but she'd only ever shot at targets before. Could she shoot a living, breathing person?

The guy took a step forward, as if he heard her thoughts and was calling her bluff. "How about you tell me why you're sleeping with one of *them*."

Her brows slashed together. "Them?"

He took another step.

Her fingers tightened around the grip. "I mean it, I'll—"

"Nylah?"

Her gaze swung toward the sound of Eleanor's voice at the mouth of the alley. The moment of distraction gave the asshole time to lunge forward and grab her wrist before twisting.

She cried out and the gun fired, causing a bullet to ricochet off the wall. He ripped the weapon from her grasp. Police sirens sounded down the street, along with Eleanor's footsteps as she ran toward them.

The guy took off in the opposite direction.

* * *

LIAM DIDN'T USE his car as he ran down the street. He didn't need to. He was fast enough on his own. And on foot, it would be easier to check every damn alley he passed.

He'd called the police to notify them about an attack in this general area. They wouldn't arrive quickly enough.

The second he'd heard the tussle over the phone—fuck, it nearly killed him.

He pushed his body to run faster, every muscle taut and his fingers fisted so damn tight, it was like they were made of granite.

Why the hell hadn't she turned around the second she'd seen the guy? She'd been uneasy. That, in combination with her being alone...unarmed...*unprotected*...

After what felt like too damn long, he saw her near the exit of an alley. She stood with Eleanor, who had a phone pressed to her ear and an arm wrapped around Nylah's waist.

He wrenched her out of the other woman's grasp, grabbing her upper arms, holding her tightly, inspecting her body for injuries. "Are you okay?" The words came out low and dangerous.

She nodded, and he tugged her into his chest. The second she was against him, some of his panic receded and he could finally breathe again.

His hand twitched to grab the Glock from his holster, though he couldn't identify an immediate threat. He pulled away from her but kept his hands on her shoulder, studying her face, searching. "Tell me what happened."

"He grabbed me and shoved me against the wall. I fought back and got his gun. When I saw Eleanor, he lunged and took the weapon back before disappearing. I'm sorry he got away."

Darkness threatened to ravage him—the asshole had tried to hurt her, *shoot* her—but he pushed it down. "Which way did he go?"

Nylah turned her head. "He ran that way, and I think he turned…"

"Left," Eleanor finished, pointing down the road. "Pierce should be here any minute. He said he already received a call."

Liam nodded. "I called nine-one-one."

Footsteps sounded behind him, and he turned to see Tyler.

"The asshole ran down there and took a left," Liam said quietly.

Nylah straightened. "He was wearing a checkered blue button-up and jeans. Dark hair. About six feet."

Tyler nodded and ran toward the end of the alley.

A police car pulled up at the end of the alley, and Officer Carlson climbed out, his partner beside him.

"What happened?" he asked the second he was close.

Nylah took a breath before rehashing the story. Hearing it out loud a second time wasn't any easier for Liam. It almost felt worse. Yes, she'd fought him off. But it could have been so different. And what if Eleanor hadn't seen them and shouted when she had? Would the asshole have attacked her?

His chest grew too fucking tight, the idea shredding him. She'd been in real danger, and he'd been down the street, unable to help.

She'd just finished describing what the man looked like when Carlson nodded and closed his notepad. "While I understand that you weren't sure who he was at first, next time you have a bad feeling about someone, best to turn around and leave the heroics to those of us who are trained."

The muscles in her back tensed beneath his fingers, and she straightened. "I wasn't trying to be *heroic*, but I can't just cower away from every single person who gives me a bad feeling."

"You can, Nylah," Liam bit out, probably too harshly. "You just turn around and walk back to safety. It's called being smart. What you did today *wasn't* smart."

Nylah's head jerked back as if she'd been slapped. Her breath stopped, her lips parting. She took a step away from him before clearing her throat. "Thank you both for your thoughts. I'll try to be *smarter* next time."

Fuck, he wasn't wording this well, but Jesus, he could barely think straight right now.

Carlson looked between them. "Okay, well…you can go when you're ready. We'll keep you informed if we find any leads on this guy."

Her back was still stiff as she turned to Eleanor and gave her a quick hug. Then, without a word, she walked away.

He hurried forward and touched her arm. "Come to the office and I'll drive you—"

"No. I can walk."

A muscle in his cheek ticked, but he followed her, staying close the entire way to The Grind. No words were spoken, the air thick with anger and frustration, and the silence was so damn loud it was deafening,

He waited until they'd reached her car to touch her arm again. "Nylah—"

"I'm going home. I'll make sure I lock my doors and windows when I get there."

When she tried to pull the car door open, he reached around

her and grabbed it, stopping its movement. "You think I'm wrong about what I said."

She whirled around. "I think you don't give me enough credit and you could have worded what you said better."

"You're right. I'm a jerk. But I said what I did because I was worried. Because I want you to trust your gut and stay safe."

"You *are* a jerk. Because you think I can't protect myself even though that shit's been drilled into me since my first steps. You're a jerk because you're doing *exactly* what my brothers do to me, even though you know I came here to get away from all that. And yes, you're a jerk because you think I make stupid decisions."

"I said what you did wasn't smart."

"It's the same thing, Liam." She blew out a frustrated breath, shaking her head as her eyes slid away, refusing to stay on his. "I need to go. Please step away from my car."

A new wave of frustration slammed into his gut. There was no part of him that wanted her to leave like this. "Let me come with you."

"No." The response was instant and firm. "I need some space tonight. Like I said, I'll keep everything locked up and my phone close in case I need to call the police."

The police. Not *him*.

The only thing that stopped him from losing his damn mind was that she'd said *tonight*. Would she allow him to see her tomorrow? Would she let him stay close?

When he didn't move, an almost anguished expression crossed her face. Then she finally turned sad eyes on him. "Please."

That one word from her lips...it sounded pained, and that pain carved itself into his chest.

It took too much fucking strength to step back. To give her space. Instantly, he hated the distance.

She ran a hand through her hair. "We'll talk later."

She met his gaze for one more fleeting moment before sliding into her car.

He turned, wanting to punch his fist through something. To kick his own ass for reacting while feeling so emotional. He'd handled this all wrong.

CHAPTER 12

*L*iam stared at the man's profile for what had to be the fiftieth fucking time. Hell, he'd read the files of every man from the shooting so many times he could probably recite their life stories. There were clues here he wasn't seeing. Something that would give him a bit of insight into their reason behind the attack.

He knew that, but...did the reason even matter when they'd made their intentions—to end Liam and his team—crystal clear?

He leaned back in his chair with a frustrated sigh. The *real* problem was that he couldn't focus. All he could goddamn think about was Nylah. The anger in her eyes this afternoon. The hurt as she'd tugged herself away from him like she couldn't bear his touch.

Fuck. It killed him.

And if the day wasn't already bad enough, they'd gotten word that there'd been an attack on Bodie in Marble Falls. He'd left the office late the previous night, and two men had just started shooting the second he was out the door. A bullet had caught him in the gut, but he'd been able to drop, roll, and return fire. The shooters were dead. Both were former military with angel and dagger tattoos.

Footsteps sounded in the hall, pulling him out of his spiraling thoughts. He knew who it was—the only other man still in the Blue Halo offices tonight.

Flynn stopped in the doorway and leaned a shoulder against the frame. "Hey. You still here because you're worried about leaving? Thinking about Bodie in Texas?"

"I'm here because I feel chained to this place until we catch these assholes."

Flynn's eyes narrowed. "I know. We have to watch our backs and those of our women."

"Carina okay?"

"Yeah, Logan and Grace are at Mom's house with Carina." A hint of a smile touched his lips. "They're cooking up a storm, apparently."

"How *is* your mom?"

A flicker of emotion passed over Flynn's face. It was heavy. "Not great. Her memory gets worse every day. I'm looking into care facilities for her. Carina's wonderful with her, though."

Liam's chest clenched for his friend. His mother had dementia. They were close, and Carina was both his partner and his mother's nurse. Before Carina, Flynn's mother was his entire family. "I'm sorry, man."

"Thanks. I hate doing it, but it's time. I'm lucky to have Carina for support. She's been my rock."

Yeah, the woman was strong. She'd come to town and worked her way into Flynn's life, then his heart. Danger had followed her, however, and the first few months of her life here in Cradle Mountain hadn't been easy.

Flynn frowned. "How's Nylah after the run-in with that asshole this afternoon?"

His hands fisted on the desk. Asshole felt like too kind a word for the guy who'd tried to hurt her. "Physically, she's okay. He shoved her against the wall, but she fought him off."

Flynn nodded, something akin to admiration in his eyes. "Yeah, I heard that. She's tough and obviously has some training behind her. I'm glad she knows how to handle herself." Then he cocked his head. "How is she emotionally, though?"

That was a good damn question. "Aside from being angry at me, I don't know. She asked for *space*." The word tasted like acid in his mouth.

There was a tick of silence before Flynn asked, "What did you do?"

Of course, his friend knew it was his damn fault. "I got angry at her for not turning around when she got a bad feeling about the asshole. Told her it wasn't smart, then I agreed with Carlson when he told her to leave the heroics to us."

Flynn's cringe confirmed just how fucking stupid he was for saying what he did.

"I mean, you weren't entirely wrong. She should have turned around. We'd prefer her safe rather than sorry. But if you said it in those words—"

"Well, I definitely said she wasn't smart. I was angry and frustrated and scared, and I just kept thinking that if something had happened, and I'd been just down the street, unable to do anything..." His chest tangled into a fucking knot.

"I can understand that," Flynn said quietly. "If Carina were in the same situation, I'd react on emotion too. But that's because it's our gut instinct to keep others safe first, especially the women in our lives. We forget that we can't always make those decisions for them."

"I know that." Shit, of course he knew that.

Flynn crossed his arms over his chest. "Is this thing between you long term?"

"Yes." The word was out before he even thought about it. "We may be new, but I know with every fiber of my being that she's mine."

Flynn nodded slowly. "Then be what she needs, not what you think you *should* be. She's here to get away from overprotective brothers, right?"

"Yeah."

"So don't push. Otherwise..."

"I'll lose her." Wasn't it the same damn advice Callum had given him?

"Something to think about." Flynn's gaze shifted to the laptop screen, then back to Liam. "Want me to stay for a while? Look over those bios with you?"

"Nah. I'm done for the night. You enjoy the evening and whatever they're cooking."

His friend's mouth stretched into a smile. "It's enchilada night. It's gonna be a good one. You're welcome to join."

He shook his head. He wasn't in a socializing mood. "I'll probably head home and have a quiet evening."

Flynn nodded and tapped the doorframe before moving out of the office.

Liam listened as Flynn's steps receded down the hallway and out the door. He looked back at the screen, so distracted he couldn't read a single word. With a curse, he clicked out, shut down the laptop, and lifted his phone.

He wrote and rewrote the message at least a dozen times before settling on two words.

Liam: I'm sorry.

* * *

NYLAH'S GAZE ran over her laptop screen as she read about the classes offered at Columbia for their Bachelor of History degree.

She'd been feeling down all afternoon, thoughts of Liam, of

the way they'd left each other, pressing against her chest, suffocating her.

She'd needed a distraction, and somehow that search had led her here. Columbia wasn't cheap, but online courses were more doable. She had some money saved up, but she'd definitely have to keep working to pay her way while studying, which would be hard. But she'd done hard things before. She was good at doing hard things.

She nibbled her bottom lip. How many times had she thought about resuming her studies to obtain a degree? So many. But as her dad's health had deteriorated, so too had his workload. It meant she'd not only been working the floor at the bar, she'd also handled accounting and scheduling...basically the entire running of the business. That had left her both physically and mentally drained.

Things were different now. She had the time and the energy to study. And Columbia, like most major universities, offered a number of online degrees in the humanities, including a Bachelor's in history. She'd already completed her first semester there, which was filled with prerequisite courses. She could use the credits she'd already earned toward an online degree.

Before she could stop herself, she found the address for the undergraduate administrator and curriculum coordinator and sent him a detailed email, asking about whether it was possible to resume her degree, this time online.

As soon as she hit send, her heart rate beat out a faster rhythm. She leaned back on the couch, excitement skittering through her veins.

There. She'd done it. Finally. It was only a first step, but wasn't that the hardest part?

She lifted her phone from the coffee table and texted Paisley.

Nylah: I did something.

Paisley: Was it dirty? Did it involve whipped cream and countertops?

Nylah: No. Not dirty. No whipped cream, although now I'm hungry.

Paisley: Tell me.

Nylah: I emailed the coordinator of Columbia's undergraduate program about resuming my studies.

Immediately the phone rang.

"Hey."

"About damn time, Ny!" Paisley squealed.

Her smile grew. "I know. It feels so right."

She rose and moved to the kitchen, taking her cell with her as she grabbed leftover Chinese takeout from the fridge.

"What instigated this? Was it Liam?"

Nylah's gut clenched at the mention of his name. She'd talked to her friend regularly over the last week, and she was pretty sure Paisley was slowly coming around to the man, even though she'd never met him.

"No. I mean, not really. You know it's something I've been wanting to do for a while, but… Maybe I did it because I needed something to distract me after my *fight* with Liam today." She hadn't been meaning to add the last part. The words just rolled out.

"You had a fight with Liam? About what?"

Nylah popped the noodles into the microwave, debating over what to tell her friend. She usually told Paisley everything, but the woman had been one step away from calling Cody the last time something had happened.

"He's just really protective, and it was feeling like a bit much." She cringed. It wasn't technically a lie, but at the same time, it kind of was.

"Oh, Ny. I'm sorry. But honestly, I'm not surprised you're falling for a replica of your brothers and dad."

Nylah's brows pulled together. "Ew."

"You know what I mean. Your brothers are good guys, and so was your dad. It's only natural that your standards are high."

Liam *was* a good guy, but he was also…a lot. She opened a drawer and grabbed a fork.

"So are you guys not talking now or what?" Paisley asked.

Of course her phone chose that moment to ding with a message. She lowered it from her ear, and her chest constricted at the text.

Liam: I'm sorry.

She put the cell back to her ear. "He just texted he's sorry."

"See, now *that's* the sign of a good man. When they can recognize the error in their ways and apologize."

Her brows flickered. "I thought you were against me hanging out with him because he's dangerous."

"Ny, you've been telling me every damn day about how sweet he is. I could only hold out on him for so long. Plus, you've reassured me that you're safe now, and I'm choosing to believe you."

Guilt swamped her at not telling Paisley what had happened.

"I really like him," she said quietly, tracing the edge of the kitchen counter with her fingers. And he *had* been right, she probably should have turned around and walked back to the coffee shop. God, that man could have shot her. But it wasn't just what he'd said that she was annoyed about. It was the way he'd said it.

Another text came through.

Liam: I should have softened my words. I reacted because all I could think about was, what if something had happened to you?

It was true. Things could have ended far differently.

"What was that sigh?" Paisley asked over the phone. "Did he write something else? Tell me now!"

She pressed the cell to her ear again. "He's just saying sweet things about wanting me to be safe."

"Okay, fine. I'm officially on Team Liam. I need to get my butt back to Cradle Mountain so I can meet him. You're gonna forgive him, right?"

"How can I not?"

As the noodles heated, she went into the bedroom to grab a sweater. She'd just opened the dresser drawer when the sound of shattering glass came from the living room.

She screamed and dropped the phone, immediately stepping toward the door to look into the other room.

A man dressed in black, wearing a balaclava, was smashing the glass from the edges of the frame.

Her heart slammed against her ribs, fear choking her. Quickly, she closed her bedroom door and clicked the lock before picking up her phone.

"Nylah? What was that?"

"Someone just broke the window in the living room," she gasped, barely able to get words out.

"*What?*"

Shit, the bedroom window. She stepped toward it, her focus on escaping, when a brick flew through the glass, breaking that window as well.

She screamed again, stumbling back. "Oh God! Someone's coming through the bedroom window too!"

"Get in the bathroom and lock the door!" Paisley said quickly. "There are no windows in there so no glass to break. Then call for help!"

Nylah turned and ran, then slammed the bathroom door and locked it. "I'm hanging up so I can call the police!"

The phone rang once before a woman's flat voice came over the line. "Nine-one-one, what's your emergency?"

"There are people breaking into my house. I need help!" Something slammed against the bathroom door. She stumbled back, her hip hitting the counter.

"What's your address, ma'am?"

She quickly rattled off the address.

The tapping of keys sounded over the line. "Police are on their way."

Nylah didn't wait to hear what the woman said next, instead hanging up and calling Liam.

The phone had rung once when she smelled it—smoke. It was subtle, but there.

Her heart stopped. They'd set a fire. They were smoking her out!

Shit, shit, shit.

She put the phone on speaker as she grabbed a towel, rushed to the sink and soaked it in water. She shoved it into the crack at the bottom of the bathroom door.

Liam answered. "Nylah—"

"People broke into the condo. I'm hiding in the bathroom, but I think they just set a fire in the bedroom!"

CHAPTER 13

$\mathcal{L}$iam swung the car around the corner and pressed his foot to the gas, pushing the GT to move a hell of a lot faster than was legal.

Rage pumped though his veins, hard and fast. It consumed him. Tormented him to the point the world around him went black.

Someone had broken into Nylah's home. Had set a fucking *fire*. Were they still there? Were they trying to force her out? Or had they just assumed the fire would kill her?

He took a left, tires squealing against the asphalt.

He wanted to kill the fuckers. Tear them apart with his bare hands. The need was so alive inside him, he could barely breathe.

When he finally reached her condo, he slammed his foot on the brake. Flames were visible through the broken glass in her bedroom window.

His chest constricted.

They didn't look big, but they didn't need to be for the smoke to get into the bathroom. For the flames to block her exit.

He shot out of the car and was halfway across the lot when a gunshot cracked. He cursed as he dropped, rolling and pulling his gun from the holster. He aimed in the direction the shot had come from and fired.

He got three rounds off, all hitting car windows, before a vehicle took off. Liam fired one more time, hitting a tire, before rising and running toward the condo.

He entered the open front door, pistol at the ready. Apart from the broken window in the living room, the space looked untouched.

When he stepped into the bedroom, his chest seized.

The fire burned all around the bathroom door.

The assholes who'd set it were going to die. Every last one of them.

Sirens sounded in the distance, but he couldn't wait. There wasn't enough time.

"Nylah," Liam yelled, making sure his voice rose above the flames. "Open the door with a towel over the knob, honey, then move to the side. I'm going to run through the flames."

There was a short pause, then the click of the lock sounded before the door opened. She met his gaze for one heartbeat before shifting out of view and calling, "Be careful."

Most wouldn't have heard her words...he did.

Yellow flames danced in front of him, but he only focused on the bathroom. He ran through the fire, heat singeing his arm hair, smoke thick against his face.

Nylah sat on the floor of the shower, a dripping-wet towel over her mouth and nose.

The air rushed out of Liam at the sight of her unharmed. He crossed the small bathroom and knelt beside her. "Are you okay?"

She nodded.

Thank God! He lifted her against his chest. "Cover yourself with the towel."

She wrapped the towel over both of their heads, leaving a gap at his eyes so he could see. He wanted to argue that she use it to cover more of herself but knew she wanted to protect him as much as he wanted to protect her.

He took off, running through the flames and the condo at inhuman speed. He didn't stop until he reached the parking lot.

Finally, he breathed his first full breath since her call. Gently, he sat her on the ground, then lowered to his haunches in front of her.

A fire truck pulled into the lot, firefighters piling out and into the condo, but he kept his entire focus on Nylah. He cupped her cheek and studied her eyes. "Did you breathe in much smoke?"

She shook her head. "The towel under the door stopped most of it."

So damn smart. He touched his forehead to hers and closed his eyes. "I'm so glad you're okay."

"Excuse me, do you know if anyone else is inside?"

Liam lifted his head to look at the firefighter, but it was Nylah who answered. "No, it was just me."

More cars pulled into the condo parking lot. Police. An ambulance. And his team.

He didn't leave Nylah's side.

It was while she was in the back of the ambulance, being checked over, that Officer Carlson, Callum, and Flynn all approached.

The officer shifted his gaze between them with a frown. "Liam. Nylah. It's been a busy day for you. Can you both take me through what happened tonight?"

Liam stepped in front of her. "She needs to be checked out first." Her health came first.

But Nylah touched his arm. "No, Liam. It's okay." She turned her attention to the officer. "I was in the bedroom when I heard the glass shatter in the living room. A man wearing a ski mask was trying to get inside. Then another guy broke the bedroom window. I went into the bathroom and locked the door to call police and Liam. That's when I smelled the smoke."

Carlson nodded. "Height of intruders? Build?"

Nylah swallowed. "I'm not sure. The guy trying to get into the living room was maybe a bit over six feet? It was hard to tell with him on the other side of the window. Build was medium—not large, but not small. I didn't see the second guy at all. Just the brick that flew through the bedroom window."

"You didn't see eye color, I assume?" Carlson asked.

She shook her head.

The officer turned to Liam. "Was anyone here when you arrived?"

"Someone shot at me from a car, but I didn't see them. I shot out a tire, though, so they might have stopped to change it or even to ditch the vehicle."

Carlson's eyes narrowed. "You get the plates?"

"Yeah, although I'm sure they'll be stolen again." He gave him the plate number and knew his team would do their own search on them as well.

Carlson turned to Nylah. "I'm glad you're okay. Have you got somewhere to stay tonight?"

"She can stay with me."

The words were out before he could stop them, but unlike the last time, Nylah didn't seem annoyed. Instead, as the paramedic checked her heart rate and blood pressure, she reached for his hand, sliding her fingers through his. "I'll stay with Liam."

A band he hadn't even noticed constricting his chest suddenly loosened. Because for once, she was letting him take care of her. And that was fucking everything.

* * *

NYLAH TIGHTENED her fingers around Liam's, the soft hum of his car engine the only noise in the otherwise quiet night.

Callum had said he'd drive her car to Liam's house. His partner, Fiona, had also offered to send over some clothes, because most of Nylah's now smelled like smoke.

Everyone had been wonderful tonight, especially Liam. He hadn't stopped touching her since the fire.

"Are you sure you're okay?" he asked quietly.

She nodded slowly. "I'm okay. Just in shock. I felt trapped in there. I've never been a claustrophobic person, but in that moment, I was. If you hadn't gotten to the condo when you did—"

"I did, though. I will *always* get to you in time."

Her heart thumped at the way he said those words, like they were a vow he'd tear down the world to keep.

She looked down and traced a vein on the back of his hand. "Tonight made it clear I'm being targeted. I just...I wish I knew why. Because of my connection to you?"

"Possibly. We don't know why any of these assholes are doing what they're doing." His voice sounded tortured and frustrated.

"Eventually they're going to slip up, and we're going to get to the bottom of this." She believed that with everything she was. She had to.

The muscles in Liam's forearms flexed. Then he seemed to take a moment to consider his next words before he spoke them. "Until then, I'd like you to stay with me, Nylah. Let me put a guy in the coffee shop while you work. Let me protect you."

More anguish in his tone. He expected her to say no. He expected her to fight him. And had he asked that same question just a few hours ago, she would have. She would have fought him down to her last breath. But she'd had time to think. Time to remember the story about his mother, and the guilt he still suffered over not saving her.

And now? Well...now she knew it wasn't just him and his team who were in danger.

"Okay."

The air whooshed from his chest. He stopped the car outside

his garage and pressed the button on the remote for the door. When they got out of the car, he asked her to wait as he checked the house.

As she waited for him, every minute felt so much longer. She almost expected to hear gunfire. To have to run and hide. That's what her life had become lately.

When he returned alone, relief flooded her chest. He took her hand again and led her up the stairs.

Without any words spoken, he led her to the bathroom connected to his bedroom. The smell of smoke from their clothes was so thick, it turned her belly. A constant reminder of what had happened tonight.

"I'll shower in the other bathroom," he said quietly. He looked like he was about to go, then stopped before stepping close and grazing her cheek. "You're still too pale."

"I think everything's just finally catching up with me. I'm also wondering how I'm going to tell Paisley about her apartment."

Her phone was off right now. She didn't have the strength to turn it back on. She knew her friend would be worried, and the chances she wouldn't call one of Nylah's brothers were getting slimmer and slimmer...but she was exhausted. A bone-deep kind of exhaustion. She'd texted her friend that she was okay, but that she'd talk to her tomorrow. It was the best she could manage tonight.

"All she'll care about is that you're safe."

Of course. She wouldn't care about the actual damage to her apartment. She'd never been a materialistic person. She'd freak out over what had almost happened to Nylah.

Her gaze moved down to Liam's lips. And suddenly, she wanted to kiss him. She wanted to become completely lost in him and let the man take her away from this place of danger and uncertainty.

She stepped toward him...but he stepped back, running a hand through his hair.

"I'll be back in a bit." He didn't look at her as he said it. Then he was gone.

With a confused frown, she slowly closed the bathroom door.

What had just happened? Was he angry at her? At the way she'd left him this afternoon? Because she'd been fighting him for so long and so hard on this protection stuff?

She stepped under the stream of water, letting the heat warm her chilled skin. Then she scrubbed her flesh until her skin was red, wanting every bit of smoke to wash down the drain. For this night to just be over. A memory that she could push to the back of her mind.

By the time she came out of the bathroom, a set of clothes sat on the bed. Fiona's clothes, no doubt.

So many thoughts rushed through her mind as she changed. Worry about Paisley's reaction to the condo fire. Confusion about Liam walking away from her so abruptly. And fear about what tonight meant. That for some reason, people were gunning for her. Wanting to kill her.

Her breathing sped up, but at the knock on the door, she forced herself to calm. "Come in."

The door opened and Liam stepped in, that same anguished expression on his face. "Do the pajamas fit? Fiona and Callum dropped them off."

"They do."

He nodded, his gaze never quite meeting hers. "I need to make up the other room. I took the sheets off when you left and never made the bed again. It'll take a few minutes, so you can just sleep in here, and I'll sleep in there. Do you need anything? Food? Drink?"

The thought of eating made her stomach turn. She shook her head.

He ran another hand through his hair. "I'll see you in the morning."

When he started to walk away, she stepped forward. "Liam."

He stopped but didn't face her. So she crossed the distance and touched his arm. "Hey. Are you okay?"

Slowly, he turned. "I hate what happened to you tonight. And I hate that it's because of me."

"We don't know that."

His jaw tightened, and he didn't have to say he didn't agree for her to know. "I'm gonna have nightmares about it."

She took a small step closer, her hand going to his cheek. "Then stay with me, and I'll pull you out of those nightmares." That wasn't an entirely selfless offer. She wanted him as close as possible. "Plus, when you're with me, I feel safe."

There was a small darkening of his eyes. His hands went to her hips and his head lowered slowly. When his lips touched hers, the kiss was soft, gentle, the touch seeping into her skin, heating her from the inside out.

The kiss wasn't sexual. It was comfort. Relief. Intimacy.

When their mouths parted, he pressed his temple to hers. "I don't deserve you." His breath brushed her face.

"You do," she whispered. It felt more like the other way around to her.

He lifted his head and tucked some hair behind her ear. "Are you sure you want me with you tonight?"

"No. I *need* you with me."

His gaze shifted between her eyes, then he nodded. "Okay. I'm going to check the house one last time, then I'll be back."

She nodded, pressing another kiss to his lips before watching him leave the room. She left a single small lamp on and climbed into bed, loving that the sheets smelled of him. A deep, earthy pine scent. It surrounded her. Calmed her.

She closed her eyes, sleep already trying to take her. But she forced herself to stay awake. To wait for him.

Footsteps finally sounded on the stairs. When the light switched off and the bed dipped behind her, she started to turn, but a strong warm arm slipped around her waist, tugging her back into a warm, hard chest.

Liam. Her new safety net. Her new sanctuary. She hadn't expected to find it in this town. Definitely hadn't been looking. And man, had she fought it. But now she was finally understanding that it really wasn't her choice.

CHAPTER 14

*L*iam climbed out of the car and scanned back and forth across the road before glancing up at the house. They finally had a lead. The getaway car from the fire hadn't been stolen. It linked back to this address, to a man named Wald Paston.

The car wasn't in the driveway, but then, he'd have to be a special kind of stupid to keep it out in the open after the windows and tire had been shot out.

Was the asshole home? Or had he made a run for it?

The door on the driver's side opened and closed, then Callum walked around to stand beside him.

His friend clutched his shoulder. "I've got a good feeling about this."

"Glad to hear it. Because we need information. We need to know if this asshole targeted Nylah because of us, and why."

Callum nodded. "I know, my friend. We'll get what we need."

At the sound of cars approaching, they both looked up to see Officer Carlson behind the wheel of a police car, another officer in the passenger seat. Another squad car followed behind, holding two more officers.

The second he stopped, Carlson was out of the vehicle and charging toward them, anger carved into his features. "What the hell are you two doing here? This is a police matter."

"We got permission from the FBI," Callum said, voice firm.

For the first time since the shooting at the engagement party, Steve had proven himself useful, getting them the time of this arrest and granting them authorization to be here.

"Feel free to check," Liam said, crossing his arms. "You should have received notification."

"Allen. Check the system."

The guy behind Carlson pulled out his phone. A beat passed before the man nodded.

Carlson's jaw clenched. He took a step forward, voice lowering. "We're making a clean arrest. You wait outside the house. You *say* nothing. You *do* nothing."

Both Liam and Callum remained silent. They weren't agreeing to shit.

Carlson huffed and turned to his guys. "Let's go. Allen—with me. You two cover the front of the house and garage in case he makes a run for it."

Liam and Callum followed Carlson but stopped halfway across the yard.

Carlson knocked. "Police! Open up."

There was the light shuffle of movement on the other side of the door. Some hushed words. Then the door opened, and a short middle-aged woman stood there, teeth stained, eyes angry. "What do you want? I haven't done anything wrong."

"We're here for a Mr. Wald Paston. Is he home?"

"No."

Something sounded from inside the house. Footsteps.

"Ma'am, this is an official police matter. If you don't cooperate, you're obstructing justice, which is a federal offense."

"He's *not* here."

Liam's eyes narrowed at the distinct sound of the back door opening.

"Round back." The words were barely out of his mouth before he was running, his feet pounding the pavement as he raced around the house, Callum not far behind him.

"Liam, stop!"

"Hey! You can't go back there."

Liam ignored Carlson's and the woman's shouts, his gaze catching on the thin middle-aged man as he jumped up on the back fence. Liam sped up his pace and grabbed the guy before he was able to throw a leg over. He threw the asshole to the grass then climbed on top of him.

"Why did you break into Nylah Walker's home last night?"

The guy growled. "Get the fuck off me!"

Police ran around the side of the house, but Liam ignored them, putting his entire focus on the scumbag beneath him. "Answer the goddamn question. *Now.*"

"I don't know any Nylah Walker! I was home all night, playing poker."

Liam backed off slightly. The asshole sounded like he was telling the truth.

He looked up at Callum, who was also frowning. But his attention wasn't on the man. Liam followed his friend's gaze to the small accessory dwelling in the backyard.

"Liam, get the hell off him," Carlson yelled, stopping beside them and grabbing Liam's arm.

"Who lives in that unit?" Liam asked, once more ignoring Carlson.

"Fuck. *You.*"

Liam lowered his voice to a deadly growl. "Unless you want to be tried for attempted murder, answer the goddamn question."

"Liam, get off before I arrest you," Carlson warned.

The guy under him was silent for a beat, uncertainty flickering in his gaze. Liam could almost hear him turning his options over in his head. "My brother Miles. He lives there. But *he* wouldn't have done that either."

Liam's muscles strained. "Did he take your car last night?"

Now the guy frowned. "Yes. He still has it. Hasn't returned it."

Fuck. "Where is he?"

The guy tried to throw him off. Liam didn't give him an inch. "I don't know! I don't watch his every goddamn move!"

Liam climbed off, and another officer immediately grabbed Wald, pulling him up while reading him his rights.

Carlson stepped closer to Liam. "You're on thin damn ice, Shore. Another stunt like that and I cuff you."

"It wasn't him." Liam's gaze went to the other house. "It was his brother."

Carlson looked to the tiny house. "Are you sure?"

"Yes." The man hadn't been lying. Liam would have heard it.

"Shit." Carlson turned to Wald, who was now on his feet and in cuffs. "Can we enter the unit?"

Anger flickered through the guy's eyes, and Liam was sure he'd say no. But then he nodded. "If it's gonna get me out of these fucking cuffs."

Liam moved over to the small building and tried the handle. When it wouldn't turn easily, he forced it open, breaking the lock. Then he stepped inside. With the curtains closed, the place was dark. There was a bed, a small kitchenette, and a desk with a computer, all in the same room, as well as a small bathroom through the only other door.

Liam crossed the space to the computer, his gaze stopping on the photos above the desk. The setup was identical to the last office they'd inspected in Murphy Reynolds's home. Photos of his team and the Marble Protection guys plastered all over the wall. But there was also another photo.

Every muscle in his body tightened at the sight of Nylah. She was walking down a street close to The Grind, totally unaware someone was watching her. And beside the photo was a scribbled note.

Without asking for permission, Callum slipped into the chair and started tapping at the keys of the laptop.

Carlson stepped forward. "What the hell do you think you're doing, Thomas?"

"Seeing if I can find out what the fuck is going on."

"Get up!"

When Callum ignored him and just kept typing, Carlson started toward him, but Liam cut him off.

"Like we said, we have permission from the FBI to be here."

"I don't care. Get out of my way before I arrest you both."

Liam opened his mouth to tell the guy to fuck off, when Callum cursed. He spun back toward the computer and skimmed the chain of emails on the screen. The last communication included Nylah's address, along with a date and time.

Last night—the night of the fire.

Callum scrolled up, and Liam focused on one of the messages in the thread.

She needs to be eliminated. She could compromise the mission.

The fuck?

Callum was scrolling up again when the screen suddenly went black.

"Shit!" he growled, madly typing.

"What's going on?" Carlson asked.

"Someone's remotely attacking the operating system." He kept typing, but after only a few seconds, he leaned back, fists slamming against the desk. "It's gone. Someone with a lot of fucking hacking skills destroyed all the data."

* * *

"YOU ARE ONE TOUGH WOMAN, coming into work today," Violet said quietly as they stood behind the counter.

Nylah smiled as she frothed the milk for a cappuccino. Her shift at The Grind was almost over. It hadn't been too crazy today, which was lucky, because a busier day would've meant instead of having one bodyguard in the coffee shop, Liam would have assigned two.

Her gaze shifted to Tyler, who sat at a table with an open laptop, before shifting back to Violet. "Keeping busy feels good. It takes my mind off things."

Liam had tried to convince her to take the day off and hang out at his office, but firstly, she needed money so she could resume her studies at Columbia. And secondly, what would she do at his office but go stir-crazy?

Eleanor brushed past them, nudging Violet. "Haven't you heard? She's made of steel."

Nylah laughed. "I'm definitely not. Maybe you guys just make this job so fun, there's nowhere I'd rather be."

"Yeah, we really do," Violet said with a smirk.

Eleanor touched her shoulder. "We're just glad you're okay."

"Thank you." Nylah smiled as she turned to her next customer.

Shifts here always passed quickly, busy or otherwise. And she hadn't been lying—being here *did* take her mind off things. Hell, she could almost forget that someone had tried to kill her last night...almost.

She swallowed, her mind never far from the call she still needed to make.

She'd briefly turned her phone on last night to text Paisley and tell her she was okay and would call her today. This morning, she'd woken to half a dozen missed calls. She'd tried Paisley before coming to work, but her friend hadn't answered.

Was it terrible that a part of Nylah was relieved? She'd left a message asking her to call back, letting her know when she was off work, and she was sure when she checked her phone after her shift, she'd have another half a dozen missed calls from her friend.

And then there were her brothers... Argh, she couldn't even think about them without her belly doing a nervous turn. They were gonna kill her for not telling them everything sooner. Then they were either going to drag her ass home or come here, guns blazing—literally.

When she next looked at the clock, it was her finishing time.

After saying goodbye to everyone, she headed to the door. Tyler was already there and holding it open for her.

She smiled at him as she passed. "Thank you."

"You're welcome."

Once they were in the car and driving, she shot a quick look his way. "Thank you for sitting in the coffee shop all day. I hope it wasn't too boring."

Boring was good though, right? Boring meant no surprise attacks or gunshots or fires.

"With all the coffee you guys brought me? Definitely not boring. Plus, I got plenty of work done on my laptop." He flicked a quick glance at her before looking back at the road again. "You doing okay today?"

"I am, actually. Your team makes me feel safe. And I love my job. Apart from waiting on my friend to return my call so I can give her the unfortunate news about her apartment, I could almost forget about what happened. Are *you* doing okay? I know there was an attempt on Blake, and one of the guys in Marble Falls."

A muscle ticked in his jaw. "Yeah. And we anticipate more attacks. But every attack gives us a chance to snag one of them." Tyler looked at her again. "I'm sorry about your friend's place."

She lifted a shoulder. "Paisley will only care about me. She'll be so worried. Maybe even push me to go home, claiming my brothers can protect me better."

"Now that we know you're a target, this is the safest place for you. With a protective detail."

"I know." But try telling that to her special forces' brothers.

When they reached Liam's house, Tyler led her inside. He nodded toward the second story. "He's up there—I can hear him on the phone. Want me to wait?"

She shook her head. "I'm okay. You go get Emerson from Blake and Willow's place. Thank you again for today."

He dipped his head. "You got it."

The door closed behind him, and she clicked the lock.

Her gaze shifted to the stairs. For a moment, she was tempted to go up there. She took a step, then stopped. If it was a work call, she didn't want to disturb him. Her attention drifted to the office, to the left of the hall. Slowly, she moved into the room. There were papers all over his desk. Some with scribbled writing. Some with photos. She was about to leave the room when one of the photos caught her eye. It was a tattoo of an angel wielding a dagger.

But it wasn't just any dagger. She recognized this one, for some reason.

She frowned, tracing the image with her finger. "Where have I seen you?" Maybe in a book? Or online?

"Talking to yourself?"

She gasped as two hands grabbed her hips. Large, warm hands. Familiar. She relaxed back into Liam, feeling the heat of his front press against her back. "I didn't hear you come in."

"I'm quiet." His lips touched her neck in a soft kiss.

The photo tugged at her again. "I've seen this dagger before, but I don't know where. I haven't seen it in person. I think in a book, maybe? It might be well known."

"Really? We thought it was just a generic dagger. All the men who attacked us at the engagement party had this tattoo on the sides of their lower backs."

"So it means something."

"Yeah, it's clearly their mark." Anger coated his words. But then he kissed her neck again, this time higher. "Everything okay at the coffee shop?"

She had to turn his words over in her head a couple of times to make sense of them. His hands on her waist, his mouth on her neck, it was all too distracting. "Mm-hmm. How's the search for the men responsible for the fire?"

There was a small tensing of his muscles. It was so subtle, she almost missed it. "We found where he lives. He wasn't there, but we have his identity and his photo. An APB is out for his arrest. He won't evade us for long."

She let that information sink in, unease spidering through her belly. He was still out there. Possibly many more just like him too.

Liam nipped her ear, and her breath caught. Slowly, his mouth moved to her cheek. The kisses were feather soft, barely a graze.

She hummed, but when she couldn't take it any longer, she turned her head. Immediately, he caught her mouth with his own. Her heart hammered, her breath catching in her throat at the heat of the kiss. The way his tongue slipped into her mouth, dueling with hers.

She turned her body, wanting more of him. Wanting everything he could give.

His hands went to her ass, and he lifted her to the desk. She gasped at the feel of him between her thighs. At the way he teased her mouth.

She felt lost. Lost in a sea of Liam. And there was no part of her that wanted to be found. She wanted the world around her to blacken and burn so that it was just them. She slid her fingers around his neck and her legs curved around his waist, tugging him closer, eliminating any space between them.

When the hand on her waist shifted up, cupping her breast,

she moaned, the sensation burning through every limb like wildfire.

She was just getting lost in him when her cell rang from her pocket.

A part of her knew she should answer it. It was probably Paisley. But the other part, the bigger part, knew that there was no stepping away from the man in this moment. Not with the way he made her feel.

He started to withdraw, but she tightened her grip on him, pulling him closer and whispering, "Don't leave me."

CHAPTER 15

*N*ylah's words rippled through Liam like little bursts of fire. Blood roared between his ears, so loud that the world deafened around him.

He lifted his mouth from hers, drowning in her ice-blue eyes. The way she looked at him like he was all she saw... He grazed a thumb over her bottom lip. "Never."

Her eyes darkened, her heated breath brushing his flesh. She swallowed and skirted her fingers through his hair. Slowly, he lowered his head once more, taking her mouth and kissing her. Losing himself in her.

He lowered his hands to her ass and lifted her into him, loving the way she curled around his body, so perfect it was as if she'd been made for his arms.

Her hands smoothed over his chest and shoulders as if she was memorizing every inch of him, as he was memorizing her. Because he wanted this woman carved into his thoughts so deep that even when she wasn't with him, she still was.

He turned and carried her out of the library, up the stairs, never separating their lips. Never letting an inch of space between them.

When he reached his room, he gently laid her on the bed, following her down, his body covering hers. Then he kissed her cheek. Her neck. When he reached her chest, he tugged the hem of her shirt up, pressing a kiss to her stomach. His mouth trailed up, the material of her shirt leading. When he reached her bra, he wrapped his mouth around her nipple through the delicate material and sucked.

Nylah whimpered beneath him, her back arching.

He continued to tug and graze her hard peak as he pulled her shirt over her head. Then his hands slipped behind her and undid the clasp of her bra. When her breasts sprang free, his gut tightened. The pink buds teased him. Tormented.

So fucking gorgeous. All of her.

Holding her breasts while taking a bare nipple in his mouth, he swirled the peak with his tongue.

Nylah writhed and groaned, her feminine whispers slipping through the room, rolling over his flesh. Her hands tugged at the strands of his hair as if she was desperate.

He ran his tongue over her bud, flicking it back and forth, becoming lost in every little sound she made. When he switched his mouth to her other breast, he was rewarded by more of those sounds. By the tumble of quick breaths sawing through her chest.

Without lifting his head, he reached down, undid the button of her jeans with one hand, and slipped his fingers inside her panties. Her moans stopped on a gasp. Her body grew so still, he was certain she wasn't breathing.

Then he swiped a finger across her clit.

Her cry whipped through the air, loud and high-pitched. He did it again. Her body trembled beneath him. Her thighs widened, giving him room, asking for more.

"Liam…" Her voice was barely a whisper now as she pulled his mouth back to hers. "I need to feel you."

She grabbed at his shirt and yanked it over his head. When

she grasped the button of his jeans, he moaned. Then she slid inside and wrapped her fingers around him.

Every limb in his body stilled, the veins in his neck pulsing. Because this woman touching him...fuck, it almost pushed him right over the edge.

With her other hand, she cupped the back of his neck, brought his mouth back to her, and kissed him, her tongue slipping to tangle with his own.

As her fingers moved over his cock, his muscles bunched, the little tendrils of sanity that remained starting to disintegrate.

When he couldn't take it anymore, he grabbed her wrist and pinned it to the mattress, then he was kissing her with a new force. Devouring her like the kiss could chase away every demon. Every shadow that had ever haunted him.

"Tell me you need this as much as I do," he growled, the words barely distinguishable.

"More...I need it more!"

Not a fucking chance that was true. Still, he let her words beat into his chest, touch every corner and crevice that existed. Then he rolled to the side and removed his jeans and briefs before tugging her jeans and panties down her thighs, his eyes never leaving hers.

He was chained to her. Two souls meant to find each other.

He leaned over to his side table and grabbed a condom out of the drawer. She watched as he sheathed himself, her breaths shortening with every passing second, her heart drumming faster.

Slowly, he returned to her. She widened her thighs, welcoming him between them. His body burned to push inside the woman. Take her fast and hard.

But he forced himself to be patient. To trace the lines of her face with his gaze. Memorize every curve. "Last chance, Ny. If you give yourself to me, I won't be able to let you go."

Hell, he wasn't sure he could anyway.

"Promise," she whispered. "Promise you'll never let me go."

Something hot and primal coiled in his gut. "I promise. You're mine, and I'm yours."

Her eyes darkened, her fingers tightening on his shoulder. Then he sank deep, and her walls clenched around him. They never broke eye contact, and that connection...God it was like nothing else.

He lowered his head and kissed her. In that kiss, he found every damn thing he'd been searching for. Salvation. Refuge. Love.

He lifted his hips and thrust harder. She groaned into his mouth, the sound twisting his gut. He did it again and again, every thrust bringing them back together. Bringing him home.

* * *

NYLAH WAS ON FIRE, the flames so hot she was sure she'd turn to ash right in front of him. The combination of his thrusts, the way he filled her so completely, and his mouth on hers was an overload of sensations. It made her lose her thoughts. Her worry. Everything. Everything but him.

She hugged her thighs tighter around his waist, lifting up on every thrust, wanting more of him. Wanting him as close and deep and connected to her as possible.

With desperate fingers, she dug her nails into the thick cords of muscle on his shoulders, as if she could somehow anchor herself to him. Because right now, in this moment, the man was shaking her foundation.

He reached down and cupped her breast, his thumb finding the hard peak of her nipple and grazing back and forth, then pinching. She whimpered, her head flinging back, eyes scrunching shut.

God, she was close. But she didn't want this to end. Every

time he briefly pulled out, another piece of her went with him. And she wanted him to have *all* of her.

She touched her head to his chest, trying to bring herself back to earth.

"I can't..." She wasn't sure what she was trying to say. Maybe that she couldn't let this moment end? Maybe that she couldn't understand the depth of this connection?

"I know, baby."

Suddenly, he rolled them so she was on top. Instinctively, her body started to move. Fast, deep thrusts, each better than the last.

As she rocked, his hand clasped the back of her neck, guiding her mouth to his. But this kiss was different. Slower and in complete contrast to her movement. It was as if he was trying to memorize her mouth. Her taste.

In the midst of the kiss, the thrusts, his hand slipped between them, and he ran his thumb over her clit.

She whimpered, but the sound was swallowed by his mouth.

He did it again and again. "Liam..." She couldn't finish her sentence.

"Fall for me, baby," he whispered, as if he were in her head and could read her thoughts.

One more swipe of her clit, one more thrust, and she fell, shattering around him. Allowing herself to break into hundreds of tiny pieces, all belonging to him.

She was still rocking and crying out when he tensed beneath her. Then he growled, his body shuddering as he flipped them over again so she was on her back, and he thrust into her three more times, hard and fast, before his body stilled deep inside her on a long moan.

For the next few moments, there was mostly silence, the roar of blood in her ears the only thing she could hear. The beat of his heart under her palm all she could feel.

She let the silence weave its way into her chest, becoming a comfort. Then she cupped the back of his neck, holding his face so close to hers that she could feel the heat radiating off his skin.

"That was…" God, how did she even explain it? "Something else."

Those words didn't do it justice, but then, none would.

He lowered his head and pressed one long kiss to her lips before whispering against her mouth, "That was us, Ny."

Her heart thudded. It was. It was what happened when they both freed the part of themselves that called to the other. When they accepted that there was no fighting this thing between them.

When he slipped out of her, she wanted to cry and pull him back. But he lowered beside her and tugged her body close. The second he was holding her, the thudding of her heart slowed. The breaths in her chest came easier.

Safety. Sanctuary. Peace. It was everything she hadn't realized she'd been searching for when she'd come to Cradle Mountain. And she'd found it…with Liam.

CHAPTER 16

*N*ylah leaned forward, studying the dagger on the screen.

Gotcha.

She'd been at the library so long, researching the damn dagger, that it was getting dark outside, and the place was almost empty…but she'd finally found it. Thank God.

Only two nights ago, there had been a near attack on Flynn. He'd been leaving the hospital with Carina and his mother when he spotted two men trying to conceal themselves behind a truck. The lights of the parking lot glinted off a concealed weapon as one man shifted, and Flynn had turned straight around and shuffled Carina and his mother back inside the hospital. When he checked the lot seconds later, the assholes were gone.

But if he hadn't been paying attention, there was every chance not only Flynn but Carina and his mother could have been seriously hurt.

Things were getting desperate.

"The athame," she whispered, her gaze tracing over the wicked-looking steel edge. The black leather handle.

Why would they all have that particular type of dagger

tattooed on themselves, though? Traditionally, it wasn't used to hurt anyone. Unless it was just a symbol of their group? Or the meaning behind it?

"Hey. You doing okay?"

Nylah looked up to see Fiona beside the table. God, she'd been so caught up in research, she hadn't even heard the woman come over. Callum sat opposite Nylah, a book open in front of him. Even though he looked like he'd been reading, she'd caught him covertly glancing around the room regularly. And his muscles were always tense, like he was ready to go.

Nylah kept her voice low so other people couldn't hear. "All the men who attacked at the event center had a tattoo of an angel wielding a dagger." From her peripheral vision, she saw Callum's head lift. "I knew I'd seen the dagger before, but I couldn't remember where."

Fiona frowned. "But you remember now?"

"I saw it in a class I took a few years ago. It's a ceremonial dagger called an athame. You see the union of fire and air carved into the handle?" She pointed to the screen and Fiona nodded. "That's apparently to safeguard people from evil. The dagger represents protection."

Fiona seemed to consider that for a moment. "So they each have the tattoo to protect themselves from evil?"

"Maybe," Callum said as he rose and came to stand behind her. "Or maybe they think *they are* the protectors, protecting *others* from evil. Maybe they're scared that we have more power than we should."

It made sense that this entire thing was a misguided endeavor to get rid of men with impossible speed and strength who, if they chose, could become formidable enemies.

Fiona's sigh was loud.

Callum slipped an arm around her waist. "It's definitely something to consider."

"Did you ever find the brother?" she asked Callum. "Miles?"

There was a small narrowing of his eyes, and Nylah knew the answer before he gave it. "The car was found deserted a few miles out of town, but police are searching for him. He won't be able to evade arrest for long."

She swallowed, praying he was right.

"All right. I think it's time for us all to get home," Callum said.

Nylah nodded and closed her laptop.

She was just getting her bag packed when the text came through on her phone.

Cody: You free to talk?

Oh, man. She'd been avoiding her brothers like the plague, especially Cody. There was no way she could talk to him and not reveal everything that had been happening. And she would reveal it all.

She'd finally told Paisley what had occurred at her apartment, and that had been hard enough. But telling her brothers?

Nylah: I'm just heading home now. I'll call you when I get there.

Just the thought made her break out in hives.

She swung her bag over her shoulder as they stepped out the back door of the library. They were halfway across the back parking lot when Fiona cursed.

"Crap, I forgot my phone. Be back in a second."

She'd just disappeared into the library when Callum's arm suddenly swung out in front of Nylah, halting her from moving forward.

Her gaze shot up. "What's—"

Before she could finish her sentence or understand what was happening, Callum shoved her to the ground and a popping noise sounded from across the lot. It took her muddy brain a second too long to realize it was a gunshot—an almost silent one.

Her breath caught in her throat, her belly clenching as Callum rolled them behind a car, all while bullets continued to fly.

They were being shot at in a public library parking lot! Were people so desperate for her to die that they'd willingly kill her out in the open now?

Callum pulled out his phone, pressed something, and put it to his ear. "I need backup behind the library!"

He was still talking when the library door opened, and Fiona stepped out. Nylah gasped, and Callum shouted, "Get inside and lock the door!"

Fiona's eyes widened but she immediately followed Callum's instructions, disappearing back inside the building.

He pulled out a gun and turned to her, his expression hard and deadly, looking nothing like the man she was used to. "Stay down," he growled under his breath.

When he poked his head and pistol around the car, her heart leapt into her throat.

He fired, his shots loud, piercing the air like little explosions.

She heard bullets hitting metal, glass shattering...then there was a different sound.

The dull thud of a body hitting the ground.

When a police officer appeared from the alley running alongside the library, gun raised, Nylah's belly cramped.

He started shooting, yelling for people to put their weapons down, when a bullet caught his shoulder and he dropped.

Oh, Jesus! Nylah's feet twitched to move. To help the man, but there were still bullets peppering the air.

When the officer didn't get up, nausea welled in her throat.

She pulled out her phone and called for an ambulance. As she did, Callum swiftly stood behind the car and leaned over the roof. He fired three more times, every bullet accompanied by the thump of a body hitting the ground.

Then...silence.

Nylah's breath stopped. Was that it? Was it over? Could she go to the officer on the ground?

Callum straightened, his pistol still raised as he surveyed the area. "They're dead," he finally said in a low voice.

The air whooshed out of her, and she sprinted toward the officer, dropping down beside him.

"Hey. You're going to be okay." She'd just pressed her hands to his wound when suddenly, a man flew out of the alley right beside her—shooting Callum in the chest before she could blink.

Nylah gasped, shock and devastation bursting through her gut.

When the gun shifted to her, every emotion blanked as her brothers' lessons kicked in.

Her foot flew into the man's knee. She followed it up with a punch to his groin.

The second he was hunched over, she took off. But not toward the library. There was no part of her that wanted to risk Callum or the officer being shot a second time.

She needed to get this man away from everyone.

She flew down the alley and opened a door to the right, a side entrance to a business. She barely got the door open and dove inside before a bullet hit the wall beside her. Slamming the door closed and locking it, she turned to see she was in an office of some kind. Desks were scattered around the space and two people were still there, packing their bags, both with surprised looks on their faces as they glanced up.

A bang sounded on the door, even as she started to weave around the desks.

"Hide!" she yelled, before running into the foyer and out the front door. She was on the street for seconds when a bullet hit the ground at her feet.

Nylah screamed, almost falling through the first door she came across that had someone inside, before slamming it closed behind her.

A shoe store. She was in a shoe store, with half a dozen tall aisles in front of her.

The woman behind the counter stared, wide-eyed. "Are you—"

A bullet cracked the glass in the door. Nylah screamed and dropped, noticing the woman at the counter do the same.

She army-crawled down the first aisle. As she reached the end, the door to the shop flew open. She crawled faster.

"Come out!" the man yelled, voice deep and angry. "You're gonna die anyway, may as well get this over and done with quickly."

Like hell she would. She'd fight to her last breath.

She moved quietly, always away from him, staying low. When his steps went silent, her heart pounded.

At the mouth of an aisle, she paused and he appeared at the other end. She rolled around the endcap, another bullet hitting the floor beside her. His steps were loud as he ran toward her. The second he was close, she kicked out, getting him in the knee again—hard. He fell down, and her next strike was a kick to the face.

He cried out, the gun dropping as his hands went to his bloodied nose.

She lunged for the weapon, but the man lunged onto her back before she could grab it, spinning her around to face him.

Immediately, she brought up a knee, nailing the bastard between the legs.

He growled, but before she could try to get away, his fingers wrapped around her throat, cutting off her air.

Panic swamped her, her chest screaming for breaths as her vision grayed.

No! She couldn't let him win.

Attack the soft points.

Cody's frequent advice sounded in her mind. She reached out to press her thumbs to his eyes, but the darkness was coming too fast.

She'd barely touched his face when the darkness won, and her hands dropped.

* * *

LIAM SLAMMED his foot on the brake in the library parking lot. He'd been at home when he'd gotten the notification, and it had taken him too damn long to get here. Paramedics were just pulling up, and Fiona was hunched over a bleeding, unconscious Callum. Liam's chest pulled so tight that it was impossible to get air, the panic like a living, breathing thing inside him.

The paramedics rushed past him, each approaching an injured person.

He forced himself to focus. The paramedics were with Callum. There was nothing he could do for him at the moment.

As an EMT shuffled around Fiona, she rose, her tear-filled eyes finding his.

"What happened?" he asked.

Fiona shook her head. "I'm sorry! I don't know...and I don't know where she is! She wasn't here when I came out."

Shit!

He ran desperate fingers through his hair as police sirens wailed behind him. Then Officer Carlson was there. He'd just exited his vehicle when the radio on his uniform squawked.

"We have reports of a shooter in the Pandemonium Shoe Store on Wight Street."

Liam was moving before the radio call finished, ignoring Carlson's shouts behind him. He pushed his body to move faster than it had ever moved before, feet pounding pavement, arms pumping.

He hit the street, his gaze whipping to the shoe store. To the shattered glass and open door.

He lunged inside. A woman peeked out from behind a desk, phone to her ear.

Sounds from the far aisle pulled him to the right. The thumping of two hearts. The rustle and thud of fighting. He grabbed his Glock from the holster and ran toward the sounds.

When he saw the man on top of Nylah, rage shot through his body like a whip.

He fired, hitting the asshole in the shoulder.

The guy dropped, but before his weight could fall onto Nylah, Liam was already there, grabbing and wrenching him away.

Nylah started coughing and grabbing at her throat. The air whooshed out of Liam. She was okay. Thank God!

Liam dropped on top of the attacker, shoving the man to the floor while pressing the muzzle of the Glock to his head.

He recognized the guy immediately. Miles fucking Paston, the man they'd been hunting.

"Why is she a target?" Liam shouted, every word so loud, they echoed off the walls of the small shop.

"Get off me!" he growled.

Not a fucking chance.

Liam lowered his head, his voice now deadly quiet. "If you don't talk, you're useless to me and I end you. And trust me, it's taking everything in me not to do that already. One more chance."

The air moving in and out of the guy's chest was loud, a mix of anger and pain swirling through his dark eyes. "I don't know. The orders were emailed by Hawk. I was told she was a threat to our objective and needed to be eliminated."

A threat to their objective? How, exactly? He needed more. "That's all you know?"

"Yes."

At the ring of truth in his voice, Liam's chest constricted, frustration brimming that this asshole couldn't be more useful.

He pressed the pistol harder to his skull. "What do *you* get out of this?"

The guy laughed. "Not money, if that's what you're thinking."

"Then what?" Liam growled.

"I get to save our nation from *you* and your fucking friends. People may not understand the threat you pose, but those of us who are trained in combat do. We understand *exactly* how dangerous it is for you assholes to remain alive when you have a background in special forces and so much fucking power."

The door to the shop opened, and three police officers rushed in at the same time as Nylah's head dropped to the floor with a thud.

Fuck!

The officers took Miles while Liam went to Nylah. "Nylah? Baby? Talk to me!"

She couldn't. She was unconscious.

Real fear sliced through his limbs, making the world darken around him. The only thing that kept him calm was the thudding of her heart.

Paramedics entered the store, but before they reached him, he lowered his head to her ear and whispered, "I'm here, baby. You're safe."

CHAPTER 17

*I*f there was ever a moment Liam wanted to go back in time and murder a man, it was now, as his gaze ran over the bruises on Nylah's neck. As he watched her still form in the hospital bed, machines attached to her.

The only thing keeping him calm was the slow rise and fall of her chest.

Noises sounded all around him. Doctors and nurses talking to patients. Footsteps in the halls. There was the beeping of machines and the thrum of wheels rolling over vinyl flooring.

It all barely registered when every ounce of his attention remained on Nylah.

It was late. She'd woken in the ambulance, then fallen asleep again a while ago, after doctors had given her some drugs. She'd been so pale, and every time she swallowed, pain marred her features. Doctors wanted to keep an eye on her for the night, which meant he was here for the night as well. Because there was no chance in hell he was leaving her.

Regret tugged at his chest. That he hadn't killed the man who'd strangled her when he'd had a chance. The same man who'd shot Callum. If he hadn't needed information, he would have.

He lifted her hand and pressed a kiss to the back of it, letting his lips linger and the warmth in her skin seep into him.

He loved this woman. He didn't care that it hadn't been that long, or that the intensity of the danger around them had sped up their relationship. Every part of him knew exactly how he felt for Nylah.

His phone vibrated, but he already knew what the text was going to say. He could hear his team talking outside in the hall.

He pulled it out anyway.

Tyler: Just got back from questioning Paston. Want us to come in there, or are you coming out here?

He hated leaving her, but this room was too small for his team, and he had to find out if letting the asshole live had been worth it.

Lowering her hand, he rose and pressed one final kiss to her forehead before moving to the hall. He didn't close the door. In fact, he positioned himself in the doorway, as close to her as he could get while still being in the hall. He wasn't letting her out of his damn sight for a second.

Tyler, Logan, Jason, and Flynn walked toward him.

"How's Callum?" Liam asked, looking at Flynn and Jason. Both guys had gone with Callum to watch his back as he'd been taken away in an ambulance.

"Good," Flynn said. "Bullet missed his vital organs and he's healing. He's awake and already arguing to get out of bed."

The corners of Liam's mouth twitched. Wasn't a surprise. Liam would be doing the same thing if situations were reversed.

Jason shook his head. "He's not impressed by the resounding *no* he keeps getting, even if the doctors are impressed by how fast he's healing."

Thank God. If his team had lost one of their own...no. He couldn't even think about that. It would annihilate him.

Jason tipped his head toward the room Nylah was in. "How's she doing?"

"She's okay. She was awake for a bit but fell asleep after the doctor gave her something for the pain and to help her rest. They didn't find any damage to her vocal cords, just a lot of bruising."

Relief relaxed his friends' faces. They were probably thinking the same thing he was. It could have been worse. So much fucking worse.

Liam looked at Tyler and Logan, his voice a thin line as he asked, "You get anything from Miles?"

Hell, even saying the fucker's name out loud made the rage resurface in his chest.

"He couldn't tell us anything about Hawk's identity," Tyler said in a low voice.

Liam cursed under his breath.

"Hawk apparently doesn't reveal his identity to *anyone*," Logan said quietly. "He sends people in his organization job details via email and with little warning. So Miles, and presumably the other guys who attacked at the library, only got about ten minutes' notice that Nylah was there and they were ordered to kill her."

Liam frowned. "How the fuck did he even know she *was* there?"

No one had an answer for him.

"There's something else...we actually have a second guy in police custody."

"Who?" he asked.

"There was an attack on Aidan as well, and he got the guy. We interviewed him too, and he knew just as little as Miles."

Fuck! "Is Aidan okay?"

"Yeah. He was taking the trash out at home when someone shot at him. He saw them in time to dodge the bullet. He grabbed the guy before he could make a run for it."

There were far too many of these attacks. There'd been more in Marble Falls too. "Does he have a military background?"

Tyler nodded. "Yep."

There was a heavy quiet among his team.

"We need to infiltrate this group," Flynn said, breaking the silence. "Get on the inside."

"How do we do that when everyone knows who we are and what we look like?" Jason asked.

"Callum and Wyatt will find a way." They always did. Liam looked over to Nylah, watching the slow rise and fall of her chest. "When they do, our priority needs to be figuring out who this Hawk is. Cut off the head of the snake."

"He must have a lot of resources at his disposal," Logan said. "Somehow, he's recruited all these assholes to kill us all the while remaining anonymous."

"And he keeps learning our locations," Tyler added.

That was one of the most concerning parts. "So maybe he's closer than we think," Liam said.

He felt the air thicken around him. That idea didn't sit well with any of them. That someone in this town could be working against them. Maybe even someone they trusted.

Flynn shoved his hands into his pockets. "When Callum woke up, he said Nylah identified the dagger in the tattoos as being a symbol for protection."

So the idiots thought they were protecting people. But that was a fucking lie, and everyone knew it. They were murderers, looking for a weak excuse to wield a gun.

* * *

WHEN A RAY of light hit the back of Nylah's eyelids, she grimaced and turned her face away to escape the glare.

Beeping sounded, slow and steady. It was loud in her ears, pinging into her skull. She wrinkled her nose at the antiseptic smell, and when she swallowed, the action brought an ache to her throat.

Suddenly, memories trickled back to her. Of the attack outside the library. The shooter who'd run after her. Strangled her.

The beeping picked up speed, growing louder in her ears, almost angry.

"Hey. You're safe. I'm here."

At the sound of his voice, her eyes fluttered open and landed straight on Liam, who sat beside the bed. His hair was ruffled and there were circles under his eyes. He looked tired...and the man *never* looked tired.

"Are you okay?" Her voice was raspy, and that pain in her throat increased with her words.

His jaw ticked. "You're asking *me* if I'm okay?" He lifted a glass with a straw and placed it at her lips. "Here, have some water."

She sipped, and again, the action of swallowing made her cringe.

A vein twitched in Liam's temple. "I'm sorry."

Why was he apologizing? He'd saved her. "None of this is your fault." Then she straightened, Callum flicking into her mind. "Callum! Is he—"

"He's okay. Pretty sure he's demanding to be discharged right now."

The air rushed from her chest. Thank God. "I was so worried. What about the police officer who was shot?"

"He's doing okay. Not out of the woods yet. There was a lot of blood loss, but I think he'll pull through."

Guilt trickled through her chest and down into her belly. She hated that innocent people had gotten hit by bullets meant for her.

Like he could hear her thoughts, Liam cupped her cheek. "Hey. The only person you should worry about is you."

She leaned into his touch, needing his warmth and strength,

allowing it to seep into her. Soothe her. "Did the guy who attacked me survive?"

Liam's eyes darkened. "He did. He's in police custody."

"Did he say why I've become a target?"

"No. He wasn't told the specific reason, just that you could compromise what they were trying to achieve."

She frowned. "That doesn't make sense."

"I know." New anger and frustration darkened his features.

She reached up and grazed the circles under his eyes. "You look tired."

"I'm fine."

There wasn't a single part of her that believed that. The man could probably have a bullet wound and a broken leg while being deserted in the middle of nowhere and still claim he was fine.

"You should go home and sleep." She was sure he had more of his guys in the hall watching the room.

"Not until you're discharged."

She opened her mouth to argue, but the hard set of his jaw told her it was a fight she wouldn't win.

With a sigh, she turned her head and pressed a kiss to his palm. Words bubbled in her throat. Words about love. But it felt so soon to put those out there, so she sucked them back in, deciding to keep them deep inside her until the time felt right.

"You got some missed calls and messages," Liam said softly, thumb grazing her cheek.

She frowned as he lifted her phone from the bedside table. Oh crap. Missed calls from Paisley, Cody, Kayden, and Eastern, as well as texts. All because she hadn't called Cody or Paisley when she'd said she would yesterday.

She quickly sent off a group text.

Nylah: Sorry I missed your calls last night. I'm okay. I'll call you later.

She hadn't even put the phone down when it rang, Paisley's

name flashing on the screen. Christ. She should have expected that.

When she didn't answer, a text came through.

Paisley: You answer this phone right now, Nylah Walker, or I'm sending the cavalry over!

Shit. The cavalry being her brothers. It started ringing again.

Liam squeezed her arm. "I'll just go talk to the guys in the hall."

She let herself have one more second to feel sorry for herself, then cleared her throat and answered the call. "Hey, Pais."

"What's wrong with your voice?"

God, her friend was like a dog chasing a bone. "Paisley—"

"Wait…is that beeping? Are you in a damn hospital, Ny?"

Nylah cringed. "Yes. I'm in a hospital. I was attacked yesterday, and my voice sounds bad because he strangled me."

The gasp whipped over the line. "Oh my God! Are you okay?"

"Yes. I stayed in the hospital overnight, but it was only precautionary, because I passed out."

The second the words were out, she regretted them, because Paisley gasped a second time. "*Oh my God!* I can't believe I agreed to keep this a secret! I knew things would escalate."

Nylah pushed up in bed, shaking her head even though her friend couldn't see her. "Paisley, I'm okay. Liam got to me in time."

"You were attacked…*again*! Strangled!" Emotion clogged her friend's voice.

Nylah swallowed. "I know. It's bad. I'm going to tell my brothers."

"Good! Because they love you. You should have told them right at the start."

"I know," Nylah said quietly.

Her friends sighed. "Ny…I'm so worried about you."

"Don't be. Things sound bad, but I still have Liam and his team protecting me."

"Things are still okay with him?"

Okay? The word didn't sound big enough. God, how did she even describe what he was to her? Her everything? Her center?

"You've fallen for him, haven't you?" she asked softly.

Head over freaking heels. "I have."

"Oh, Ny."

"And, not only that, despite the danger, despite everything that's being thrown my way, Cradle Mountain feels like home. That's why I haven't told my brothers. Because I need to be here, and they would try to drag me away."

"They want you to be happy." Paisley sighed. "Just...tell me again that you're okay."

"I'm okay."

Well, except the sinking feeling churning in her gut. Because now, she really would need to tell her overprotective, military-trained brothers that people were trying to kill her. And there was no part of that conversation that would end well.

CHAPTER 18

*L*iam's gaze ran over the police report from Marble Falls PD. He was trying goddamn hard to keep his cool. The team in Texas had caught a man who'd tried to shoot Luca when he stepped outside his home.

They'd taken him in and questioned him, but yet again, he'd known next to nothing. Hell, the attack hadn't even been organized by the Hawk guy who was targeting them. The man was part of the group, but he'd gone rogue, claiming he was sick of waiting for orders.

Liam leaned back in the booth, gaze catching on Nylah behind the counter. Only two days had passed since her latest attack, and she was already back at work. It was too soon, but no matter how much he'd pushed for her to rest, she'd claimed she had to get out of the house, and she was in just as much danger at home.

His teeth ground together. The woman was damn stubborn, and her need for independence was strong. It was one of the things he loved about her, but also…it frustrated the hell out of him.

She pushed a drink across the counter to a customer, then

lifted her gaze to him. He forced his features to soften. For a hint of a smile to stretch his mouth as he winked at her.

She returned the smile before turning to the next customer. Everyone loved her here. That was something he'd realized pretty damn quickly. Customers were always genuinely happy to see her, some even seemed to wait specifically for her to serve them.

Because of her high-necked shirt, the bruising on her neck wasn't visible. Every time he looked at her though, it was all he saw, all he could think about, covered or not. Seeing her under that asshole...fuck, it would haunt him forever.

His phone rang, pulling him out of his thoughts, Wyatt's name popping up on the screen. "Hey."

The wind was loud over the phone as Wyatt spoke. "You get the report?"

Liam's gaze shifted back to the laptop screen. "Yeah, seems the guy you caught knows just as little as everyone else. And if he went rogue, others from the same group could as well. We need to be on the lookout even more now."

Which made everything that much more dangerous.

"We're thinking the same thing," Wyatt said quietly. "What's interesting, though, is that local law enforcement worked with us to keep his capture a secret. We forced him to email this Hawk and ask him for an update on the next attack. And the response we got..."

Liam's gut clenched. "What?"

"Hawk already knew we had the guy."

He ran a hand through his hair, the air hissing through his teeth. "He has eyes everywhere."

"Yep. Resources and spies."

Goddamn. They already suspected as much, what with his ability to recruit people undetected. But this was more than that. This was a mole within law enforcement.

"We made a decision amongst ourselves," Wyatt said quietly. "We catch another one of these guys, we won't be telling *anyone*."

So Marble Protection was also going rogue. That's what they'd been forced into. They could get into trouble, but it was worth the risk—this wasn't just about their lives, but the lives of their families as well.

"I'll talk to my team about doing the same."

"Smart. How's Callum?"

Liam almost laughed. "He was out of the hospital the second he convinced a doctor to sign off. Since then, he refuses to stay home and rest."

It was like *everyone* around him refused to give their bodies a damn break. First Nylah, then Callum. But at the same time, he understood Callum's refusal. The guy was angry. Angry that the shooters had attacked him and Nylah. Angry that she'd been hurt while under his protection. Liam would have felt the same way.

"Good," Wyatt said. "I'll talk to you later."

"Watch your back, Wyatt."

"Always."

He hung up and scanned the coffee shop once more. Nylah was talking to one of the other waitresses, Eleanor, while Courtney served coffee down at the other end of the counter.

Every time he looked at his woman, his chest grew tighter. He had someone to lose now. And that terrified him.

"How you doing, Liam?" Courtney asked, voice soft as she stopped at his table. "You look ready to kill someone."

That was a true damn statement if ever he'd heard one. "I am."

The corners of her mouth tilted down. "I'm sorry. But with all the resources of your team, the Marble Falls team, and the FBI, there's no way you won't win this."

Yeah, but *when*? After they lost one of their own?

He gestured toward Nylah. "Did she seem okay today?"

"She was great. She's just finishing now. Honestly, she's such a people person that when she steps behind that counter, customers gravitate toward her. She even put up with me asking her a million times if she was okay without whacking me."

Liam's mouth twitched. "I think she was going stir-crazy staying home all day yesterday."

Courtney laughed. "I don't blame her. I would too."

Nylah looked at him, nodding toward the back room to indicate she was getting her bag. He nodded back. She'd just turned toward the back when the door to the coffee shop opened.

A man stepped inside, tall and wide. He had military written all over him, scanning the space like he was looking for a threat.

Then his focus narrowed in on Nylah's back.

Liam's muscles tensed, his world reducing to just that one man. When the guy started across the room toward her, Liam was up and out of his seat in a heartbeat. He caught the asshole just before he reached the counter, grabbing his arm and spinning him.

"Who the fuck are you?" Liam growled.

The man's eyes narrowed, anger darkening his features. He shifted slightly, settling into a balanced stance like he was ready to fight. "Get your damn hand off me or I'll break it."

Not a chance. "Tell me who you are." There was something familiar about him.

"I don't have to tell you shit. Now get your hand off me before I make you."

* * *

When a customer stepped up to the counter, Nylah was about to assist, but Eleanor stopped her with a touch to her arm. "I've got it. Your shift's finished. Get out of here. Go home and rest."

She looked up at the clock. Eleanor was right. Damn, that had gone quickly. She almost didn't want to leave. Because when she was home, not only was she basically forced into bed rest, she had nothing to take her mind off what had happened. Also, what *could* happen.

Liam was talking to Courtney at one of the tables. When his gaze met hers, she indicated she was heading to the back and he nodded, one side of his mouth lifting. Even though he'd been hovering a lot, he'd also been pretending he was fine. Like everything that was happening wasn't affecting him. But in the moments when he thought she wasn't watching, she saw the flickers of concern on his face. She wasn't sure if it was concern for her, his team, or dread over what may come. Probably all three.

As she walked toward the back, the bell on the coffee shop door dinged, but she kept moving. If she didn't, she'd stay and help serve, and she was pretty sure Liam would throw her over his shoulder and storm out of the place. He was the one who'd insisted on a short shift today.

Honestly, she felt a bit bad. Every time something happened, and she had to take time off, the pressure was on Courtney to fill her shift and replace her. Yes, the woman understood and was good about it, but Nylah had always been a hard worker, and when she committed to something, she followed through.

She stepped into the back room and grabbed her bag. When she pulled out her phone, she wasn't surprised to see a message from Paisley.

She opened the text, then frowned.

Paisley: I'm sorry. Please don't hate me. I thought you'd already done it.

Done it? What was she—

"Get your damn hand off me or I'll break it."

Her head shot up, the familiar voice trickling down her spine, making her belly do a nervous flip. It was a voice she'd know anywhere. A voice she'd grown up with.

"Tell me who you are," Liam growled.

She rushed back into the coffee shop to see the back of her

twin brother, standing opposite Liam, the two powerful men facing off. "I don't have to tell you shit. Now get your hand off me before I make you."

She was running before she could stop herself. She reached for Cody's arm, but Liam saw her coming and grabbed her first, tugging her behind him.

Fury glittered in her brother's eyes, and he stepped forward. "Don't you fucking touch her!"

"Cody, stop!"

Liam's gaze swung to her. "Cody? As in—"

"My twin brother," she rushed out, pressing a palm to Liam's chest, trying to calm some of the anger.

Understanding swept through his eyes. She looked up to see her brother's brows slashed together, his gaze on her hand, where it still rested on Liam's chest.

She cleared her throat. It wasn't exactly the meeting she'd pictured between two of the most important men in her life, but it would have to do.

"Liam, this is my brother, Cody. Cody, this is Liam. We're dating."

CHAPTER 19

"*T*ell me what's going on, Ny."

She swallowed and avoided looking at her brother, still not sure how she'd been able to convince him to come here before she told him anything. Hell, still not sure how to word everything that had happened since she'd arrived in Cradle Mountain. How did you tell your twin brother that someone had tried to kill you multiple times?

She glanced down the hall, almost wishing Liam hadn't disappeared to his office to give them some space, but at the same time appreciating that he had. "It's a long story."

"I have nowhere to be." His words were short and clipped.

With a sigh, she faced him. "What did Paisley tell you?"

She wasn't mad at her friend. It was *her* fault this had happened. She'd told Paisley she'd tell her brothers and just... hadn't.

"That someone tried to kill you." The veins in Cody's neck pulsed, and she didn't miss the way he clenched his fists like he was about to hit someone. The blue eyes that matched her own were direct, unyielding. "I pushed her for more information, but she told me to ask you myself. She was surprised *you* hadn't told me yet."

She took a deep breath. "My first night working at the event center, there was an engagement party for Liam's friends. His team and the guys from Marble Protection in Texas were there."

If possible, Cody's expression darkened further. "You're talking about the shootout that was all over the news. You were there?"

She cringed. She hadn't watched the news but wasn't surprised it had been reported. "Yeah. I was. That's how I met Liam. And ever since, I seem to be a target, but we don't know why."

The anger on her brother's face was so clear that she barely recognized him. Usually, he was the calm one. The brother who was good at keeping his emotions in check.

"People have been targeting you for that long and you never told me?"

"I wanted to. But I knew you'd freak out. Convince me to come back home."

"Of course I would! And would that be so bad?"

"Yes." The word came out quickly and with no hesitation. "I needed a break. From you and Kayden. From family watching my every move. And I didn't want you to come here and put yourself in danger."

His brows flickered. "First of all, I can protect myself. Secondly, we do it because—"

"You love me. I know. And since Mom died, I've been the only girl in the family, and you guys are all protectors. I love you for that. But I also need to breathe. Even when you guys were all gone and Dad was sick, he was still Dad. He still watched over me. You and Kayden came home, and the overprotection got worse. When Eastern said he was coming home too... I needed to learn who I was without family trying to protect me from every little thing."

For a moment, Cody was quiet, his brows still drawn like he was piecing her words together and trying to make sense of them. "I'm sorry if we made you feel like you needed to leave."

She reached over and tightly wrapped her fingers around his hand. "No. I don't want you to be sorry. I am so grateful for you and everyone else in the family. I know how lucky I am. Coming here was just…"

"Something you had to do."

"Yes." She breathed the word, feeling it so deeply, it ran through her veins.

He gave a slow nod. "Despite everything…are you happy here?"

"Yes. It feels like home. *Liam* feels like home."

Cody's chest rose and fell on a sigh. "I'm glad. I want that for you. Is he treating you well?"

"The best."

He nodded. "That's good, because otherwise I'd have to kick his ass."

She laughed. Always her protector. "Again? Pretty sure you've sent most men I've dated running scared."

"If they scare that easily, they're not good enough for you."

He was right. And Liam definitely didn't scare easily.

The humor left his eyes. "Tell me everything that's happened."

She blew out a breath and started at the beginning. Every word she spoke had the anger on Cody's face deepening.

"The entire Blue Halo team is protecting me like I'm their own," she said quietly.

"And now you'll have me too."

She was shaking her head before he finished speaking. "You can't stay here, Cody. It's too dangerous."

"I told you, I can take care of myself."

Oh, she knew how well her brother was trained. The man was skilled. That wasn't her concern. "You're not bullet or fireproof.

Please. Trust Liam and his team to protect me, and once it's over, everyone can visit. Hell, I'll bring Liam back to visit."

A muscle in Cody's cheek ticked. "No."

"Cody—"

"I'm not leaving. The best I can do is try to hold off the others from coming. But even then, I don't know if they'll listen."

The others being her brothers. Argh.

At the resolution in her brother's eyes, she knew it was a battle she wouldn't win. "God, you're stubborn."

His brows rose. "*I'm* stubborn?"

She rolled her eyes. "Okay. We're both stubborn. Let's blame it on genetics."

He laughed, and man, that sound was so familiar.

She slid her fingers through his. "I love you."

He turned serious. "I love you too, Ny."

"How's the bar?"

"Barry's giving me a damn headache with his bossiness. Anyone would think *he* was the owner. And the new guys don't know what hard work is."

The thought of Barry made her grin. He'd worked in the bar since their father had taken over the place and was always on someone's ass about something. "I'm sorry about the new guys, but I'm sure Barry will whip them into shape." She sighed. "I miss Barry. And Mrs. Sandler's cupcakes."

Man, those cupcakes. She'd lived off them her entire life. The older woman had a little shop that was Nylah's personal heaven. It was all pastel colors and served cupcakes and sweet drinks. Sometimes Barry left one of those cupcakes on her desk at the end of a particularly long day.

"Everyone misses you too," he said quietly. "And if you come back and visit, I'm sure Mrs. Sandler will give you a dozen cupcakes to take home."

A dozen? Ha. She'd go through that in a week. She needed ten dozen and a deep freezer to stash them in.

She leaned into Cody's shoulder, and immediately his big strong arms wrapped around her. *This* was what she'd missed the most. Hugs from her twin. Her best friend.

When she pulled back, he wiped a tear from her cheek that she didn't realize had fallen.

"You staying for dinner?" she asked quietly.

"Definitely. I need to vet this boyfriend of yours."

Nylah laughed. "Any other guy and I'd be worried. Fortunately, Liam can hold his own."

"Good. I've been waiting for you to meet someone as strong as you."

* * *

LIAM LIFTED the plates from the table as Nylah and her brother stood to do the same. The dinner had been spent with Nylah and Cody regaling him with stories of their childhood. Stories of their brothers and the headaches they'd given their father.

He'd learned about the entire family. Kayden, the oldest brother, who was slow to trust and didn't joke often. He'd grown up wanting to help people so had joined the Air Force's Special Warfare pararescue team

Eastern, who'd become a Navy SEAL but was now returning to Misty Peak to spend more time with his daughter. He was also running for town sheriff. Jace, the easygoing brother, was still in the Air Force as a tactical controller.

And Lock, the intense brother, part of an Army Ghost Ops team, couldn't reveal what he did.

Liam absorbed every detail of Nylah's life, wanting to know her and her family and all the things that had made her the woman she was today. He couldn't get enough of her. Everything she was, he wanted.

Even though conversation flowed easily, he'd felt the intense looks from Cody. Knew every time he spoke, his words were carefully analyzed. Every time he touched Nylah, it was noted.

Good. Liam wanted her brother to look out for her. He was glad she had other protectors in this world. People who loved her and had been looking out for her since she was a kid.

While they busied themselves in the kitchen, Liam smiled as Nylah started telling her brother about the men of Blue Halo.

"There are eight of you, right?" Cody asked, directing his attention to Liam.

"Yep."

"Going through Project Arma, being taken and held and changed…that had to affect you in ways you never expected."

Liam looked Cody in the eye. "It affected every single one of us. Made us stronger in more ways than one, as the entire world knows. But it also created a brotherhood. We're family. We'd each die for the others, and for each other's loved ones."

And fuck, he was grateful for that. His team and the men from Marble Protection were the only good things to come out of the project. Not a day passed where he wasn't grateful for them.

Cody's eyes stayed on him for a moment, studying, the former Delta soldier easy to see. The man had a hardness about him that only came from seeing intense military action.

"I'm glad," he finally said.

"What made you get out?" Liam asked as he put their leftovers in containers. Nylah moved past him, her side grazing his as she set to work on putting dishes into the washer.

"My team and our missions always came first."

Liam nodded. When you were in the military, especially special operations, that was your world. It had to be, with the life-or-death nature of the job.

"But back home, Dad was getting sicker, and it wasn't fair that Nylah was shouldering all of that and the bar. So, both Kayden and I were discharged almost at the same time, and we came home for the last six months of Dad's life. Certainly don't regret it. And I don't feel any pull to go back."

Cody continued to ask questions about Blue Halo, Nylah filling a lot of the silence as they cleaned. They were just about finished when her phone rang. She lifted it and sighed. "It's Paisley. I need to take this."

She leaned up and pressed a kiss to Liam's cheek before moving past Cody and squeezing his arm.

"Go easy on her," Cody said before she left the room. "She really did think you'd already told me."

Nylah dipped her head. "I know."

When she stepped away, Liam looked back at Cody. "You grew up with Paisley too?"

"Yeah, the woman's like a sister to me."

"I look forward to meeting her one day." He set another cup into the dishwasher.

"You gonna protect Ny?"

He'd been expecting the question or something like it. Liam straightened and looked the man straight in the eye. "With my life."

There was another of those pauses, where Cody stared at Liam as if trying to decide if he believed him.

When Cody seemed to accept the words as truth, he nodded. "Good. Thank you for watching over her."

"Always. But you should know something," Liam added, crossing his arms. "Your sister's tough. She fought off numerous attacks on her own."

And he was so proud of her for that. For her strength. Her smarts. Her courage and ability to not fall apart in the face of danger.

The corners of Cody's mouth twitched. "I'd hope so. She's only had five brothers and a veteran father to ingrain self-defense into her throughout her entire life."

Liam was grateful. Every person should have a basic knowledge of how to protect themselves, and he was glad Nylah had a bit more than most.

When she returned ten minutes later, she sighed. "Oh good. You two haven't killed each other."

"Not today," Cody said with a wink. "I should get back to my motel."

Liam stepped forward. "You could always stay here."

He shook his head. "Thank you, but I'll give you two your space. At night, that is. During the day, I'm gonna be the shadow Nylah *wishes* she could get rid of."

"That'll make two of us," Liam said.

Nylah rolled her eyes as Liam stepped forward and held out his hand. "It was good to meet you, Cody."

Cody shook it. "Likewise."

Nylah walked her brother to the door, and Liam watched as he gave her a big hug. Wanting to give them some privacy, he went back to the kitchen and was wiping down the counter when she returned. She wrapped her arms around him from behind and pressed a kiss to his back.

"Thank you. I know Cody can be a lot."

He turned, curling his arms around her waist. "He's the perfect amount. I like that he looks out for you."

"Oh, he definitely does that." She slid her hands up his chest, then into his hair. "Maybe one day you can meet the rest of my brothers."

His heart thumped. "I'd like that. I want to know everyone you love."

Her eyes softened. "I want that too. But, be warned, they've scared off a lot of men from my life."

"I don't scare easily." Especially not when it came to this woman.

"I know. That's what I told Cody." She tugged his head down so their temples touched. "Thank you for being so perfect."

No. He wasn't the perfect one.
She lifted to her toes and kissed him.

CHAPTER 20

"*Y*ou're really playing the 'I can't remember' card?"

Nylah laughed at her brother's question as they stepped into The Grind. For once, she wasn't here for work, just a coffee with Cody. "I can't remember because it never happened."

He shook his head as they headed to the back corner booth. She sat facing the wall, knowing he'd want the corner seat so he had a full view of the coffee shop. That was something important to all her brothers, the situational awareness they constantly "encouraged" her to maintain.

She turned her head, spotting Jason stepping inside and moving straight to the counter toward Courtney. He'd followed them today so Liam could sit in on a meeting at work. She knew how safe she was with Cody, but having a second guy on her didn't hurt.

Her brother leaned forward. "Ny, we were ten. Dad ordered a dozen hot cross buns, left them on the counter. *You* ate half of them and tried to blame it on me."

"Cody, I think I would remember if I—" Oh God...it *did* happen. "I remember!"

"So you *did* eat six hot cross buns. I knew it!"

She laughed. "No. I ate two, Jace ate three, and we fed one to Beans." Oh, Beans...she still missed their childhood dog.

Cody frowned. "I don't believe you. If Jace was involved, you would have ratted each other out."

She lifted a shoulder. "We made a deal. Eat the buns and lay the blame on you. It was actually his idea."

He scowled, but there was a hint of a smile on his face. "I should have known. Jace loved to blame shit on me."

Nylah chuckled. It was true. He was the troublemaker of the group.

Courtney came to stop at the table. "Hey, how're you doing today, Ny?"

"I'm good," she said with a smile. "I don't think you officially met my brother yesterday. This is my twin, Cody."

Cody dipped his head. "Good to meet you."

"You too." Courtney shook her head. "Man, you fit right in with the Blue Halo guys. What are you? Marines? Navy?"

One side of Cody's mouth lifted. "Army."

"Figures. Everyone's so badass in this town." Her smile grew. "Lucky for me, I love serving people who have protected our country. How do you take your coffee?"

"Black. Thanks."

"Double shot latte, please," Nylah said quickly. Probably too quickly. It was three in the afternoon, and she was at that midafternoon, zero-energy point.

"You got it."

Courtney had just left the table when Nylah's phone rang. She pulled it out and groaned.

Cody raised a brow. "Eastern or—"

"Kayden. What did you tell him?"

"The truth. I actually thought he'd call much earlier."

If he knew what was going on here in Cradle Mountain, she

was surprised he hadn't called sooner too. With a sigh, she answered the phone. "Hey, K."

"Are you okay?"

"Yes."

"You should have told me."

She traced a finger over the edge of the table. "You know why I didn't."

"You should have come home after that first shootout."

That earned him a frown. "According to you."

"Yeah. According to me."

"Kayden—"

"But I'm glad you're okay. Cody told me you have a small army protecting you and I should keep my ass out of that town."

Her lips twitched. "Yeah, I do. The guys here are awesome. Does this mean you're trusting Cody on that and staying away?"

"I'm staying away for *now*."

Relief washed over her limbs. She'd expected a fight from Kayden. For him to be completely inflexible about wanting to be here. She looked over at Cody, mouthing a silent thank-you. He'd clearly worked some kind of magic.

"What's this I hear about you dating someone?"

Suddenly, she felt a bit less gratitude toward Cody. "His name's Liam Shore. He works at Blue Halo Security."

"Is he good to you?"

Did her brother really think she'd date a guy who wasn't? She almost rolled her eyes. "Better than good." There weren't words to describe how he treated her. "What about you? Are you doing okay?"

There was a small pause, and for a moment she thought he wouldn't answer and instead keep asking questions. But then he spoke. "I'm keeping busy. A lot of tourists think they know everything there is to know about the mountains by reading a bit of information online."

Nylah cringed. Working search and rescue in the Smoky

Mountains was a busy job, and trying to navigate without knowledge of the area could be dangerous.

"Saving lives, as per usual."

"You go back to school yet?"

Her heart thumped. She'd thought her brothers had forgotten. "Actually, I've made contact with some people at Columbia. They've let me know that my degree can be transferred to an online program if I want to get back to it."

Cody's brows lifted.

"I'm proud of you, Ny."

The corners of her lips tugged up. "Thanks, K. Right back at you."

"Stay safe, okay? Otherwise, I'll have to drag my ass across the country and come save you."

"I think Cody has that covered."

"I'm counting on it."

She hung up just as Courtney returned with their coffees. "Here ya go."

Cody frowned, lifting his mug and reading the text on the side. "There are two types of people in the world...those who love coffee, and liars."

Nylah smiled. "Courtney's cups are awesome. They each have their own quote." She glanced at her own mug. "What's the difference between coffee and your opinion? I asked for coffee." She chuckled. "This is a good one."

Courtney lifted a shoulder. "They're all my babies."

El stepped up beside Courtney. "I'm done and Pierce is here to get me. Vi's taking care of the counter." She looked at Nylah with a smirk. "You just can't stay away from this place, can you?"

Nylah lifted a shoulder. "Not when it's the best coffee in town."

El grinned. "It is, isn't it? See you both later."

"See you tomorrow," Courtney said, squeezing the woman's arm as she headed to the counter and Eleanor went to the door, where Pierce was waiting for her. He nodded toward Nylah before heading out.

"He a police officer?" Cody asked.

She turned back to him. "How'd you know? He wasn't in uniform."

"They have a look about them."

Over the next half hour or so, Nylah smiled so much her cheeks hurt, laughing at Cody's latest stories about the family bar. God, she'd missed her brother.

When a text came through from Liam, her heart rate sped up.

Liam: Just heading to the coffee shop now. Be there in a couple minutes.

The man had woken up with her. He'd seen her a few short hours ago. Still…

Nylah: Good. Because I miss you. See you soon.

They were rising from the table when Cody looked out the window behind her. His eyes narrowed.

She frowned. "What—"

Suddenly, he threw his body on top of hers.

Glass shattered as bullets peppered the coffee shop.

* * *

"BRYCE BURGER. A Canadian-born systems administrator and hacker. Suspected of hacking over fifty US military and government databases in just the last five years."

Liam frowned at Steve's words. The suspect's image briefly appeared on the video screen in the office, but Liam, Tyler, Flynn, and Blake all had their eyes on the man's bio.

"You really think this could be Hawk?" Tyler asked, shifting through the printed files in front of him.

"It's possible," Steve said. "He has the ability to manage untraceable forms of communication. To hack into the profiles of US citizens and identify people who would be interested in joining his cause. He's been on our watch list for a while but went underground about a year ago. Now it's just a matter of locating him."

Liam ran a hand through his hair. "I don't know, Steve. Firstly, he's not American, and these men who want us dead seem to be really territorial over their country. I get the feeling they think they're saving our nation from us. Secondly, it says here he was specifically looking for information on UFOs and antigravity technology."

Flynn leaned forward. "A profiler also made a comment about him having poor communication skills. I can't see this man convincing dozens of people to fight in his war."

Steve scrubbed a hand over his face. He looked tired. But then, he always looked overworked. "I know. It's not optimal, but it's the best we have at the moment. We'll keep searching for other possibilities on our end. In the meantime, we're also going to keep looking into Burger. The guy may be off in his own world, but he's incredibly intelligent and a big threat regardless. And now that you have his photo, you can keep an eye out for him too."

The guys all nodded, but Liam still wasn't convinced. Everything in him said this was the wrong guy. Hell, just looking at the man's photo made him think they were wrong. Call it gut instinct.

"Liam, how's Nylah?" Steve asked.

"Good." He lowered the profile to the table and leaned back in his chair. "Everything's been quiet for a few days, but we're making sure she's always protected."

"I'm glad she's safe. Any idea why she might be a target?"

He shook his head, his jaw grinding. "No. And I don't think we'll find out until we catch this Hawk guy and make him talk. We just have to keep her safe until that point."

It was frustrating as hell that their entire plan was to just watch and wait. He felt like she was a sitting duck, and they were trying to be the wall around her.

"We'll get there," Steve said quietly, determination in his eyes.

"I know we will."

"In the meantime, watch your backs. There have already been too many attacks for my liking, both on your team and the guys in Texas."

Even one attack was too many, dammit.

When the meeting ended, Liam shot a look at the time to see it was his turn to take over from Jason. If it was up to him, he'd be guarding Nylah every goddamn minute of the day. But he knew that would risk suffocating her. Plus, she needed some time with her brother.

As he passed Blake's office on his way out, he stopped to see his friend reading over Burger's profile again.

"You on the same page about this?" Liam asked.

Blake set down the papers. "He doesn't fit what we're looking for. And more than that, my gut says it's not him."

"Exactly what I'm feeling."

"The FBI has obviously profiled the guy and decided he fits the parameters, and because they have no one else—"

"They're desperate."

"Yep."

He shook his head, hating that they pretty much had nothing. "How's Willow and Mila?"

Blake's family was his whole world. He'd gone through hell when he and Willow were separated and he was forced to be a part-time father. Things were different now, and his friend was finally happy again.

"They're good." A pained expression came over Blake's face. "Willow's been keeping Mila home from school for her safety. But we're both worried."

"Nothing's gonna happen to them."

A part of him knew he couldn't guarantee that. But the other part, the part desperate to keep his people safe, knew that anyone who tried to hurt their loved ones would have to go through Liam's team, and that would be a wall that wouldn't break easily.

"Thanks. Nylah's really doing okay?"

"She's a fighter, man. If there was ever a woman who I felt was made for me, it's her."

One side of Blake's mouth lifted. "Then hold on to her. Because that only ever comes once in a lifetime."

"I know." He tapped the doorframe. "I'll see you tomorrow."

He headed out of the office, saying a quick goodbye to Cassie and Aidan, who were talking in the reception area. Another couple who'd gone through hell to find each other again.

As he trotted down the stairs, he sent a quick message to Nylah.

Liam: Just heading to the coffee shop now. Be there in a couple minutes.

Nylah: Good. Because I miss you. See you soon.

His heart clenched. He'd started to realize that his heart moved to an entirely different rhythm when it came to Nylah. Faster. And so out of sync to what he was used to.

He slid behind the wheel of his car and drove toward The Grind. He could have walked, but being off the sidewalk and not out in the open felt safer. One day soon, he'd make sure he could hold his woman's hand and go anywhere without having to look over their shoulders.

The coffee shop had just come into view when he saw an arm stretch out the window from the car in front of him, gun in hand.

Bullets hit the glass, smashing it right before his eyes.

Three shots fired, then the vehicle took off.

Black rage spiked though Liam's veins. He pressed on the gas and took off after the asshole.

CHAPTER 21

*T*he engine roared, Liam's foot almost to the floor as he drove. He pressed a button on the steering wheel, and the phone only rang once before Jason picked up.

"Tell me she's okay," Liam growled as he swung the car around a corner, never letting the shooter out of his sight. If his friend said no, if he said Nylah was injured, Liam would turn the car around and go to her. Losing this asshole would hurt, but he couldn't *not* go to Nylah if she wasn't okay. "Tell me *everyone's* okay."

"Cody covered Nylah and I covered Courtney. No one got hurt, bar a couple grazes from dropping to the ground and the glass."

The air rushed from Liam's chest, the panic and fear shifting over to his fury, fueling it. "Good. I'm behind the asshole now. He's in a Ram pickup. Get the guys to track the GPS on my phone to find my location and ask Callum to run these plates." He rattled off the numbers in front of him.

"Got it. Someone will be there soon."

"Before you go, could you tell who he was shooting at? You or her?"

There was a small pause. "Definitely her."

Fuck. He pushed the car to move faster. "Stick close to Nylah for me."

"I'm not leaving her side."

Another rush of air moved through his lungs. He wanted to call Nylah. Hear her voice. Know firsthand that she was okay. Breathing. Safe. But he trusted Jason. And right now, he needed to put everything he had into catching this guy so he didn't hurt anyone else or go after Nylah again.

When the shooter's car swerved into oncoming traffic to pass someone, he almost collided with another vehicle. Liam waited for the Ford to pass and stayed on the guy's ass. The shooter took a hard right, and Liam followed, tires squealing against asphalt. He sped up again. His GT was faster than the guy's pickup. He closed the distance so there wasn't even the length of a car space between them.

That's right, asshole. I've got you.

He pressed his foot to the floor, hitting the guy's pickup with his GT. The pickup skidded, but the driver maintained control.

When a dead end became visible ahead, Liam waited, staying close, knowing the guy would have no choice but to turn left or right.

The second he started to turn right, Liam yanked his wheel and shot forward, hitting the side of the pickup midturn, hard enough that the vehicle spun out, hit the curb, and overturned before smashing into a building.

Liam was out with his Glock in under a second. When he threw open the driver's-side door, the guy tried haphazardly to lift a pistol, but Liam grabbed his wrist and squeezed so hard that a bone snapped. The guy cried out, pistol dropping.

Liam hauled him out and pressed him against the truck, muzzle of the Glock to his head. "Who are you?"

The guy groaned, blood dripping from his temple. "I hit my fucking head!"

Liam pressed the muzzle of the gun harder to the guy's skull, voice lowering. "We can do this the easy way or the hard way. The easy way is you answer every goddamn question I ask. The hard way? I hurt you. Broken bones are only the start of the pain I can cause. Do you understand?"

"That's why I joined this organization," the guy sneered. "You're a fucking monster! An abomination!"

"You're right. I am. I'm the worst fucking nightmare you'll ever come across. But only to people who wrong me—and that's *you*. Now who the fuck are you?"

The shooter's chest heaved with his rapid breaths, the hate in his eyes so thick, Liam could almost feel it.

"Alex Page," he finally growled.

"Who were you shooting at in the coffee shop?" Liam had Jason's confirmation, but he wanted this guy to admit it. He needed to hear the words out loud.

"I was ordered to shoot and kill Nylah Walker." Ice dripped through Liam's veins. "I was sent a photo so I'd know what she looked like. And I was told exactly where she'd be sitting."

The asshole who'd sent this guy had known where she'd be *sitting*? "When did you get the order?"

"Half an hour ago."

Liam breathed through his rage, running every word over in his head. Trying to make sense of it. "How did Hawk know where she'd be?"

"How the hell should I know? I don't know how he gets *any* information. I just know that, out of everyone, he wants you dead the most. And he'll do anything to accomplish that."

Liam ground his teeth. "You're willing to kill an innocent woman without knowing why?"

"I *do* know why. I'm not gonna just shoot some random person."

Liam frowned, muscles tensing. The moron shot into a coffee shop—he *could* have killed a random customer. "Why?" The guy started to sag in his hold, but Liam shoved him against the truck harder. "*Why?*"

"He said she can expose our leader's identity and destroy everything we've worked toward."

The air stalled in Liam's lungs.

No. That wasn't possible. If she knew who Hawk was, she'd have told him. Hell, she would have exposed him at her first opportunity.

Cars pulled up behind him. He glanced over to see not only Tyler and Flynn but also the damn police. Fuck! Someone local must have called.

He moved back and let the police swoop in, taking Page with them. Tyler and Flynn came to stand beside him.

"He give you anything worthwhile?" Flynn asked quietly.

Anger and confusion swirled inside him. "Someone knew exactly where Nylah was sitting in the coffee shop, down to her table. They gave Page the information half an hour ago."

Tyler frowned. "So either someone was watching her, or—"

"Someone she knows is part of this," Liam finished, hating every fucking word from his mouth. "Someone who saw her this morning, in the coffee shop."

Flynn cursed under his breath.

"There's more," Liam said quietly. "He knew why Nylah's been a target this whole time."

Both men stilled, the silence so thick around them it was almost hard to breathe.

"He said she knows who Hawk is."

* * *

EVERY MINUTE that passed had Nylah pressing her nails deeper into her palms. She barely felt the cool air on her skin. Barely heard the sounds of movement and chatter around her.

Liam had chased the man who'd shot up the coffee shop. Had

he caught him? Was Liam okay? God, she felt like her heart was going to burst through her chest. She needed to know he was safe.

"He'll be okay."

She looked up at Cody. Her brother hadn't left her side. Not while the police had interviewed her. Not when the paramedics wanted to check her over, even though she was fine.

She knew the bullets had been meant for her. They'd hit the wall right behind her head. It was like the guy had known exactly where she'd been sitting. If Cody hadn't seen the car and thrown her to the floor...

"I just need to see him," she said quietly, wishing she had her brother's confidence. "What if the guy had backup? Or leads Liam to some compound or into a trap?"

"Liam's smart. He won't let that happen."

She blew out a shuddering breath as Courtney and Jason came to stand with her. Jason's arm was around Courtney's waist. And just like Cody, his gaze hadn't stopped shifting around the parking lot the entire time they'd been outside, as if he were moments from flinging his body onto Courtney again, just like he had during the shooting.

Courtney touched her arm. "Hey. I'm sorry I haven't had much of a chance to check in. I wanted to make sure all the customers were okay. You doing all right?"

"I should be asking *you* that. I'm so sorry about your shop." She couldn't help but look at the broken glass.

Courtney squeezed her arm, drawing her attention back. "That's all just stuff. Windows and walls. It's fixable. Lives are a lot more fragile. I care about *you*. And I'm glad that none of those bullets hit you."

Nylah's throat thickened. "Thank you. I'm glad you and everyone else in the shop are okay, too."

Courtney tugged her into a hug that was firm and warm and

comforting. Nylah leaned into it, wanting to stay exactly where she was for as long as possible.

When they finally parted, Nylah looked up at Jason, trying to keep the nerves out of her voice as she asked, "Any word on Liam?"

"Actually, he should be here right—"

A car screeched to a stop on the street. Liam's car. Then he stepped out. And despite the chaos around them, the hustle of so many people, Liam's eyes cut straight to her. Like she was all he saw. Like he'd spot her in a crowd of a thousand.

His gaze shifted down her body, probably searching for injuries, even as he was moving toward her with long, determined strides, practically daring someone to get between them.

When he reached her, he cupped her cheeks and studied her face. "Are you okay?"

She nodded, already feeling the wave of calm wash through her body at his mere closeness. At his warm touch. "Yes. Are you?"

"I am now."

He folded her into his chest, her cheek pressing against his heart so the steady rhythm beat into her. And finally, every muscle in her body, even the little ones she hadn't realized were so tight, relaxed, and she let him be the warm to her cold. The strong to her weak.

She wasn't sure how long she stayed in his arms. Whatever it was, it wasn't enough. When she finally stepped back, she didn't go far, because his arm wound around her waist to keep her close.

Tyler and Flynn came to stand with them, neither man looking happy.

"Did you catch him?" she finally asked, almost scared to know the answer in case she didn't like it.

"I did."

She frowned when something she couldn't place flashed through his eyes.

"Did he have any useful information?" she asked.

His jaw tightened. "He was given the exact location of where you'd be sitting in the coffee shop thirty minutes before he did the drive-by."

Her mouth dropped open. How was that—

"Someone saw her in there," Cody said, anger rippling through his voice.

Liam nodded. "Highly likely."

She shook her head. "That doesn't make sense. Wouldn't Jason or Cody have seen someone watching me?"

The guys shared a look between them before Cody answered. "Unless it was someone you know."

She studied her brother, his words replaying in her head.

"Someone with resources," Jason added.

Who were they—

Suddenly, it hit her. She shook her head, voice lowering to a whisper. "No. You're talking about Officer Carlson, right? No." She shook her head again, as if to confirm how much of a no it was.

Liam frowned. "You saw Carlson today?"

"Yes, he picked up El."

"When?" Liam asked.

"Half an hour before the shooting," Cody said, Jason nodding to confirm it.

Her chest tightened, an uncomfortable pit forming in her belly. "There could be another answer to this," Nylah whispered, even though Officer Carlson wasn't even on the scene. "I think El would be smart enough to see that side of him if it existed." She turned to look at Courtney. "Don't you agree?"

The woman lifted her shoulders, uncertainty rolling over her features. "I don't know. Unfortunately, I think it's pretty easy for people to hide their true nature."

"What about the tattoo?" Nylah tried. "If he's part of this group, he'd have a tattoo."

"We can ask El," Courtney said. "Maybe ask her if Carlson has a tattoo without giving away why we're asking."

It felt wrong, like they were tricking their friend. But if it would help?

When she saw the expression on Liam's face, she frowned. "There's something else, isn't there?" At the small click of his jaw, she knew she was right. "What?"

For a moment, he was silent, and that silence killed her.

She touched his chest. "Liam...tell me. Please."

"He said the reason you're a target is because you have the ability to expose their leader and destroy whatever they're planning."

She almost stumbled back a step. Liam's arm tightened around her.

"That's not true," she argued. "I don't know anything about any of this!"

When Liam remained silent a beat too long, when his eyes ran over her face and his entire focus seemed to center on her voice, her features... Nylah's heart cracked.

He was looking for a lie.

She stepped out of his arms, her next words whispering out of her. "You think I'd lie about this?"

He blinked, and that motion seemed to snap him out of it. "No."

She swallowed, wanting to believe him. But he *had* been listening for a lie.

"Is there any way you know but aren't aware of it?" Tyler asked, pulling her attention away from Liam.

She looked at him, frowning. "I don't know how that would be possible. You all know everything I've been through and every man I've seen."

"You've been a target since that first night at the engagement party," Courtney said. "It must be someone from that evening."

"I've told all of you everything that happened that night. I got Willow and Mila out. I was going to go back into the main room, but that guy came into the supply closet. We fought. He ran off when the doorknob rattled."

"Did you see his face?" Cody asked.

"Yes, but when I offered to give a description to Carlson, he told me I didn't need to. That the man had been shot and killed."

There was a clear shift of energy in the group, and when she realized why, her gut clenched.

Because maybe she *had* seen the leader of their organization that night. Maybe she'd seen Hawk...and maybe Carlson *was* a part of this after all and had lied to protect the man.

CHAPTER 22

"I've shown Nylah photos of the guys who attacked and were killed at the party," Liam said to his team over video chat. The entire team was on the call, except Tyler, who'd just left Liam's. "None of them are the guy she fought that night."

The guys cursed loudly.

"You have the description she gave me, so you know it doesn't give us much," Liam continued, leaning back in his office chair while Nylah showered upstairs. He wanted to be up there with her, but he needed to talk to his team first. He ran a hand through his hair. "She's gonna sit down with Emerson tomorrow and see if they can sketch the guy."

Emerson was Tyler's woman, and she was also an artist. If anyone could put a good sketch of the perpetrator together, it was her.

Logan nodded. "Good. Because you're right—medium height, slim build, dark eyes, and late thirties is nothing to go on."

"I know. And she knows that too." He'd seen the frustration brimming in her eyes. She'd wanted to help more. "She said her first reaction to seeing his face was that he wasn't what she thought he'd be. He was too clean-cut."

The guys nodded.

"Did you speak to Steve?" Liam asked.

It was Jason who answered. "We raised our suspicion about Carlson, highlighting his position in the police department and the resources he'd have at his disposal. Also mentioned the timing of his visit to the coffee shop and the attack."

"We also told him why we think it would be someone close to us," Logan added. "And mentioned that Carlson just started dating a waitress who works with Nylah."

"It obviously won't be enough to arrest him, but maybe to bring him in for questioning," Jason said quietly.

Liam nodded. "Did you tell him about Carlson neglecting to get a description of the guy who attacked Nylah in the closet at the function center?"

"We did," Logan said. "It was a risk, when we don't know if there's a leak in the FBI, but if we didn't—"

"Then there wouldn't even be enough to have Carlson taken in for questioning," Liam finished. Fuck, it was a bad situation. But they really didn't have any other lead.

"I was thinking," Aidan started slowly. "You said the guy used the word 'leader,' and he claimed that info came from Hawk. Sounds like there are two people running the show here."

Liam frowned, rolling that around in his head. He was right. Liam hadn't picked up on it at the time, too full of rage because Nylah had almost been killed *again*.

"At this point, nothing would surprise me," Callum said. "And if fucking law enforcement are in on this, *anyone* could be."

The anger and frustration that pummeled through Liam's veins shone back at him from every man on the team. They were ready for this to be over. Past ready.

The guys talked security for a few minutes, then Liam leaned forward. "I've got to go check on Nylah. Watch your backs, okay?"

They all nodded, the same hard expressions slipping over their features. Because they all knew the same thing he did...that more attacks were coming.

When they ended the call, Liam leaned back in his seat and ran his hands through his hair.

Nylah had almost been hurt yet again. And for the second time, the attack had been brazenly public. At least half of his team had also been targeted since the engagement party, and most of the men in Marble Falls.

He closed his laptop and rose to his feet. Then he spent the next ten minutes checking that every window and door in the house was locked. That the alarm was activated.

When there was nothing else to do, he looked up the stairs. Nylah had gone straight up there the second they'd gotten home. She'd barely eaten this afternoon. Barely spoken to him. And he knew why.

A flicker of doubt from him...one mistake. And she'd seen it. Been hurt by it.

Damn, he'd fucked up. Maybe it was because he'd seen so much scum in the world that trusting was harder than it should have been. Maybe it was because he was used to listening for lies. But Nylah deserved his trust. Out of everyone in this goddamn world, she deserved it the most.

His feet thudded against the stairs as he headed to his bedroom. When he stepped inside, he saw the bathroom door was closed. Fuck, he even hated *that*. She never closed the door between them.

Slowly, he moved forward. He wanted to walk straight into the ensuite. Take the woman into his arms and ask for her forgiveness. Beg for it. But he didn't want to risk pushing her further away. She needed slow right now. Gentle.

So he forced himself to knock and wait.

There was a beat of silence on the other side of the door. He was pretty sure even her breathing stopped. Then, "You can come in, Liam."

He stepped into the bathroom to find her standing in front of the mirror, robe on, hair wet and hanging at her shoulders. She was smoothing moisturizer over her face, watching her reflection.

And the only thought in his goddamn head was how fucking gorgeous she was. How completely she annihilated him.

He moved behind her, lightly touching her hips. Then his mouth lowered to her ear. "I'm sorry."

She lowered the small tub of moisturizer to the counter. Her fingers wrapped around the edge, her chest moving up and down with a big sigh. The minute of silence that ticked by felt like a fucking lifetime.

Then, finally, her gaze lifted to look at his in the mirror. "You thought I was withholding information from you."

"No." His answer was instant.

She tilted her head. "You did. Otherwise, you wouldn't have studied my response so closely. You wouldn't have needed to hear me say I didn't know anything. You would have just known."

The hurt in her voice carved a hole in his chest so damn deep that he wondered how he was still standing and in one piece.

She moved away from him and into the bedroom.

He followed. "Nylah—"

"I would *never* have questioned you like that." Her words were quiet, but the force of them slammed into his gut as if she'd shouted across the room. "And while I can see that you really are sorry, it doesn't change what happened."

There was no anger in her words, and if possible, that made it worse.

She swallowed, a thin sheen of tears coating her eyes. "I would never have questioned you, because I—"

When she stopped, his heart thrashed against his ribs. He stepped closer. "You what, Nylah?"

She wet her lips, gaze moving around the room before settling on him again. "I love you. And I would have trusted you, no lie detection needed."

Her words narrowed his world to just her. Shifted him. Changed him.

"You love me." He wasn't sure if it was a question or a statement or just words said out loud to convince himself they were real.

"I love you." A tear fell down her cheek. "And I thought you might feel the same, but after today—"

He crossed the room in a second, placing a hand on her hip and the other to her cheek. Gently, he swiped away a tear with the pad of his thumb. "Nylah, I'm sorry. I'm so damn sorry, and I know words aren't enough. You're right. I *was* watching you for a lie. It was a moment of weakness that says more about me than it does about you...but *nothing* about what I feel for you."

Her brows flickered, her gaze shifting between his eyes.

He stepped closer, his front pressing against hers. "I lost my mom when I was a teenager and have trusted very few people since. My team became my family, but it took me a while to even trust in *them*. I need to work on that. I *want* to work on that. And I will. Every day. Because I love you too."

Her breathing faltered. "Love?"

"Yeah, Ny. I love you. It feels both exciting and scary, kind of like falling over the edge of a cliff and relying on the other person to catch you. Today, I didn't catch you. And I'm sorry. Next time, I swear to you, I will."

Her eyes continued to shift between his, searching. And the silence felt heavy.

He lowered his head, lips hovering over hers. "Tell me you forgive me, Ny. Tell me we can move past this."

* * *

HE LOVED HER. This man, who she'd fallen for so quickly and with so little hesitation, loved her.

Today had hurt. Had cracked her chest wide open. But now, standing in a room with the man she loved, hearing that he loved her back, that he wanted to be a better man for her, for them...

"I forgive you," she whispered. Then she shrugged. "If we're going to love each other, we're both gonna screw up every so often. Today it was you. Tomorrow, it'll probably be me."

The words were barely out of her mouth before he swooped, his head dropping and his arms wrapping around her as he lifted her off her feet and kissed her.

Being held by this man, having his lips on her...God, it was everything. It made the moments of fear and pain over the last few weeks feel like distant echoes of the past. Just stepping stones necessary to get here, to Liam.

She wrapped her arms around his neck and sank into him. When he slipped his tongue into her mouth and tangled it with hers, her heart thudded, beating to a faster, desperate rhythm.

She ran her fingers through his hair, tugging. Desperate to hold him just that bit closer.

When her robe fell open, she wasn't sure if he'd moved it or if it had separated on its own. She didn't care. Because immediately his hand slid over her skin, grazing up her side, fingers spanning over her rib cage. When he spun and pressed her to the wall, his hand shifted the final inch to cup her breast.

A wild, uninhibited cry tore from her chest. She arched, pressing herself farther into him as he palmed her.

The dull throb in her lower belly intensified, her skin burning wherever he touched.

When his mouth moved to her cheek, then her neck, she turned her head, giving him more access. Wanting everything he could give. He sucked and nipped at her, tormenting her, before moving his mouth down her chest.

Her breath caught, and when he took one pebbled nipple between his teeth, she threw her head back. His tongue swirled around the bud, his teeth grazing her flesh.

She squirmed in his hold, her heart racing so fast she swore it was beating right out of her body. The blood roaring between her ears was all she could hear. Liam's hands and mouth on her all she could feel. Her world narrowed to just those sensations.

When he switched to her other breast, she grabbed his shoulders, digging her nails into his skin. It was an overload of pleasure. It consumed her. Tortured and teased.

His hand slipped to the apex of her thighs, and his finger ran over her clit. Her entire body shuddered. He did it again and again, exploring her. Causing her body to tremble in his hold. When his finger touched her entrance, her breath stalled. Then he pushed inside.

She couldn't have stopped her whimper if she tried. The way her core ground against him, begging for more. His mouth never stopped teasing her breast, his finger moving rhythmically inside her as his thumb worked her clit.

"Liam," she gasped, the word barely tearing from her chest. "I need you."

His head lifted and he started to step back, but she gripped his shoulders tighter. "Here," she whispered.

A growl, so low and guttural it sounded painful, fell from his lips. He slipped his finger out of her and fought with his jeans before lowering them just enough to release his cock from his briefs.

He opened a drawer beside them and tugged out a foil, quickly slipping it on before lifting her higher. Nylah's legs automatically wrapped around his waist, and when she felt him between her thighs, so large and hot, her entire body tingled.

He didn't slide straight in, instead pausing at her entrance and looking so deeply into her eyes, she swore he saw every little crevice of her soul.

"I love you, Ny. And I'm gonna tell you that every single day."

Those words shredded her. Cut her into pieces shaped just for him. "I love you too, Liam."

Then she tightened her legs, pulling him inside her.

He growled again, gripping her thighs tightly, holding her in place once he was deep inside her. "Nylah…"

She touched her lips to his ear. "Take me, Liam. I'm yours."

It was as if her words flicked a switch. One more of those deep growls beat through the room, and he began to thrust… long, slow thrusts that took her right to the brink.

His mouth crashed back to hers, and she lost herself in him. In the taste of his tongue. The feel of him inside her, filling her so completely. She allowed this moment to become her entire world.

She wrapped her arms around his neck, her fingers sweeping through his hair. When he reached for her nipple and began to roll it between his thumb and forefinger, she wanted to crumble. To break for him.

He whipped them around and moved to the bed, where he placed Nylah on her back. Liam's feet were on the floor and her legs remained locked around him, keeping him bent at the waist. He drove into her faster. Harder.

Her breaths shortened, her lower abdomen throbbing.

His thumb ran over her nipple again, and he nipped her bottom lip with his teeth. That broke her. She let herself shatter, trusting this man to put her back together later.

Her cry was so loud it echoed throughout the room.

Then Liam groaned, the noise rivaling her own, and she felt him tense above her, continuing to drive into her until finally his body shuddered, and he broke right along with her.

Then, there was stillness.

She sucked in deep breaths, reminding herself to breathe. To allow the air to flow in and out of her lungs.

That had been... God, she didn't even know how to describe it. There were no words.

He lifted his head and looked at her like she was *it*. Like she was all he needed, and together they had everything. "I'm going to show you how much I love you every damn day, Nylah Walker."

Then he kissed her again, and she let herself fall, without hesitation, without fear.

Fall into Liam.

CHAPTER 23

"*H*is eyes were a bit more almond-shaped," Nylah said, tilting her head to study the sketch from a new angle.

Emerson nodded and moved the pencil over the paper. She sketched quickly but with ease, like she'd done it a thousand times before. They sat in Liam's office in the Blue Halo Security building while some of the guys were in a meeting in the conference room.

She hadn't spent much time with Emerson before today, but just like the other women who were partnered with the Blue Halo guys, she was friendly and easy to talk to. And so talented. She'd already sketched the mouth and a million little details of the face. The shadowing and lines she added made the image look incredibly real.

"Are you doing okay with this?" Emerson asked quietly, her hand continuing to move. "If watching this guy come to life on paper is too much, please tell me."

Nylah shook her head. "It's not too much. It feels good that I might be able to help the guys in a small way."

No, she definitely didn't feel fear. If anything, she felt anger.

That this man might be the leader of their sick organization. That he might be responsible for everything that had taken place up to now, including the target on her head.

"I feel awful that I didn't mention it earlier," she added quietly, the words slipping into the air.

Emerson stopped and looked up, already shaking her head before Nylah finished speaking. "Don't. That cop told you he'd already been killed, so you thought the information wasn't important. That wasn't your fault."

She swallowed. She knew it was true. But, still, there was guilt there. That she'd had this guy's description the entire time and hadn't given it to anyone.

"Hopefully," Emerson said quietly, as she turned back to the sketch and continued to bring the eyes to life, "Callum or the FBI can run this sketch through whatever fancy system they have and find a match."

"I really hope so. I hope they find this guy, confirm he's Hawk and put an end to all this."

Emerson nodded. "That would be good. I hate all the attacks that have already taken place. The men have had a lot of enemies to fight over the last few years, but this feels different. This feels…"

"Bigger," Nylah finished when the other woman couldn't.

"Yeah." Emerson cocked her head. "How's that?"

Nylah nodded slowly. "Yep. Those are his eyes."

"Good." Next, she started on the nose.

Nylah shifted forward. "A bit thinner."

Emerson quickly thinned out the nose.

"Actually, maybe a couple more lines around the eyes, too. He didn't look old, but not young either. Late thirties."

Emerson's hand shifted, adding age to the man on paper. "How's everything going with you and Liam?" she asked as she added more shadowing to the face.

"I don't even know how to explain what we have. It's unlike

any other relationship I've been in." She pulled at a loose thread on her top. "It's so strange that I came here wanting to live on my own, without anyone watching over me…and I found Liam."

Emerson smiled. "The world has a funny way of giving us what we need rather than what we ask for. I came here wanting the team to find and detain my stepbrother. I wasn't expecting love or a happy ever after. And certainly not with any of the Blue Halo guys. But once you fall, you can't un-fall."

"That's so true." Nylah's mouth stretched into a smile. "You and Tyler seem happy together."

"This is the happiest I've ever been." Emerson smudged the outline of the man's jaw. "How's that?"

"I think his face was a bit thinner." She frowned, the pressure of getting this right sitting so heavy on her chest that she could barely breathe. She needed this sketch to be perfect. It was her only contribution. The only way she could help end this.

"Hey."

Nylah's gaze swung back to Emerson at the sound of her voice. She hadn't even realized the other woman had stopped drawing and was looking at her.

Emerson touched her arm. "It's okay. Whether this sketch leads to an identification or not, the guys will find him and end this."

"I know, I just…I really hate that this could have led to an arrest sooner."

Again, Emerson shook her head. "Like I said before, not your fault. You were told what you were told."

Nylah exhaled a long breath. Emerson sounded so sure, and that dulled some of the guilt niggling at her mind. "Thank you."

"You're welcome. Now…hair?"

Nylah studied the image, racking her brain to remember all the fine details. "It was short and dark. Not quite long enough to fall into his eyes, but a bit over his forehead. It had some grays in it, but I'm not sure if you can capture that in a sketch."

Emerson got to work. Every so often, Nylah stopped her and asked for a change or addition, and Emerson implemented everything. When they were finally finished, Nylah nodded, feeling the first whispers of confidence. "That's him. That's the man who attacked me. And the more I think about it, the more it makes sense that he was the leader. He told his guys to get out of there when things went to shit."

"Good. Let's get this asshole, then."

Nylah grinned, tugging out her phone. "I'll text Liam that we're done."

Nylah: We just finished. We'll wait for you in the office.

Liam: Come in. We're just wrapping up. You can show us the sketch.

"He wants us to go to the conference room."

Emerson stood. "Great. Let's go."

* * *

"He wasn't happy when he was brought in for questioning."

Liam shook his head. "Of course not. But did he cooperate?"

Tyler, Callum, Aidan, and Flynn sat with him at the conference room table. He was making sure to listen for other sounds in the office as well, safety for Nylah at the forefront of his mind.

Steve ran a hand through his hair, dark shadows under his eyes. "He did. Once he got over the fact he was a suspect in the shooting, he answered all questions and gave us full access to his laptop and home."

Liam frowned. Did he do that because he had nothing to hide? Or because he was smart enough not to have any connection to the group in his home or office?

Steve cleared his throat. "He also allowed my guys to do a body search...he didn't have the tattoo."

Liam fisted his hands, wanting to ram them into a damn wall. He'd wanted evidence. Something to link him with this group.

"Just because he doesn't have a tattoo and there's no evidence in his house, doesn't mean he's not involved," Liam said through gritted teeth, although everyone in the room was smart enough to know that already.

Steve ran a hand through his hair. "We're not dismissing him entirely. He's still our best suspect, we just have nothing to hold him."

"It's frustrating as hell," Aidan bitched, saying what every man was thinking.

"We'll get there," Steve pressed. "We're still searching for Burger. And the tech team here is working overtime to infiltrate this organization. Trying to get an invite into this little community of theirs."

Liam's muscles tightened. At this point, the FBI had achieved nothing, and he had given up relying on them. That was why Callum was currently doing the same thing in secret. His friend had created a fake profile that was so solid, no one would know it wasn't a real person. Now he was scouring the web, looking for any Project Arma hate groups.

"No information has come up on why Nylah's being targeted?" Steve asked.

Liam opened his mouth to respond, but his phone vibrated with a text.

Nylah: We just finished. We'll wait for you in the office.

Good timing. "Sorry, Steve, that's her."

Liam: Come in. We're just wrapping up. You can show us the sketch.

"I assume she's at your house, Liam?" Steve asked.

At the sound of footsteps in the hall, Liam leaned forward. "Actually, she's not. Steve, before you go, Emerson's done a sketch of the guy Nylah saw at the function center."

Steve's brows rose. "She has?"

"Yes. And we'd like you to run it through your system and see if you can identify him."

Liam rose to his feet and moved to the door. He opened it to find Nylah on the other side, her smile so sweet, it made the tight muscles in his body soften.

Emerson stood behind Nylah, sketch pad in hand with the image facing away from him.

He stepped back, giving them room to step inside.

Nylah smiled up at the screen. "Hi, I'm Nylah."

The agent dipped his head. "Steve."

Emerson stepped in after her.

"How'd it go?" Tyler asked before Liam could.

"Good," Emerson said with a nod. "I think we've got a good idea of what he looks like."

Nylah nodded too. "At least, as close as we're going to get."

Emerson turned the sketch pad and showed the team first, then Liam, and finally Steve. Liam nodded, not recognizing the guy at all.

There was a quick intake of breath from the screen, so quiet that Liam almost didn't hear it. He turned to see the FBI agent suddenly looking pale.

Liam frowned. "Steve?"

He cleared his throat and shook his head. "Sorry, one of my guys just informed me of a fire I need to put out. I'll call back soon." Then the screen turned black.

CHAPTER 24

They couldn't get through to anyone in the goddamn intelligence department. The second Steve ended the call, Liam's team became alarmed. They'd been trying unsuccessfully to get him back on the phone. They wanted to know why he'd gone so pale. Why he'd ended the call so abruptly. Liam didn't believe for a second that an emergency had popped up.

Over the last hour, they'd talked to one low-level agent after another at the Idaho field offices, trying to connect with Steve, or hell, *anyone* in intelligence. So far, no one had been willing to help.

Fuck. What was going on? He was so goddamn sick of not having answers. Was Steve part of this? Was that why he'd signed off in a rush? Did he know the guy? Was he friends with him?

Liam shot to his feet. He couldn't sit anymore. He had to move. Go. *Do something.*

He left the conference room and walked down the hall to his office. His team would keep working on making contact, but he needed a few minutes to calm the hell down.

He slammed his office door closed and ran his hands through his hair, almost pulling the strands out by the roots.

He leaned his palms onto his desk and was still working on controlling his breaths, trying to calm his damn heart rate, when soft steps sounded from the hall outside his office. Then the quiet creak of the door opening. He didn't have to look up to know it was Nylah. He knew her heart. *Felt* her presence.

She'd been sitting with Cassie and Emerson. The second Steve had ended the call, the team had begun trying to re-establish contact. Nylah and Emerson, clearly aware something was going on, had gone to sit at the front desk.

He wanted her to go back to the other women. For the first time, he wanted her to stay away—because no part of him wanted her to witness him unravelling, threatening to come apart altogether.

Two hands touched his back. Small, warm hands that were so familiar. Then the heat of her forehead pressed to his back. "I'm sorry you don't know what's happening with Steve right now."

Whispered words that twisted his insides. Pulled him back from the brink and anchored him.

He swallowed, forcing his voice to work. "Why are *you* sorry?"

"Because everyone you love is in danger, and you've been working overtime to solve this. But every time we take a step forward, it feels like we also move two steps back."

She was right. Fuck, she was so right. He was scared shitless of losing one of his friends, and now, he was forced to doubt one of their few allies.

Slowly, he turned and looked down into his woman's eyes, letting her ice-blue gaze calm some of the storm inside him. "We need to know why he ended the call like that. Why he looked so shocked at the sight of that sketch."

She cupped his cheek, her touch spreading over his skin like wildfire. "We will. We'll connect with him or another member of intelligence, and we'll find out what's going on."

He let those words settle, begging them to drown out the other voices in his head. The ones that told him she was wrong.

That their enemy would remain a step ahead of them until he got everything he wanted.

"Liam…your team's got this. I know they do."

When her breath brushed his face, he lowered his head and touched his forehead to hers. "God, I love you."

"I love you too."

He lowered his mouth and kissed her. Let the softness of her lips, the warmth of her touch, sweep inside him. And there it was…the peace he'd lost an hour ago.

Her hands slid up his chest, fingers wrapping around his shoulders, holding him together.

The minutes ran into one another as the dust of his anger began to settle. When they finally came up for air, he didn't let her go. He couldn't. He felt chained to this woman. Desperate to have her in his arms. "Thank you."

A new set of footsteps sounded in the hall. Then a knock.

He lifted his head, arms still wrapped around Nylah. "Yeah?"

Tyler popped his head in. "We're finally being put through to Steve."

Nylah grazed her hand down his arm, her fingers slipping through his before they followed Tyler down the hall.

When they stepped into the conference room, Callum had his phone in hand, the call on speaker.

"Callum."

A vein in Liam's temple throbbed at the sound of Steve's voice.

"What happened back there?" Callum asked, voice a thin line.

"I told you, I had an emergency with one of my guys. Sorry I ended the call so abruptly. Have you sent the sketch?"

Liam wasn't sure if he believed the guy. And since it was a phone conversation, there was no way for him or his team to detect a truth or a lie.

"We'll send it through now," Callum said slowly. "You'll run it through the system? Figure out if it can lead to an identification?"

"Yes. I'm going to do everything I can to assist your team on this, Callum. I promise."

Liam wanted to believe him. He *sounded* like he was telling the truth.

God, Liam's head was a mess.

The only thing that kept him calm was Nylah's touch. The way the pad of her thumb stroked over the back of his hand. It was what he had to focus on to stay whole.

* * *

NYLAH LOOKED at Liam from beneath her lashes.

A couple of days had passed since they'd sent the sketch to Steve. So far, he hadn't been able to identify the man…but Liam and his team weren't sure they believed him.

Liam was incredibly angry about no longer feeling like he could trust Steve. They all were. He tried to hide it from her—smiles when she looked at him, gentle touches—but she felt his rage. It bounced off him hot and heavy, even now, as they walked to The Grind to check on the progress of the new windows.

God, her heart bled for him. For his entire team. They deserved answers.

"You okay?" she finally asked as they crossed the road.

There was a short pause. "Yeah. I'm okay, Ny."

She frowned, not believing him for a second.

"One good thing to come out of the last few days," Liam added. "There've been no recent attacks."

It was true. And in the calm, she could almost forget she'd been a target at all.

She forced a smile to her face. "You're right. Maybe you might not have to worry about me anymore."

His fingers tightened around hers. "I'll always worry."

And she'd always worry about him. It seemed that was how love worked.

She ran her thumb over the back of his hand. As they neared the coffee shop, Nylah saw the hustle of contractors moving around. Courtney was talking to a couple of them, with Jason close beside her.

When Courtney saw them, she stepped up to Nylah and tugged her into a hug. It was a warm, all-encompassing hug, and Nylah was used to them by now. This woman wasn't just a boss. She'd become a good friend.

Courtney pulled back, but her hands remained on Nylah's upper arms. "I haven't seen you for a few days. How are you doing?"

"Really good."

She gave a slow nod, almost like she was considering whether to believe her or not. Until finally, she gave a small smile. "Good." She looked up at Liam, and the same concern skittered in her eyes. "And how are *you*?"

"I'm okay." He nodded toward the windows. "They installing today?"

Nylah sighed. And by the look on Courtney's face, she didn't miss his avoidance tactic, either. She didn't call him out on it, though. She turned to watch the contractors at work. "Yeah. I'm so grateful for them squeezing us in. Thank God Jason weaved some kind of contractor magic."

Jason slid an arm around her waist. "I'll always weave my magic for you."

"Anything we can do to help?" Nylah asked.

"Not today. But after we patch the bullet holes, I was going to ask you, El, and Vi to come over to help me paint. Maybe we could order some pizza. Drink some cider."

Nylah grinned. "I wouldn't turn down a pizza and cider night."

"Great."

Jason frowned at Courtney. "Girls' night?"

She rolled her eyes, but there was a hint of humor there. "I guess you can come too."

Jason opened his mouth to respond but stopped when his gaze caught on something behind Nylah. She turned to see a blue Honda parking at the curb across the street. Violet was in the back, and Eleanor was behind the wheel.

It was the person in the passenger seat, however, who had Nylah's heart thumping...Carlson.

"What's he doing here?" Jason asked through gritted teeth before anyone else could.

Carlson climbed out of the car, his gaze never leaving Liam and Jason. He crossed the road with so much anger on his face that Liam grabbed her arm and pushed her behind him. Jason did the same with Courtney.

Eleanor rushed forward to try to stop him, but he shook her off and kept walking.

"What the hell was that?" Carlson shouted, shoving Liam in the chest. Liam didn't move an inch. "You tell the fucking *FBI* to take me in for questioning? That I'm trying to *kill* you?"

"Pierce, stop it! You said you wouldn't do this." Eleanor tried to pull him away, but again, he extracted his arm.

Violet stood back, worry on her face, arms wrapped around her waist.

"Someone knew where Nylah was sitting in that café before the shooting," Liam said quietly. "Right down to the exact booth. The timing matched when you left."

"So you just assumed it was me with no other evidence?"

"No." Jason stepped closer. "*Not* with no other evidence. Nylah saw the face of a man at the engagement party shooting— and *you* didn't bother getting a description when she offered one. You also didn't ask her to identify whether he was one of the assholes who'd died."

Carlson's eyes rounded and his lips snapped shut. It took a

moment for him to speak. "Because everyone who was there *did* die. It would have been a waste of time. It was more important to question you guys—you had more information than her."

"You're wrong," Liam said between gritted teeth. "That asshole *lived*. And seeing his face is the reason she's been a target this whole goddamn time."

Some of the color leached from Carlson's face.

Nylah frowned, wondering for the first time if it really had just been a big mistake on his part. Maybe he couldn't be bothered with the paperwork. Or he'd just been in such a rush to question the guys, he'd disregarded her.

"I didn't know," he said quietly.

Liam's hands fisted, watching the guy like he was studying for a lie. "Now you do."

Carlson stepped back, scowl firmly etched on his face. Without another word, he turned and stalked back to the car.

"Pierce!" Eleanor called. She cringed, turning back to them. "Sorry. I came to check on the shop. He asked to come, and I made him promise not to do anything like this if he saw any of you."

"It's okay, El," Courtney said softly, stepping up beside Jason.

"You're in a tough position," Nylah added.

Violet slipped an arm around Eleanor's waist and looked at Courtney. "Everything going okay here?"

"Yeah, I was just saying I might get you ladies to help me paint so we can be up and running again in a week or so."

Violet smiled. "I'm great with a paintbrush, so that sounds good to me."

"Me too," Eleanor said, but she sounded a bit less enthusiastic. She glanced over her shoulder at Carlson, who was already back in the car. "I'd better get back to him."

Violet gave them a small smile. "I'll see you guys later."

The second they were back in their car, Nylah cringed. "I feel bad for Eleanor."

"He was telling the truth," Liam said quietly. "He didn't know the guy was alive. It sounded like it was just a big fuckup on his part."

So they were back to square one.

CHAPTER 25

*M*usic was loud in the bar. Voices and the clinking of glasses. Nylah scanned the space, moving over every person and seeing nothing out of place.

Another week had passed, and in that week, there'd been nothing. No attacks. No shootings. And no sign of Steve. But in truth, she'd barely been anywhere other than home and Blue Halo since the shooting at Courtney's shop. All the Blue Halo guys and their women had been on lockdown.

Tonight was Courtney's birthday. She'd insisted she didn't need to do anything, because she didn't want to put anyone at risk, but the women had pushed, arguing that she deserved at least a short night out.

The guys, of course, had fought them on it, arguing that it was safer for everyone to stay home. But it hadn't taken much for them to cave and agree on a quick celebratory drink. Nylah knew part of it was that everyone understood they couldn't just keep their lives on hold indefinitely.

Courtney, Jason, Grace, Logan, and Cody all stood around the tall bar table with her and Liam, while the others were at the next table over. Every time she looked at her brother, she felt a bit sad, because she knew her time with him was coming to an end. He didn't want to leave until the danger was gone, but he had a life in Misty Peak. A business to run. He couldn't stay forever. They had no idea when they'd catch this group.

Liam leaned down, his lips grazing her ear. "I'm gonna get a beer. Would you like anything?"

She smiled up at him, watching the specks of black dance in his gray eyes. "A red wine would be wonderful."

"You got it." He kissed the side of her head, and she felt that kiss right down to her toes.

Cody squeezed her arm from the other side, then she watched as her two favorite men crossed to the bar.

"It must be nice having him here," Grace said quietly from beside her.

Nylah turned back to the other woman. She hadn't spent a lot of time with Grace, just a few interactions when she'd popped into the café, but so far, she was nice. She was a therapist who ran her own practice in Cradle Mountain, so it was no surprise that when she asked questions, Nylah really felt like she was truly listening to the answers.

"It is. I'm a bit sad that he'll be going soon."

Grace nodded. "I can understand that. Does he live far?"

"A little town called Misty Peak. It's in Tennessee."

Courtney's brows rose. "Ooh, near the Smoky Mountains?"

"Yep. The forest runs straight through the town. We've even just built a skywalk through a portion of it. It's pretty cool."

Grace cringed. "Nope. Skywalks are not for me. I don't do heights."

"I think I'd like it," Courtney said with a nod, like she was convincing herself. "I have fears, but heights ain't one of them."

Nylah lifted a shoulder. "It's not too bad. You just have to trust in the infrastructure." Her gaze shifted back to Liam at the bar, drawn to him, before turning back to the women. "How have your guys been with everything?"

Concern flashed over Courtney's face. "Jason's been worried about what's coming. He tries to hide it, but I see it."

"Logan too," Grace said quietly. "I keep reminding him that whatever it is, his team can handle it, like they handled the shooting at the engagement party."

Nylah sighed. "So it's not just Liam."

"Definitely not," Courtney replied.

Nylah bumped her shoulder. "I'm glad you got to celebrate with everyone here tonight."

A genuine smile curved Courtney's lips. "Thanks to all you guys. I would have been happy with a cake at home."

Grace scoffed. "Absolutely not. This year has hit everyone hard, and you deserve drinks out." She turned to look at Nylah. "Now, tell us the truth…how's Courtney as a boss?"

"Eh, she has her moments." She laughed at Courtney's gasp. "I'm kidding. She's amazing. She even told me that if I re-enroll at Columbia, she'll work around my study hours." If that wasn't worthy of a boss award, nothing would be.

Grace's eyes softened. "That sounds like our Courtney."

The guys returned to the table. Liam placed wine in front of her and slipped an arm around her waist, then his lips moved to her ear. "Dance with me."

She shuddered at the way his breath whispered over her skin. At the heat that penetrated her side.

A soft smile spread her lips. "How can I say no to that?"

He tugged her to the dance floor, and the second she placed her hand on his chest, she felt his tense muscles. Saw the way his eyes continued to watch the bar. It wasn't busy tonight, which was probably the only reason he'd allowed them to come.

Against her palm, his heart beat in strong, steady thumps. "How are you doing?"

His gaze lowered, and she could see the effort he put into smoothing out his features. "Better now that I have you in my arms."

He pressed a kiss to the top of her head—and when his head rose again and he suddenly stilled, she frowned and glanced over her shoulder to see Carlson stepping into the bar with two friends.

She turned back to Liam and lifted a hand to his cheek. "Hey. He's allowed to be here. He's done nothing wrong."

For Liam, she knew that was debatable. His mistake after the engagement party had been a big one, but Liam had agreed the guy wasn't lying when he'd said he hadn't known her attacker had survived. So it seemed like it *was* just a mistake.

She sighed and leaned her cheek against Liam's chest. Bit by bit, his muscles eased and his breathing became steadier. Slower. And his arms pulled her closer.

She wasn't sure how long they remained on the dance floor, swaying to the music, getting lost in each other. But eventually she lifted her head and smiled at him. "We should get back to the table."

"How do I let you out of my arms, though?"

Her heart melted. "The second we get home, you can hold me all night long."

A guttural sound vibrated from his throat, something between a growl and a groan. "I'm holding you to that."

They headed back to the table, but before reaching their friends, she touched his arm. "I'm just going to the bathroom."

His gaze flicked toward the restrooms, then back to her. "Okay. Don't take long."

"I won't."

The thin crowd was easy to maneuver through. When she stepped out of the stall to wash her hands, her reflection revealed eyes that were wide and cheeks that were flushed. It was crazy that in the middle of danger and chaos, she could feel such happiness because she'd found Liam.

As she left the bathroom, she noticed Carlson moving to an

unoccupied corner of the bar. Something about the look on his face caught her attention.

Without thinking, she moved toward him, stopping at the end of the long bar, which was just close enough to hear his hushed voice.

"Can you hear me?" he asked, his back to Nylah. "Shit, the music's too loud in here. Hang on, I'm going outside. You need to hear this. It's about the Blue Halo, Project Arma case. Don't hang up!"

She sucked in a breath as he strode toward the back exit. Liam would hate it if she followed, and yeah, it would be stupid...but she had to hear what he said.

With gritted teeth, she followed, hoping like hell Liam would forgive her. When Carlson stepped outside, she hesitated for only a second before following.

"Can you hear me now?"

He faced the parking lot. There were a handful of people outside, standing several feet away.

"I found something today. At first I didn't think anything of it, but the more I sit on it, the more I think it's important." There was a pause, and Nylah held her breath as she waited. "I have a lead on someone who's been in Cradle Mountain since before the first shooting. It's—"

Suddenly, a loud bang exploded.

Immediately, Nylah recognized the sound as a gunshot—but the bullet was already in Carlson.

She didn't have time to scream before a big body hit her from behind, sending her to the ground.

* * *

LIAM TRACKED Nylah as she crossed the bar to the bathroom. Not only did he watch her, he also watched everyone around her, making sure no one's eyes lingered. That no one paid her more attention than they should.

"Hey. She's okay."

Liam glanced at Cody. He'd gotten closer to Nylah's twin brother over the last week. The guy was intense and protective of his sister. Liam liked it. The more people looking out for her, the better. "She doesn't seem to feel any fear about what could happen."

One side of Cody's mouth lifted. "Because she's stubborn. She's decided that everyone's going to be okay and the bad guys are going to be arrested, so that's obviously what's going to happen."

"She told you that?"

"Yeah. She was very convincing too. Told me this guy you have a sketch of is going to mess up and get caught, then he and all his minions will never see the light of day again."

Liam shook his head.

Some of the humor left Cody's eyes. "Also, she can sense your unease, and she's trying to be calm for you."

A muscle in Liam's cheek twitched. He wasn't surprised. "I'm guessing she told you that too?"

"Nah, I can see it. She reads people well. Probably from working in a bar and having five overreactive brothers."

Liam frowned, checking the bathroom door again. "How do you feel about her being here and not back home?"

"I hate it. I want her where I can see her, especially after this entire fucking mess."

"Understandable."

"But...she's happy here." He lifted a shoulder. "Plus, she found herself a man who's actually more protective and overbearing than me and all my brothers combined. So I feel like she's safe with you."

Liam couldn't even muster a smile at that. "She is."

"I know. I see it."

Liam frowned when he saw Nylah walk out of the bathroom, pause…then head toward the far end of the bar.

He straightened when he saw Carlson close by.

The officer's head was down as he walked outside. When Nylah left the bar, Liam's gut coiled. She was following Carlson toward the exit.

Fuck! What the hell was she doing?

Liam rushed toward the door, but not before she pushed outside. He growled and moved faster.

He'd just stepped out behind her when the shot fired.

Liam lunged, grabbing Nylah around the waist, spinning and dropping to the ground. He rolled on top of her, covering her body with his own.

He looked up, but it was too late. The car with the shooter was gone.

Nylah's heart thudded loudly. Screams and cries sounded from the group of people standing a few feet away, some on the phone to police or paramedics already.

Liam leaned to the side and rolled Nylah to her back, checking her quickly for injuries. "Are you okay?"

Her mouth was open, face pale. "Yes."

She turned her head, and he followed her gaze to see Carlson still on the pavement. The police officer was on his back, head turned away from them. Liam didn't need to get any closer to know he wasn't breathing. Kill shot to the heart.

"I think I'm going to be sick."

He tugged her face back to him. "Don't look at him, honey."

She swallowed and sounded like she was on the verge of hyperventilating. He tugged her to her feet, then held her shoulders. "Breathe."

She nodded, sucking in deeper breaths, staring at him like he was her lifeline. "I'm okay now," she said finally.

He cupped her cheek. "What were you thinking, following him out here?"

"I—"

The door to the bar opened, and his friends rushed outside, surrounding them.

Cody grabbed Nylah's arm, his gaze moving over her body. "Are you hurt?"

She shook her head, face still too pale. When Cody pulled her into his arms, Liam wanted to growl at having to let the woman go.

"Have police been called?" Logan asked.

Liam nodded.

Five minutes later, everyone had arrived—police, paramedics. No one caught the damn registration plate, which was frustrating as hell. When it was Nylah's turn to talk to police, a bit of color had returned to her face, but not much.

"And why did you follow him outside, Miss Walker?" the officer asked.

She wet her lips, gaze shifting to Liam, then back to the officer. "I was just curious where he was going."

Liam watched her carefully. She'd just lied. Why?

"Do you know who he was talking to?"

"No." She shook her head.

Truth.

"I could barely hear what he was saying."

Another lie.

The officer nodded. "And what happened when he came out here?"

"He was still on the phone. I'd only just stepped out when the gunshot fired, then Liam threw me to the ground."

The officer turned to Liam. He looked angry. But then, all the officers looked angry. Because one of their own had been killed tonight. "Is there anything you'd like to add, Mr. Shore?"

Liam shook his head. He'd already given his statement.

Frustration crossed the guy's face. "If you remember anything else later, please let us know."

When the officer walked away, Liam looked down at Nylah, voice lowering. "Why did you lie to him?"

After scanning the area around them, she lowered her voice. "I didn't know if your team wanted people to know this."

Dread spidered in his gut. "Know what?"

His team joined them, but Nylah only had eyes for Liam. "Carlson was saying he had a lead on another person from this organization. He said they've been in Cradle Mountain since before the first shooting."

CHAPTER 26

*N*ylah wrung her hands together in her lap. Emotions swirled inside her, spilling out for the world to see. Nerves. Guilt.

They were almost at Courtney and Jason's apartment. An apartment Eleanor would be visiting. Courtney had invited her over to make sure she was okay. Give her some company during this hard time. But that wasn't the only reason.

They had an ulterior motive. They wanted to know if Carlson had been with her the day he'd been shot, and if so, what that day had looked like. Basically, they were fishing for information from a woman who was grieving, and Nylah felt awful about it.

Her fingers were digging into her palms as Liam's warm hand covered hers. "Hey. Everything's gonna be all right."

"I know. I just feel guilty about us inviting Eleanor over for selfish reasons. At the same time, I feel anxious that she won't actually know anything. She's our only lead."

His fingers tightened around her hand. "First of all, you don't need to feel bad. You're still supporting a woman who's lost someone she cares about. Secondly, there's no pressure on you to learn anything. Eleanor either knows something that will help, or she doesn't." He shot her a quick look. "You don't have to do this if you don't want to, though. Courtney will talk to her on her own."

Nylah shook her head. "No. I want to be there. I need to check on her anyway." The woman was a friend, and even though she'd only been dating Carlson a few weeks, the loss would still be significant.

Liam stopped outside Courtney's building. Eleanor's car was already parked on the street. As soon as they got to Courtney's apartment, Liam would disappear with Jason to give them the illusion of space, but of course he'd be listening to everything.

"Ready?"

Was she? She had to be. She nodded. "Let's do this."

They'd just knocked when Liam lowered his mouth to her ear. "Remember, I'm just in the office."

Then he kissed her, and some of the guilt and nerves pitting her belly calmed.

Jason opened the door. "Hey." He didn't smile as he stepped back.

Nylah passed him, offering a small, tight smile before spotting Eleanor on the couch beside Courtney, face tearstained. Courtney stood and Nylah didn't hesitate to take her place, lowering to the couch beside Eleanor and tugging her into her arms.

"I'm so sorry," she whispered.

Eleanor's arms wrapped around her waist, her head digging into Nylah's shoulder as silent tears wet her shirt. Courtney squeezed Nylah's arm before moving into the kitchen. She also heard the dull footsteps of Liam and Jason walking toward the home office.

When Eleanor finally pulled back, Nylah touched her knee. "Tell me what I can do."

Eleanor swallowed. "You and Courtney just asking me over

means everything. I don't have many people here in Cradle Mountain, except you guys and Violet."

"Where is Violet?"

"She hasn't left my side since I received the news, so I told her to go and do something for herself today. Have the day off babysitting."

"It's not babysitting when a friend's in pain," Nylah said quietly.

Courtney returned, handing out glasses of juice before sitting on the couch on Eleanor's other side. "Have you thought any more about talking to Grace? She's an amazing therapist. You feel like you're talking to a friend."

"I have," Eleanor said quietly. "I probably will. I'm just trying to take it one day at a time right now. Pierce and I were so new, but…I felt like he was it, you know? Like he was my person. I was already falling in love with him."

Nylah felt the tears build in her own eyes at the sorrow behind the woman's words. "I could see that. And I have no doubt he felt the same way."

Eleanor shook her head. "After he found out about the mistake he made, not getting a description of the perpetrator after the shooting, he was determined to help with the case. He was acting like he needed to prove himself, even though he didn't."

Nylah sent a quick look Courtney's way before turning back to Eleanor. She spoke softly and carefully. "Do you know if he learned anything?"

Eleanor shook her head. "Not as far as I was aware."

"Were you together that day?" Courtney asked.

"Yes. We went out for lunch, then he took me home. We watched a movie. When he left, he seemed completely fine."

Courtney shuffled forward. "So he spent the whole day with you?"

"Yes. Well, from about lunch until late afternoon."

"Did he message you after he left?" Nylah asked.

"He did." A tear fell down her cheek. "To ask if he could come back to my place after the bar. I said yes...then never heard from him again."

Nylah's heart cracked for the woman. She'd really cared about Carlson.

Courtney rubbed Eleanor's arm. "I'm so sorry, El. Was he at the bar with friends?"

She sniffed. "Yeah, some old high school friends. One of the guys is a firefighter, another a lawyer. He catches up with them often, but I don't think they'd have anything to do with what happened."

No. Whatever he'd learned that had gotten him shot, he'd learned it earlier that day. That was what he'd said before he was shot. Day...not night.

"I know this is hard," Courtney said softly. "But could we get the names of the guys and look into them, just in case? And perhaps anyone he interacted with during the day? Even who served you at lunch...anything could help. We want to do everything we can to find out who did this."

She nodded vigorously. "Yes. I'll do whatever I can to help catch his killer. They took someone from me, and I want them to pay for that."

Nylah swallowed. "We want them to pay too, El."

* * *

"They took the bait," Callum said quietly over the video call. "I got an email."

Liam's chest tightened. Was this it? Could they finally be a step ahead of these assholes?

Callum had scoured the web for countless hours before finally discovering a Project Arma hate group, and the second he did, he'd known it was the break they'd been waiting for. Little things gave them away. Like on the day of the engagement shooting, there'd been vague posts about something going down and the world being safer. And the day after, angry comments about needing a plan B. Someone had even mentioned the name Hawk.

Each member of the group was also former military.

They didn't think Hawk had started the hate group. But they'd already identified some of the dead perpetrators as members, so it was at least a recruiting ground.

Callum had used his fake profile to leave subtle footprints of hate on the web for any survivors of Project Arma before even joining the group. Once he was approved, he participated in several chats, hating on himself, his team, and the Marble Protection men.

Conspiracy theories had been thrown around in various conversations, some even insisting the men involved in the project had their own secret agenda. That they'd *wanted* what had happened to them. Every member thought no man should have the abilities Liam's team possessed; that they were too dangerous to exist.

"And there's no way they'd know who you really are?" Jason asked.

"If they dig, they'll find a full background for a Marshall Fawkes from Salt Lake City. A forty-five-year-old former soldier. It's solid and will check out."

"What does the email say?" Liam asked.

"It's vague, and it asks more than it tells. Basically, they want information about me. They also ask if I want to be part of something great and what lengths I would go to in order to protect my country."

Liam cursed. "Assholes."

Jason's hands fisted. "Okay. What's next?"

"I'm responding today, giving them everything they're asking for and making sure they think I'm all in for whatever they're planning. That I'll go to any lengths necessary to protect my country." There was a dangerous edge to Callum's voice.

Liam nodded. They talked details for another ten minutes, figuring out the basics of what would be in the response email. When Liam heard movement in the other room, he stood. "Keep us updated and let us know if there's anything more we can do."

Callum nodded. "Will do."

When Liam walked into the living room, it was to see the women on their feet and moving toward the door. Nylah brought Eleanor into a hug, then Courtney did the same. When Courtney pulled back, she kept her hands on the woman's shoulders. "Remember, if it's too much for you, you don't need to come help at the shop."

Eleanor shook her head. "No. I do. I need to keep busy and keep my mind off what happened, otherwise it'll just swamp me. A girls' night will be good for me."

"Well, girls' night plus Jason," Courtney said.

Eleanor aimed a small smile toward the guys before turning to the door.

Liam stepped forward. "I'm sorry about Carlson."

Jason nodded. "Me too."

Tears began to build in Eleanor's eyes, but she blinked them away. "Thank you. If there's anything I can do to help figure out what happened that night, please let me know."

The second she was gone, Nylah went to Liam and laid her head on his shoulder. "I ache for her."

He slid an arm around her waist, pressing a kiss to the top of her head. "Me too."

"She didn't know anything, unfortunately. She and Carlson went out for lunch, watched a movie together, then he went to the bar with his high school friends. She gave us the names of those friends and everyone they interacted with during the day, so you guys can talk to them. Also the name of the restaurant they went to, and the time they were there."

Courtney handed a piece of paper to Jason. "Here's all the information. How'd the meeting with Callum go?"

"They reached out to him."

Courtney's eyes widened.

"Really?" Nylah gasped. "So he's in? Do you think they'll actually tell him about their plans before anything happens?"

Liam shifted some hair from her face. "They're asking for more information first. But, if that goes well, then hopefully."

Her face fell a little.

"But we'll get there," he added. "If they're reaching out, it means they're still recruiting, so there's time to stop whatever they're working toward before it happens."

Nylah nodded but didn't seem convinced. He looked up at Jason and Courtney. "Thanks for today. We'll see you later."

They nodded, and Liam led Nylah out of the apartment. When she reached for the handle of his car door, he tugged her into his arms. "Hey. It's gonna be okay."

Just days ago, she'd told her brother the same thing. Now...

"You don't know that. A few days ago, Carlson just stepped out of a bar and was shot. Somehow this guy knew where he'd be and that he had vital information. It's like he has ears and eyes everywhere. It's all so dangerous."

"*We're* dangerous. And we're also the best. We will *not* let them win this."

That was a fucking vow.

She swallowed. "I want to believe you—"

"Then do. Trust me."

She sighed and leaned her head against his chest. "Okay, Liam. I trust you."

Those words...they sank deep inside his chest, lifting some of the heaviness of the past few weeks.

He wrapped his arms around her and held her close, letting the simple touch be enough to make him feel almost at peace.

CHAPTER 27

"*W*hat do you think?" Courtney asked, stepping back, paintbrush in hand.

Nylah's lips stretched into a smile "It's soothing. I love it. And I think your customers will, too."

Courtney had chosen a beautiful sage green for the walls, which really brought the coffee shop to life. They'd already finished the first coat on one wall, and between the four women, she was sure it wouldn't take them long to finish the next.

Jason and Cody were here too. Because of the newspaper blocking the windows, they were alternating who guarded the front of the shop. Right now, it was Jason, which meant Cody had the great fortune of painting with them.

Nylah was glad she was here. It was taking her mind off the fact that Liam was at Blue Halo with a few of the other guys. It was almost closing time, and though they'd been waiting anxiously all day, Callum still hadn't received a response email from this group.

Violet nodded. "Nylah's right. It's beautiful. Good choice, Courtney. You have an eye for color. Imagine how good this place will look after the rest of the walls are done."

"And of course, my painting's the best," Cody said, always one to inject humor into a situation. She shook her head, a smile on her face.

Eleanor just nodded, her own small smile not quite reaching her eyes. As if sensing her mood, Violet inched closer to Eleanor, slipping her fingers into her friend's. "You okay?"

Eleanor shook her head like she was trying to pull herself out of a trance. "Sorry, I've been a bit of a downer tonight, haven't I?"

"No," Courtney said quickly. "Absolutely not. We're glad you're here. We're all running a bit low on energy, though, since we haven't eaten all night. You know what we need? That cider and pizza I promised."

Nylah's stomach growled at the thought. "I wouldn't say no to that."

Cody scoffed. "When do you *ever* say no to pizza?"

She whacked him on the shoulder.

Courtney just laughed before pulling her phone from her pocket. "Done." Then she stepped into the back room to call the pizza place.

Nylah dipped her brush in the paint and looked at Eleanor. "Have they set a date for Pierce's funeral?"

Eleanor swallowed. "I'm not sure. His family lives in Utah, so they want it there. Maybe next week. They haven't kept me in the loop much. They didn't even know we were dating. We were so new, Pierce hadn't told them yet."

"I'm sorry."

"When we know a date and time, we'll be there," Violet promised.

Courtney returned to the room. "Done. I'll go pick up the pizza."

Nylah frowned. "They can't deliver?"

"Nope. I asked. Two of his guys are sick, so he can't offer delivery tonight. But it's fine. I'll go. I just need to convince my big, broody protector to let me go get our sustenance. You guys okay if I pop out?"

"Uh, yeah, if you're returning with pizza," Violet said sarcastically.

Courtney laughed and left to talk to Jason just as Nylah's phone buzzed in her pocket. She tugged it out to see Liam's name.

Liam: Almost finishing time. I'll come straight to The Grind after. You okay?

Nylah: Don't stress. Cody and Jason are here. We're all doing great. Stay safe.

She pushed her phone back into her pocket just as Violet clapped her hands. "I'll get the cider."

Nylah chuckled. The woman had wanted to crack into the cider the moment they'd all arrived but had promised Courtney she'd wait. Nylah was more a wine girl, but she wouldn't turn down a cold hard cider.

Violet disappeared into the back room while Nylah and Eleanor resumed their work.

"Painting's actually kind of therapeutic," Eleanor said quietly. "Maybe I'll ask my landlord if we can paint the apartment."

"Ooh, call me over to help. I'm always happy to paint a wall."

Eleanor smiled, and this time, it looked a little less forced.

Nylah managed a couple more strokes before Violet yelled from the back room. "Cody? Can you help me reach the cider?"

As he headed to the back room, Eleanor shuffled closer. "I've been meaning to ask how you're doing. Everyone keeps asking *me*, but you're the one who saw him get...shot." She stumbled over the last word.

Nylah swallowed, hating the memory of that night. For a moment, she didn't know how to answer. Yes, it had been traumatic. But honestly, she'd had so much support from Liam that she hadn't focused on that awful moment. The truth was, despite everything, she was happier than she'd been in a long time. But there was no part of her that wanted to flaunt her happiness at being in a loving relationship with a woman who'd just lost someone.

"I'm good," she started slowly. "I'll be better when we catch this person who's targeting the guys."

Eleanor nodded. "Right?"

"I'm really glad you've had Violet to look after you."

"She's amazing." Eleanor quickly glanced over her shoulder, obviously checking for her roommate. "I actually think she's been secretly dating someone, so I feel bad for using up all her time."

Nylah's brows rose. "Really? And she didn't tell us? Heck, she didn't tell *you*?"

Eleanor lifted a shoulder. "I think it's because she might have met him through her dad? He might even work with him, and she always swore she'd never date anyone from the FBI."

Nylah paused mid-swipe, her arm lifted, iciness slipping over her skin. She turned to face Eleanor. "What?"

"Well, I'm not certain, but I've heard her talking to someone in a hushed voice in her room a couple of times. I heard the word FBI thrown around, and I know her dad works for them."

Nylah's breath started to shorten. It had to be a coincidence, right? That she was so closely connected to the FBI...the organization Liam and his team had suspected of having a mole. "Do you know what her dad's name is?"

Eleanor wrinkled her nose. "Steve, I think?"

Now the breath caught in Nylah's throat, every muscle in her body locking.

Footsteps sounded from the back moments before Violet stepped into the room, ciders in hand. "Got 'em! We have cider, and soon we'll have pizza. If anyone calls this work, I'm calling their bluff."

Nylah's gaze flicked to the back room before returning to Violet. "Where's Cody?"

"I think he popped out the back to check on Jason." She didn't look at them as she spoke.

Nylah swallowed, the thudding of her heart so loud, she could barely hear anything else. Eleanor went back to painting, but Nylah's finger had developed a shake. She almost wanted to hide her hands behind her back in case Violet saw.

When Violet handed her a cider, Nylah had little choice but to take it.

The woman's brows flickered. "Is everything okay?"

"Of course." Shit. Her voice came out too high. But dammit, every part of her wanted to go into the back room and check on her brother. To call Liam and tell him what she'd just learned.

They'd suspected Hawk was close. How much closer could you get than Violet dating him?

Her coworker was still frowning as she handed a cider to Eleanor before opening her own. Violet took a sip, then lowered to the floor and lifted her brush. When she leaned toward the wall to begin painting, her shirt pulled up in the back...and Nylah's gaze caught on a tattoo.

The world darkened around her. Even though she could only see half the tattoo, it was enough for her to know what it was—the same tattoo on every one of the perpetrators. But in Violet's, it wasn't an angel wielding the dagger.

It was a hawk.

Oh God! She wasn't feeding Hawk information...she *was* Hawk!

It took every scrap of strength Nylah had to remain still. To not show the shock, fear, and anger on her face. She had to remain calm and contact Liam. She had to check that Cody was okay.

"Hey. You all right?"

At Eleanor's question, she nodded quickly...maybe too quickly. "Yes. Of course. I actually feel like juice instead of cider. I might go and grab some from the fridge."

She felt Violet's gaze on her as she set down her cider. She'd almost made it to the door leading to the kitchen when the click of a gun sounded.

"Stop. Or I shoot."

Nylah's lungs seized. Violet's voice was different...harder.

Eleanor gasped. "Vi! What are you doing?"

Slowly, Nylah turned to find Violet holding a pistol, pointing it right at her chest, features blank.

"Really?" Nylah said quietly. "All this time, it's been you?"

Her brows rose. "Surprised?"

"Yes." She hadn't suspected Violet for a second. She was too kind and sweet.

Violet cocked her head. "Because a woman couldn't do this?"

"Because it was a *man* I fought off at the engagement party shooting, and people suggested *he* was Hawk."

She nodded. "That makes sense. And yeah, I knew I needed help. Someone with resources. But my partner isn't the person behind everything."

"No...Vi..." Eleanor shook her head, voice trembling. "Tell me this is some sick joke!"

"Afraid not." Violet never took her eyes off Nylah. She took several steps, almost closing the distance between them. "You think I don't know what they are? What they can do? Guess what? I'm *intimately* familiar with the depths of their inhumanity. Because I dated one of them."

Nylah frowned. Who did she—

"His name was Carter. And he was normal. Until Project Arma stripped him of every goddamn moral he had."

Nylah's throat closed, recollection hitting her like a ton of bricks. Of Liam talking about a Carter. The man who was a monster, who worked alongside the Project Arma leader, Hylar.

"No," Nylah said quickly. "These guys aren't like Carter. He was everything they were fighting against."

"But they could be *exactly* like him!" she yelled, her composure suddenly crumbling, the hand on the gun trembling with her words. "He thought he could do whatever he goddamn wanted! Hurt me whenever he felt like it! Kill whoever pissed him off. He was *dangerous*, and he scared the hell out of me!"

Nylah shook her head. She had to get through to this woman. "Violet—"

"When my father discovered how Carter had treated me before he died, he was outraged. He used his connections to get close to the Blue Halo team. But he decided they were good men!" she barked with a laugh. "That they could never possibly turn. He didn't seem to understand that even if just one of them did, the consequences would be devastating."

"Your father...Steve...he's not part of this?"

She scoffed. "No. Although, he's been frantically trying to get in contact with me since you did your little sketch of Trey."

"Trey?" Nylah breathed.

Violet's watch beeped. She glanced at it before looking up, a small smile on her face. "He's here now, actually. Ready to watch this all come to a perfect fucking finale?"

The door opened, and Nylah stumbled back a step. It was the man from the event center...the one who'd fought her in the closet.

Violet smiled wider. "Hi, honey."

He approached her and leaned down, kissing her on the cheek. "Hey, baby."

"What did you do to Jason?" Nylah demanded, anger and dread rivaling inside her.

"He won't be helping anyone tonight," Trey said, voice cold.

Violet scowled. "Trey knows all about the vile things Carter did to me. Not to mention how he used to brag about the kills he'd made, how unstoppable he was."

"Too much power for any man is dangerous," Trey said quietly.

"You don't even know them," Nylah whispered. Had this man

been seduced by Violet, or did he really believe he was doing the right thing here?

Trey looked at his watch. "Almost time."

Bile crawled up Nylah's throat. "Time for what?"

Violet smiled, pure evil on her face as her brows rose. "*Boom.*"

Nylah heart stopped. "There's a bomb? Where?"

"You know where," Violet said quietly.

Oh God…it had to be at Blue Halo. Almost the entire team was there right now.

A choking noise sounded from Eleanor.

Devastation and rage fought for dominance in Nylah's chest. She ruthlessly pushed them down. "You're going to pay for this. Both of you."

"Wrong. We're going to be fucking *heroes,*" Violet hissed. "Now, unfortunately, both of you have to die. It was only gonna be Nylah, but she kind of put you in a shitty position by figuring it out while you were in the same room, El."

Nylah's entire body trembled.

She was a second away from diving behind the counter when Trey suddenly cursed and dove on top of Violet as a gunshot blasted from somewhere behind Nylah. She looked up to see Cody standing in the doorway to the back room, gun in hand, blood dripping from a cut on his head.

His gaze flew to Nylah. Trey took advantage of his second of distraction and jumped to his feet and lunged for Cody. The two men dropped to the floor, fighting over the pistol.

Violet rose to her knees and swung her weapon around, but before she could shoot, Nylah dove forward, grabbing her around the middle and sending them both crashing back to the floor. The gun went off, hitting the newly installed window, the shattering of glass loud in the otherwise quiet night.

There were loud sounds of fighting behind her from Cody and Trey, but she put her whole focus on Violet, grabbing her wrists and keeping the gun pointed over the woman's head.

"You're not gonna win," Violet growled before lunging up to headbutt Nylah.

Pain ricocheted throughout her skull, her head flinging back. Violet took advantage, rolling them until she was on top. The woman was struggling to maneuver the gun when something smashed into her so hard that she flew sideways off Nylah and thudded to the floor.

Nylah gasped at the sight of Eleanor holding a chair. She dropped the heavy piece of furniture and grabbed the pistol, hands shaking as she aimed it at Violet's chest.

"Are you okay?" Eleanor gasped.

"Yes," Nylah said, voice trembling.

Then the ground beneath her shook violently, and a massive *boom* overtook every other sound.

Nylah's heart stopped.

No! She was too late!

Devastation tried to drown her, but she refused to let it take over. Liam *wasn't* dead. No part of her felt capable of accepting that. He'd gotten out. He had to.

Eleanor nodded toward the door. "Go check on Blue Halo. We'll check on Jason."

Nylah's gaze swung from Violet, who was groaning beside her, to Cody, who was straddling Trey on the floor, furiously punching the man over and over.

The door flew open and Courtney ran in, eyes wide. "What's going on? I just heard—"

Nylah pushed to her feet. "It's Violet...she's Hawk. I need to check on Liam at Blue Halo. You go find Jason. He's outside hurt somewhere!"

Courtney gasped and ran back out, Nylah right behind her.

CHAPTER 28

*L*iam's eyes narrowed on the screen. He leaned forward as if that could somehow slow the text down. The chat was moving so damn quickly, he and Callum could barely keep up, even with their enhanced vision.

It was while waiting for any response to their email that they'd clicked into the chat forum. The posts had been fast and furious, and they hadn't stopped.

"You following this, Wyatt?" Callum asked quietly to their friend who was on speakerphone.

"Yeah. Why's there so much activity?"

Liam didn't fucking know, but he didn't have a good feeling about it. The people on the chat had worked themselves into a frenzy, upping their hate for Liam and his team. Talking about why they needed to be eliminated. Why there was a sudden sense of urgency.

Liam was just about to flick to the emails on his own computer when a comment had his eyes narrowing on Callum's screen.

He leaned forward and used the keypad to go back up and highlight the comment. Callum tensed beside him as Liam read the post out loud in case Wyatt had missed it. "Blue Halo and Marble Protection won't know what hit them."

"What the fuck does that mean?" Wyatt growled.

Dread started to gnaw at Liam's gut. Something was coming, and it was coming soon. "Wyatt, is your team with you at Marble Protection?"

"Yeah, six of us are here."

More comments started to filter down the page. More hate and slander. A particular one caught Liam's attention.

They built those businesses with government fucking money. It's only fitting we hit them where it'll hurt most—their pocketbooks.

Hit them?

Then the next…

Guns at the ready, men. Two minutes until we light up the fucking night.

Liam shot to his feet as the next guy wrote one single word.

Boom.

"Get out," Liam said—but not nearly loud enough. "Everyone fucking out! Wyatt, get your team out of the building!"

He moved through the hall, knocking on every office door and yelling the same damn thing. That they had to get the hell out of Blue Halo.

His teammates were up and moving, grabbing their weapons and racing to the front, then down the stairs. Liam made sure every man was out of the office before he followed. On the way down the stairs, he pulled his Glock.

He'd just run out the front door when the bomb detonated, so loud it deafened the world around him and with so much force that he flew through the air and hit a car on the other side of the road.

Pain surged through his body at the brush of flames. The impact with the car. He barely had time to feel it before a man rose from behind a parked car down the street.

"Shooter!" he shouted, in case his team hadn't seen him. He

slid over the car he'd just crashed into. Callum dove beside him as bullets hit the metal of the old Mazda.

"You okay?" Liam asked without looking at his friend.

"Yes. You?"

"Yeah." He poked his head out to see his team had all found cover. Good. "Let's end this quickly." Because all he could goddamn think about was Nylah. Was she okay at The Grind? He needed to get to her. Get confirmation that she was okay.

"Agreed," Callum growled.

Bullets continued to fly through the mostly deserted street, flames lighting the dim sky from his right. Liam waited. He needed a small lull in gunfire so he could move. Shoot. Kill.

When it finally came, no words were spoken. Both he and Callum rose simultaneously, backs to each other as they fired in opposite directions.

Three rounds from Liam, three kill shots. He saw more of his team doing the same around them.

When more men rose with weapons aimed, Liam lowered at the same time as Callum. "Three dead on my side. I counted eight more."

"Two dead, one injured over here. Five to go."

His team together could easily take care of that number.

The bullets were loud around him, small concussions competing with the roar of the flames. Beneath that, he heard footsteps. Some of the assholes were getting closer.

Good. They'd lose their cover and Liam or his team would be able to kill them at close range.

He dropped to a prone position and fired at a man's feet, then another in quick succession, sending two guys to the ground before shooting them in the foreheads.

Suddenly, two men rounded the car.

Liam kicked out a foot, sending one to the ground while shooting the other in the heart. When the asshole on the ground fired at Liam, he rolled, narrowly missing the bullet.

He lunged, grabbing the guy's wrist before pushing the muzzle of his Glock to the man's head and firing.

Liam swung one quick look around to locate his team, seeing them all rising from behind cover, weapons at the ready...but there were no more enemies to shoot.

Then he was running before he could stop himself. He needed to get to Nylah, and he needed to get to her fast.

* * *

NYLAH HAD JUST CROSSED the street when a man suddenly appeared from behind a car, gun in hand. She stumbled back a step, gaze colliding with his. He frowned—like he wasn't sure if he was supposed to shoot her or not.

Before he could decide, the door to The Grind opened and Violet stepped out, rage on her face and gun in her hand.

Oh God! Eleanor!

Concern for her friend blasted through her system even as Violet took aim.

Nylah ran, slipping into the alley to her right, ignoring the bullets that ricocheted off the bricks. She didn't stop. She ran so fast that her lungs burned.

Near the end of the alley, another gunshot roared through the night, the bullet grazing her skin, causing pain to radiate up her side. She cried out and stumbled, her knees almost collapsing. It was only through sheer determination that she was able to force herself to remain on her feet. To keep moving as she rounded the corner onto the next street. Storefronts were dark around her, each closed up and locked, leaving her nowhere to hide.

When a single lit business came into view, hope flared in Nylah's chest. She recognized it. The museum where Liam had taken her for their first date. Was it open?

She forced her feet to move faster, her arms to pump harder.

When her fingers wrapped around the door handle, she said a silent prayer that it wasn't locked.

The door opened, and she all but fell inside just as another bullet hit the glass door, causing her to gasp and stumble as it shattered.

The interior of the building was dimly lit, with only small amounts of light from exit signs and exhibitions. She ran through the first gallery. When she heard the front door open, her breath stopped.

Then she heard another voice. A new one.

"Hey, what are you—"

The man's words were cut off by a gunshot. Nylah pressed a hand to her mouth to stifle her cry.

Quickly, she slipped from one gallery room to the next, every step as silent as the last.

"Get the fuck out here, Nylah!"

She crept into the room with the old train and tried the door leading to the next gallery. When it didn't open, her skin iced.

Shit. She was cornered.

There wasn't even anything in here she could use as a weapon, not without breaking glass and making Violet aware of her location.

She slipped behind the old train, her breathing too fast.

"You know I shot El, right?" Violet called. "Disarmed her quite easily, actually. She'll die because *you* were too much of a coward to stay in the café and fight me."

Nylah's heart broke for her friend, and she barely stifled a whimper.

"I would have shot your brother too, but he found his fucking gun and turned it on me, so I ran out the door instead. Luckily, I don't care about Trey. Cody can kill him. I only slept with him because I needed the resources of the FBI."

Cody wouldn't kill the man. He'd make sure he was arrested and never saw the light of day ever again.

"This thing between you and me has turned quite personal, Nylah."

As the footsteps crept closer, Nylah tugged out her phone with a shaking hand to see a missed call and a text from Liam. She turned the screen brightness down and covered the screen with her hand.

Liam: Where are you?

She shot a glance to the time it was received, the air rushing from her chest, her heart finally beating with a bit more ease. He'd sent it only a minute ago—*after* the explosion.

Alive. Liam was alive!

Tears of relief built in her eyes, and she blinked them away.

Nylah: Hiding in museum. Violet's here with a gun. She's Hawk.

"Maybe I've become so fixated on killing you because you've been so good at evading death. We sent some of our best guys to end you, and none of them succeeded." The footsteps continued to move closer. "My respect for you definitely grew...to the point I wanted a go at you myself."

Nylah crept to the end of the train, shoving her phone into her pocket. Liam might respond, but if the woman stepped into this room, Nylah couldn't risk her seeing the light.

She swallowed, trying to silence her breaths.

"Do you know the hell my life became thanks to Carter? He hurt me. Terrified me. Once, he killed someone right in front of my eyes, just to make me suffer. A friend of mine. A guy who was helping me get away from him."

Bile rose in Nylah's belly, and for a fleeting second, there was just a hint of sympathy for the woman. But that quickly passed.

No. She didn't deserve sympathy. Not after everything she'd done.

When Violet stepped into the train gallery, Nylah's skin turned cold, and she willed the fear inside of her to remain silent. To not burst out of her in loud breaths and trembling limbs.

"You might not understand why I do what I do. And if that's

the case, I'm actually glad for you. It means your soul hasn't been broken. No one's hurt you beyond repair."

As Violet neared the train, Nylah lowered her body, muscles tense. There was no escape, not when the woman had a gun, which meant she had no choice but to fight. And she *would* fight. Her brothers had trained her for this her entire life.

She forced her mind to focus, her breathing to even.

The second the woman started to inch around the back of the train, Nylah kicked—hard.

Violet cried out and stumbled, half falling on a display cabinet, glass shattering and the pistol hitting the floor.

Nylah grabbed for the weapon, ignoring the pain of glass cutting into her skin. Before she could wrap her fingers around the grip, Violet was there, digging her fingers into the wound on Nylah's side.

She screamed, clutching Violet's hand even as the woman climbed on top of her. The punch came before Nylah could turn her face away, Violet's fist connecting with her cheek.

Her head whipped to the side, and her vision went dark for a second. The woman raised her arm a second time, but Nylah dodged her fist, then rolled them over the shattered glass.

Violet screeched. Nylah grabbed the gun and held it to her head.

The grimace on Violet's face turned into a laugh that sounded all wrong. "You gonna shoot me, Nylah?"

"I should. You deserve to die for everything you've done."

"No. I'm rising up, from victim to savior. I should be *rewarded* for my strength and courage. Those men are abominations who shouldn't be alive! You don't see the threat they pose and the damage they could cause if they choose to, because they haven't turned on you yet."

"That's the key, though. If they *choose*. But these men have something Carter didn't—integrity. Something your own father recognized after working with them. They would never hurt good people. They *save* people."

"Until they choose differently."

At a small sound from the entrance, Nylah's focus shifted only for a second, but it was enough for Violet to flip them and smash Nylah's wrist to the floor with one hand while grabbing the gun with the other.

Suddenly, she was dragged to her feet by her hair, and the pistol was held to her head this time.

Liam stood in the doorway, radiating fury and danger as he aimed his Glock at her and Violet.

CHAPTER 29

$\mathcal{L}$iam's feet pounded the pavement. The second he'd stepped inside The Grind to see Nylah wasn't there, the blood in his veins had iced. A man lay unconscious on the floor, possibly the man in Nylah's sketch, but he'd been beaten too bloody for Liam to be sure.

Cody knelt on the floor, trying to save Eleanor from an obvious gunshot wound. Liam had barely taken in the scene when Cody yelled at him to find Nylah.

The second her text came through, his heart damn near stopped in his chest. She was hiding from a woman trying to kill her...and he wasn't there to protect her.

When he finally reached the museum, he stepped inside to find Ned on the floor, bullet wound to his gut.

Fuck.

He stepped closer, hearing the man's faint heartbeat. He pulled out his phone and dialed nine-one-one, speaking quietly and quickly to the operator. "I need an ambulance at the Cradle Mountain Museum. Man with a GSW to the abdomen."

He hung up before they could respond. Then he stopped and listened. When he heard movement in one of the farthest galleries, he took off toward it, only stopping when he reached the train room. What he saw made anger rush through his veins like wildfire.

Nylah, held against Violet's front, gun to her head.

"What the fuck are you doing alive?" Violet cursed. "We blew you up!"

The two women were the same height and similar in size, so he could barely see Violet. He couldn't take the risk of shooting.

Instead, Liam took a small, measured step forward. "We found the online hate group you've been recruiting from. The assholes gave us a two-minute warning before the bomb detonated. That was all we needed. Everyone's alive."

"No." Disbelief coated that single word, and Violet visibly pushed the muzzle of the gun harder against Nylah's skull, causing her to cringe. "That can't be true. I need everyone like you dead! Just like Carter!"

"Carter?"

"From Project Arma," Nylah said through gritted teeth. "They were together."

The muscles in Liam's body tightened.

"He was a *monster*," Violet growled. "And he showed me exactly how immoral you are. The danger in any man possessing so much strength and speed and power."

The man was a fucking animal. But that didn't mean they all were. "Violet—"

"You've decimated every opponent with ease. That's proof enough!" She took a step back, forcing Nylah to move with her. "There's only so much time before all that power goes to your heads. And just imagine if you collectively decide you want to kill innocent people. Seize control of our government."

"That wouldn't happen," Liam said quietly, slowly closing the distance.

"It *could!*"

Footsteps sounded from the entrance. Paramedics?

When they didn't stop at the entrance, Liam growled, "Who's here?"

"The militia who are loyal to me, of course. I messaged them when I arrived, in case I needed backup."

Fuck.

Suddenly, Nylah threw her head forward, simultaneously launching a fist back into Violet's nose, causing her grip to slip just enough...

The second Nylah dropped, Liam shot Violet in the stomach. Before she hit the floor, he was running forward and grabbing both Nylah and the pistol, pulling her behind the train. He heard her heart racing as he pushed Violet's gun into her hand.

"Stay down. If anyone gets past me, shoot."

She gave a quick nod but grabbed him before he could rise. "Be careful."

"Always."

The footsteps rushed into their gallery. Liam swung his weapon around the side of the train and fired, getting the first three guys in the head.

The others stopped and took cover behind the wall. Three more men.

The silence only lasted for a second before bullets began to pepper the train. They were moving forward.

Fuck! He couldn't let them get close to Nylah.

The second the first asshole came into view, Liam grabbed his arm and twisted, hearing the pop of his shoulder detaching from its socket before tugging him into his body and shooting him in the head. Liam quickly followed it up with a bullet to asshole number two when he came around the corner.

When he heard a gasp from Nylah, he spun around to see asshole number three stepping around the train. Before he could shoot, Nylah put a round in his leg.

Liam dropped the man in his arms and shot Nylah's guy in the head.

Then there was silence, broken only by Nylah's heaving breaths and her racing heart.

He dropped to her side and cupped her cheek in his hand. "Are you okay?"

She nodded, her gaze moving over him. "Yes." She scanned his torso. His legs. When she looked back up, there were tears in her eyes. "You're alive! When I felt the ground shake, I knew it was the Blue Halo building. I was so scared for you!"

Her voice cracked on the last word, and he tugged her into his chest, holding her so tightly, he barely gave her space to move. "I'm here. We're both here."

She dug her face into his chest.

That's when he heard it…the rustle of movement on the other side of the train, followed by more footsteps moving through the museum.

God, would these assholes just die?

He pushed Nylah down once again, pressing a finger to his lips. When he stepped around the train it was to see Violet standing, one hand to the bullet wound on her stomach, the other holding a gun dropped by one of her men.

"I'm going…to kill you." She coughed, the sound wet in her throat.

Liam was about to pull the trigger when a new voice rang out. "Violet!"

The woman gasped and turned to look at Steve, who was standing in the entrance to the gallery.

"Dad?"

Liam's blood ran cold. *Dad?* Steve was Violet's fucking *father*?

"You need to put the gun down, Violet. Now."

"No! He—"

"Is *not* Carter. None of them are." More guys appeared behind Steve, all wearing vests declaring them FBI, all pointing their weapons at Violet and Liam. "I told you that. I told you to drop this obsession. That Carter was dead and we needed to leave him behind. But you wouldn't listen."

"I'm trying to save people from the same fate as me!" Violet's voice shook.

Steve was shaking his head before Violet finished. "No. You're trying to get the retribution that was stolen from you because you didn't get to kill Carter yourself."

Violet glanced back at Liam, tears raining down her cheeks, and her expression shifted from anger to something else... Pain.

"Put the gun down, Violet."

It took her several heartbeats. Then, finally, she lowered the pistol to the floor, and the men behind Steve stepped forward and took her.

Dark circles shadowed Steve's eyes, pain etched into his features as he watched his daughter being led away. She'd need medical attention, but after that, she'd be going away for a long time, and her father knew it.

When Steve looked at Liam, it was obvious he was trying to pull himself together. "Are you okay?"

Liam nodded as Nylah came to stand by his side. He wrapped an arm around her waist as Steve shifted his attention to her. "I'm sorry. After I saw Trey in the sketch, I tried to find and secure him, but he'd already disappeared. I knew he was close to Violet, but...I was hoping I was wrong. I was hoping they weren't in on this together."

He took a deep breath, then nodded at Liam. "I'm going to make sure she gives me the names of every person involved. They'll all be arrested. That's a promise I'm making to you and your team."

* * *

"THIS MAY STING."

Nylah swallowed and nodded at the paramedic, barely feeling

the pain as he sterilized her wound. Just about all of her attention remained on Liam. The way his gaze flicked up and down the street, so alert she expected him to reach for his gun at any second. His team would be here soon. He'd just made contact with every man, made sure they were all uninjured.

When pain shot down her side and Nylah cringed, Liam's attention returned to her, his breath hissing through his teeth as he shifted closer. "Are you okay?"

She nodded.

"Maybe we should go to the—"

"No. I'm okay. He said the wound is superficial and he can take care of it here. That's what I want." The sooner this night was over, the better.

Liam's eyes narrowed, but he didn't argue with her. He hadn't left her side. Not while the bodies had been wheeled out of the museum. Not as the paramedic began to inspect her wounds. Not as the police asked a million questions. His hand was permanently touching her—leg, arm, back. And that was exactly what she needed. The reassurance that he was with her and not going anywhere.

"Do you think Ned will be okay?" she whispered. She wasn't sure if she was asking the paramedic or Liam. Maybe both.

"I don't know," Liam said quietly. "It will depend on whether the bullet hit any of his vital organs. But he was breathing when they wheeled him away, and his heart was beating. That's good."

She nodded, guilt trickling through her chest that he'd been shot because she chose to run into the museum.

"Hey."

Liam watched her closely. "What happened to him is not your fault."

"I know I didn't pull the trigger, but I led her right to—"

"It's all on *her*, Nylah. All of it."

So much anger laced his voice. She knew part of that anger

was him feeling like he should have known who Violet was. That all of them should have known.

They couldn't have. There was no way for them to know. Even her own father hadn't known she was here in Cradle Mountain.

She nodded slowly, gaze returning to the street. She really wanted to see Cody. He'd messaged to say he was okay, but nothing would calm the panic in her chest like seeing him.

As the paramedic worked on her side, she forced the air to move in and out of her lungs. To not let the weight of everything that had happened tonight press down on her. She'd come so close to losing Liam. Too close. And that left a wound that would take a while to heal.

Finally, the paramedic stepped away. "All done. But remember, if you feel significant pain or have any issues, I would encourage you to visit the emergency room to make sure it's not infected."

She nodded and was just opening her mouth to respond when two cars pulled up.

Jason was the first to step out of a vehicle, then Courtney. When she saw Cody climb out of his rental, she quickly thanked the paramedic, then rose from the ambulance and started moving. The second he was within reach, she flung her arms around her brother's middle, ignoring the ache to her side and hugging him hard.

Cody's arms wrapped around her just as tightly. "You okay, sis?"

She breathed him in, letting his familiar scent comfort her and the fact that he was standing here slow her speeding heart. "I'm okay. Thanks to you and Liam."

"Why were you in the ambulance? And why is your shirt bloody? Were you hurt?"

She pulled back, gaze moving over his face. "A bullet grazed my side." His eyes darkened, and she hurried to add, "But it was *just* a graze, and the paramedic bandaged it up himself."

"You need a hospital."

"I'm okay. How's your head?"

He paused before answering, clearly not wanting to let up on the hospital thing. "It's fine. The second I turned my back on her, she hit me. I only lost consciousness for a few minutes."

Thank God. "Is Trey—"

"He's been arrested."

Relief loosened the band around her chest even further.

Callum, Fiona, Logan, and Grace arrived next and came over to stand with them, as well as Jason and Courtney. Liam inched closer to her, wrapping an arm around her waist.

"The rest of the team have checked on their families and will meet us back at Blue Halo," Logan said quietly. "The building is destroyed, though, along with Marble Protection's office."

Nylah's heart dropped. These were businesses they'd built from the ground up, and this hate group had targeted them. Destroyed everything they'd worked for.

"It's just a building," Liam said, as if reading Nylah's mind. "Everyone's alive and the assholes have been arrested. That's what's important."

She eased back against his chest. He was right. Alive. Everyone was alive. God, she was grateful.

She looked to Courtney. "How's El?"

At the sad turn of Courtney's mouth, Nylah's stomach dropped. "Violet shot her in the stomach, but she was breathing when the paramedics loaded her into the ambulance."

God, the poor woman. She'd already lost Carlson, and tonight she was shot by her roommate, a woman she considered her best friend.

Nylah turned to Jason. "You're okay?"

His jaw clenched, rage transforming his expression. "A syringe was shoved into my neck from behind. I assume it was

Trey and can only guess he chose not to shoot me because the bullet would have been too loud. He was probably planning to come back and finish me off in the chaos after the explosion."

Courtney smoothed a hand down his arm, obviously trying to soothe some of the anger. "We're all alive and safe."

But Jason was a protector. It probably killed him that tonight, he hadn't been able to protect anyone.

"You all got my message about Violet being Steve's daughter?" Liam asked.

The men's features hardened as they nodded.

"I'm relieved he wasn't part of it," Jason said.

Nylah's heart thumped. She couldn't even imagine the level of betrayal if he'd known. That would have cut deep into Liam's entire team.

"I'm glad he's on our side and that he'll help us find everyone who was part of her group," Logan said quietly. "We're all safe now."

Nylah leaned against Liam while slipping her fingers into Cody's. Safe. It was a word she had to keep repeating in her head. The building they ran their business in was destroyed, but it was the lives that counted. And tonight, somehow, everyone they cared about was still breathing.

CHAPTER 30

$\mathcal{L}$iam moved around his kitchen as he prepared dinner. He had a pot roast on but was extending his skills to make an apple pie for dessert. Nylah had let slip a week ago that it was a favorite of hers, reminding her of her childhood. Usually, he'd just buy a pie from Courtney, but she still hadn't re-opened The Grind, so he was doing it himself.

So far, it didn't look terrible...but it also didn't look great.

The events of a few weeks ago were never far from his mind. The explosion. The fact that Nylah had been chased through the damn streets with a gun. Even Violet being both Steve's daughter and Hawk was a shock he was struggling to accept. But at least now, they knew why Steve had been blocked at every turn when he'd tried to get them access to things on the case. It had been Trey all along. A man Violet had seduced and used. Hell, it had even been Trey who'd put Bryce Burger forward as a suspect. He was a decoy. A weak attempt to distract and keep the attention off himself.

Liam layered the pastry on top of the pie, his jaw grinding at the memory of the list of names Steve had given them. All the men who'd been part of that online hate group, and everyone Violet and Trey had made contact with. They'd all been arrested, and it would be a long time before those directly involved saw the outside of a prison again, if ever.

Liam could finally sleep well, knowing his loved ones were safe.

Voices sounded from the bedroom. Nylah was on a video call with her brothers. Cody had left a week ago, but Liam would forever be grateful to the man for his part in keeping Nylah safe that night. He had no doubt that had he not attacked Trey, Violet would have shot Nylah, then walked outside and finished off Jason.

His gut clenched at the thought, acid filling his chest.

He'd just slotted the pie into the oven when his phone rang from the counter. A small smile stretched his face when he saw Callum's name.

"Hey, Cal. How's Vermont treating you?"

Callum and Fiona had decided to get away for a week and had rented an Airbnb on the East Coast.

Hell, a lot of his team were either away or actively planning a trip. They all needed some down time with their loved ones after the events that had taken place, before they began to rebuild Blue Halo.

"It's good, except for the damn house cat, Toby."

Liam frowned. "What's wrong with a house cat?"

"Fiona's now convinced we need our own cat. A black one with a white stomach, exactly like him."

Liam laughed. "I'm surprised an Airbnb has a house cat."

"Technically, it doesn't. The owners live close by, so this cat thinks it has two homes. I don't blame the thing. Fiona feeds it, pets it. Hell, she let him sleep in our room last night. I'd be confused too."

Liam shook his head, the smile still on his face as he checked on the pot roast. Steam billowed when he removed the lid to the slow cooker. "Other than that, everything okay?"

"Yeah. I just got off the phone with Wyatt. His team's doing well. They've started to rebuild Marble Protection."

Relief splintered through Liam. Relief that they'd only lost their places of work and not any lives. That they *could* rebuild. "Good."

"I wanted to check in on El and Ned. You visited them today, right? They doing okay?"

Liam's muscles tensed. He fucking hated that innocent people had gotten caught up in the crossfire of a war that had nothing to do with them. "They're both doing okay, El better than Ned. She's being discharged tomorrow. Ned's gonna need a bit more time, but hopefully he'll be okay to go home soon."

Callum sighed. "I'll try to visit him when I get home tomorrow."

"He'd like that."

Callum cleared his throat. "Also, got some good news. I found a new location for Blue Halo."

Liam's lips twitched. "You telling me I have to get my ass into the office again already? I can't even get a month off?"

"You *want* a month off?"

His friend knew him too well. He loved being home, especially because this was where Nylah was. But he also lived and breathed his job. Taking assholes down. Protecting innocents from the bad guys.

"Nope. Send me the address."

Callum chuckled. "Thought so. I'll send it through and see you there bright and early Monday morning to check it out."

"Done."

When the call ended, Liam briefly checked the pie before heading to the bedroom. *Any* time Nylah was out of his sight was too damn long. Hearing her wasn't enough.

He stopped at the door just in time to hear her brother Kayden saying, "I want to know more about this Liam."

Nylah laughed. "You've spoken to him on the phone half a dozen times."

"I know. It's not enough."

"All you need to know is that I love him." Her voice was soft. "And he treats me well."

Liam's heart thudded. He'd never tire of hearing those words. Not if they were spoken a dozen times a day for the rest of his damn life.

* * *

"You sure you're okay out there, Ny?"

Nylah smiled at Eastern's question. Somehow, her brothers had performed a miracle and scheduled a video call where all five of them could be on with her at the same time, even though Jace and Lock were still on active duty.

"I'm better than okay. I'm the happiest I've been in my life."

Her brothers studied her closely. Another person may have squirmed under the assessing looks, but she was so used to it she'd be more surprised if they *didn't* look at her like that.

"So you're out of Misty Peak for good, then?" Lock asked.

"For now, yes. But I'll come visit on holidays." She ran her finger over a crease in the bedsheet. A part of her heart would always miss home and her brothers. But the rest of her knew that Idaho was her new home and where she wanted to be. But then, wherever Liam was would always be where she wanted to be.

"How's the side healing?" Kayden asked. He'd wanted to come out and see her, but she'd insisted that right now, they just needed some time to get back to normal after the chaos and danger. Then he could visit.

"It's healing really well. I barely feel it." She cocked her head. "How's the search and rescue business going?"

Kayden scowled. "People are idiots. I rescued two twenty-year-olds from out of town the other day. They thought they could navigate the mountains when they've never stepped foot in them in their lives. I had to drag their asses out."

Safety. It was something her brothers were all serious about, but Kayden in particular. Each of them could navigate those mountains with their eyes closed. To them, it was the backyard they'd grown up in.

"Lucky they had you."

He scoffed.

Well, *safety wise* they were lucky. She was sure her brother, who had a tendency to be grumpy, had chewed their asses out good.

She smiled at Eastern. "And how's my favorite niece, Avery?"

"She's good. Since I got back to town, she's been spending a lot more time with me, which I'm loving."

Nylah grinned. She loved her niece, although she hadn't spent nearly enough time with her, mostly because Nylah and Avery's mother hadn't gotten along. "And I heard you're the new town sheriff."

He dipped his head. "Yep. It's been good, taking down assholes but in a different capacity."

A way different capacity to being a SEAL. But she could see her brother fitting into the role well. He'd always been a stickler for the rules.

"What about you two?" Nylah asked her other brothers, Jace and Lock. "You guys ever gonna retire and go home?"

Jace lifted a shoulder. "Maybe. I'm not bored enough yet."

God, if Jace was waiting to get bored, he'd never be home. He was the definition of an adrenaline junkie.

Lock leaned back in his seat. "Nope."

She smirked. Lock...forever a man of few words. Which was probably why he was so well suited to the supersecret Ghost Ops team he was a part of.

Finally, she settled her gaze on her twin. "You still taking good care of the bar, Cody? You know Dad's watching and making sure, right?"

At the frustrated look on his face, Nylah straightened. "What happened?"

"I had to let two of the new guys go last week, Travis and Dayne. Barry caught them red-handed stealing from the register, one right after the other."

"Oh my gosh..." They'd never had issues with employees before, and certainly not with theft. Misty Peak was a small town that attracted small-town people. Good people.

Cody ran his fingers through his hair. "Yeah. And now I need to find new bartenders, fast."

He did. It would be tourist season soon, and being the only bar in town, it got very busy.

"What about you, Ny?" Cody asked. "You just gonna work in that coffee shop forever?"

"I could. I love it there." Her lips twitched. "Although, I'm gonna have to amend my hours because I'm picking up where I left off with my history degree at Columbia. I just received information on the course work last night, actually."

The second the words were out of her mouth, her brothers cheered, Lock even throwing his fist into the air and hooting.

"Good on you, Ny," Cody said quietly.

Eastern nodded. "About time."

It really was.

Kayden cleared his throat. "I want to know more about this Liam."

She chuckled. "You've spoken to him on the phone half a dozen times."

"I know. It's not enough."

"All you need to know is that I love him. And he treats me well."

"Good. Because you deserve the best, Ny."

God, she loved her brothers. "So do you. So I'd like you all to hurry up and find women so I can have some sisters-in-law."

They all laughed like she'd just announced the sky was turning purple tomorrow. Okay, so maybe sisters-in-law wouldn't be happening for a while.

She sighed. "All right, I have to go. It's getting close to dinner-time here. But let's do this again soon, okay?"

They all nodded, and after the goodbyes and the call ended, all Nylah wanted to do was pull them back to her.

The door opened and Liam stepped in, his smile soft.

She cocked her head. "Hey, you."

He crossed the space between them slowly and lowered to the bed beside her. "Hey. You okay?"

She lifted a shoulder. "I miss them." Heck, she'd only said goodbye to Cody a week ago, and she missed him so much her heart hurt. "And...I don't know...they're all slowly moving back home. Their lives are changing. I'll miss it."

Liam cupped her cheek. "We can visit Misty Peak anytime you want."

"Thank you." She leaned into his touch. "I don't know what I did to deserve you, Liam Shore, but I'm so glad you're mine."

"I should be the one thanking you. You've changed my entire world."

"In a good way?"

"The best."

She ran her hands up his chest. "Have I told you I love you today?"

One side of his mouth lifted. "Yeah. But you can tell me again."

"I love you."

Slowly, he leaned closer until his lips hovered over hers. "Nylah Walker, I have never loved another person the way I love you. It's almost an obsession."

Obsession...that was a good way of describing what she felt for him.

Then his mouth lowered, and he kissed her, proving she was well and truly chained to this man.

Order Cody's story - book one in the Reckless Series, RECKLESS HOPE now!

ALSO BY NYSSA KATHRYN

Declan

Cole

Ryker

BEAUTIFUL PIECES

(series ongoing)

Erik's Salvation

Erik's Redemption

Erik's Refuge

SHORT CHRISTMAS STORY

Hidden Shadows

RECKLESS SERIES

(series ongoing)

Reckless Hope

Reckless Trust

JOIN my newsletter and be the first to find out about sales and new releases!

~https://www.nyssakathryn.com/vip-newsletter~

ABOUT THE AUTHOR

Nyssa Kathryn is a romantic suspense author. She lives in South Australia with her daughter and hubby and takes every chance she can to be plotting and writing. Always an avid reader of romance novels, she considers alpha males and happily-ever-afters to be her jam.

Don't forget to follow Nyssa and never miss another release.

Facebook | Instagram | Amazon | Goodreads

9 781922 869111